I0604215

Derek Jones and the Dark Mirrors: Book 1

By Eugene Ingram Jr

Copyright

Library of Congress Cataloging-in-Publication Data is available.

Manufactured in the United States of America.

21 20 19 18 17 16 15 14 13 12 11 10 9 8 7 6 5 4 3 2 1

First Edition

The paper used in the print publication meets the minimum requirements of ANSI/NISO Z39.48-1992 (R2009) Permanence of Paper for Publications.

ISBN 978-0-9987730-3-2

For more information, visit: *EugeneIngramJr.com*

Dedication

*D*edicated to Lynn, my parents, my beloved lovebirds Indy and Mindy, and my loving dog Daisy.

"Never tell a young person that anything cannot be done. God may have been waiting centuries for someone ignorant enough of the impossible to do that very thing."

— G. M. Trevelyan

Table of Contents

Prologue: Dark Mirror Prequel

*T*he monastery's granite courtyard shimmered under the moonlight, casting a silvery glow upon two figures standing beneath an ocean of stars. One billion years ago, simple life was developing on Earth, and over twelve thousand light-years from Earth, in the Milky Way Galaxy, an advanced civilization thrived on Venaticora. The predominant language spoken among them was English.

"Our only hope, Sister Clara, is there," said Sister Mona Beacon, pointing at the celestial light accentuating the deep richness of her skin against the folds of her azure-blue hood. Her eyes sparkled with wonder as she gazed at the cosmos, her voice imbued with quiet reverence.

"Are you looking at Venaticora's future home planet in your vision?" Clara asked, curiosity threading through her words. "How can you be so certain it is our only hope?"

"I dreamt it," Mona replied, her tone edged with certainty. "It lies on the other side of our galaxy."

Clara hesitated. "Will they speak our language, Sister Beacon?"

"Yes," Mona assured her with unwavering conviction. "I see a civilization that evolved. A future time when a young Pentillion who had been born just twenty-three years earlier—an incomprehensibly young baby by our standards—answered the same question you did! A darling and handsome boy, he memorably said, 'I'll make the conceptual overview short and sweet. Extraterrestrials 'seeded' specific linguistic ideas long before humans consciously developed languages like English. These seeds might have been embedded in early human cognition or culture, influencing the evolution of proto-languages. For example, the Alpheratz called English the Great Whisper—a subtle, ancient code that would echo across time, whispered into early humans' dreams. It wasn't English back then; it was just a pattern, a rhythm, and a foundation for a language that would one day emerge on Earth. English wasn't our invention. It was inevitable. We encoded it in the stars, our earliest songs, and our thoughts' structure. What we call Old English, Middle English, Shakespeare—it's a human iteration of a much older design.' Sister Clara, this boy speaks a billion years into our future."

"How do you know this? How could a distant planet on the far side of our galaxy ever become our home? How do you know this dream is from the far future?"

Mona turned to Clara, her dreamy gaze locking onto her sister's eyes. "I know because the Lord has spoken."

Another sister, Mary, had been listening quietly. She whispered, "How long did you say, Sister?"

Mona's gaze drifted upward again, a knowing smile on her lips. "In almost one billion years."

A gentle breeze stirred, carrying whispers of something unseen, something unknown. The two sisters, clad in their azure blue robes, stood still as the wind wove between them. Then, Mona turned suddenly toward the horizon, where moonlit rock formations loomed beyond the monastery walls.

"What is it, Sister Beacon?" Clara asked, a hint of unease threading her voice.

Mona's face was alight with an almost divine certainty. "I know where it is."

"You know where what is?" Mary echoed, glancing between them.

"One of the openings we will escape through when the time is right—an opening to everywhere. Follow me," Mona whispered, stepping forward with purpose.

They descended the monastery's stone steps, their robes trailing behind them as they crossed the moonlit terrain of basalt and granite.

"Sister Beacon, we're heading toward the forbidden canyon," Clara warned.

Mona only smiled. "I know. But follow me if you wish to witness something extraordinary."

"Why are you doing this?" Clara pressed. "You never wanted to go there after we were warned to stay away."

Mona's steps never faltered. "Because, Sister Clara, God has revealed the truth about that place to me."

Mary hesitated, but the pull of curiosity was more potent than fear. She followed Mona, who moved like an unseen force and guided them into the narrow slot canyons. The eerie howl of wolves echoed around them.

"Those are wolves," Mary whispered. "I've heard they're enormous—larger than horses."

"I know," Mona replied calmly with a gleam in her eyes.

"Aren't you afraid?" Mary asked, her voice barely audible.

Mona turned to her, her expression serene and resolute. "No."

They emerged into a vast open space encircled by towering canyon walls. A single black surface gleamed ahead, its polished face reflecting the starlight like an obsidian mirror lying on the ground. On their approach, its mirrored face looked like liquid silver and perfectly reflected the ocean of stars above.

Mary took an uneasy step forward, mesmerized by the dark surface. Gazing down into it, her reflection shimmered—then vanished.

The reflective surface shifted instantly, revealing lush, vibrant green grass stretching into infinity. The sky above was impossibly blue, untouched by clouds or shadow. A herd of zebras grazed nearby, their forms both familiar and surreal. They stood upon a vertical plane that seemed to defy gravity. The strangeness of this scene was that it appeared sideways, with the grass to the right and the sky to the left.

Mary gasped, stepping closer, and felt vertigo. The sensation was dizzying—gravity no longer felt fixed. She reached out a trembling hand and lost her balance, tumbling forward, only to land gently on the grass in a perpendicular sideways position to Mona, a thick carpet of grass beneath her. Her perspective pivoted, and suddenly, she was flat on the ground, covered with thick grass.

Mona's head appeared above her as if sideways, peering down from what should have been an impossible angle.

The sunlight warmed her skin. The zebras turned their heads nearby, acknowledging her presence as if she had always been there. The emerald green world stretched infinitely before her, an untouched paradise beyond reason. The sound of a river punctuated the gentle breeze.

Mona extended her hand. "Come back."

Mary hesitated, glancing at the endless horizon before grasping Mona's hand. As Mona pulled her up, the world around them twisted. Relative space and gravity reoriented itself. The vibrant field snapped back into darkness, the mirror again solid and unyielding.

Mary staggered, breathless. "Where was I?" she asked, looking at Mona with wide, astonished eyes.

"Paradiso," Mona whispered, her voice barely above a breath. "It is somewhere beyond this universe, in another universe."

And somewhere, far beyond their understanding, a door had been opened—one that could never be closed.

Chapter 1 Awakening

"The most beautiful thing we can experience is the mysterious. It is the source of all true art and science."

— Albert Einstein

Derek and Jenna

*O*ne billion years after Sister Mona Beacon's time, in the present day on Earth—deep within the Milky Way Galaxy—a civilization of humans flourished, unaware that their distant ancestors had once lived across the galaxy on the planet Venaticora.

Derek drifted through the lingering haze of a dream that clung to him with an almost tangible weight. It was Jenna. But before she appeared, another woman — a mysterious black figure draped in an azure-blue hooded robe — stood serenely in a luminous corridor of solid translucent blue. The high, curved ceiling gave the space an almost sacred quality, as though time had paused in reverence.

She smiled, a knowing, benevolent expression that sent a ripple of unseen energy through the air.

"Derek Jordan Jones." Her voice carried both an intimacy and a gentle command. "Go to your bride, Derek."

His pulse quickened. "Who are you?"

"My name is Mona Beacon."

And then the dream shifted.

The door before Derek opened, and he was struck motionless.

The room — if it could even be called that — was otherworldly. Blue jade, white marble, and polished rock shimmered under soft, ambient light while the translucent blue stone of the walls seemed to pulse with a life of its own. The massive window framed a brightly moonlit landscape so lush and breathtaking that it felt stolen from another realm — where reality bent to desire.

And at the center of it all, Jenna.

She lay back on the crisp white sheets, the fabric concealing and highlighting her curves. Shadows and moonlight danced across her bare shoulders, accentuating the smooth lines of her skin. Her dark hair fanned out around her, tousled and inviting, as if she had been waiting for him in a dream that defied the boundaries of time. Derek's breath caught in his throat.

A flicker of movement caught his eye, drawing him to the mirror on the wall. He saw his reflection there — his bare chest and torso wrapped only in a plush towel. The image was familiar yet foreign. Every muscle and definition of his body appeared perfectly chiseled, sculpted not out of vanity but by fate itself. He had never viewed himself this way — intense, confident, radiating a presence that transcended mere physicality, a man poised on the brink of something profoundly significant.

As he turned back to Jenna, his periphery caught the hallway behind him disappearing. He looked around to see, in its place, a wide corridor carved from solid rock stretched into infinity. The dream was changing.

Jenna's gaze met his, dark and unwavering. There was no coyness in her stare — only invitation.

Derek felt gravity shift around him, his entire world narrowing to the space between them. He took a step closer, drawn to her, to the unspoken promise lingering in the air.

Then — he woke up.

Moonlight pooled across his sheets, the dream dissolving into the quiet reality of his bedroom. But the feeling remained engraved in his memory, as tangible as the cool air against his skin.

Jenna's lips brushed against his cheek — real, this time. His memory was punctuated by sunlight that warmed the space around them as they sat together on a soft picnic blanket, the grass beneath them contrasting with the dream's vast expanse.

Derek turned to her, his pulse still uneven.

She smiled a slow, knowing smile that sent energy rushing through him.

Jenna Collins wasn't just beautiful — she was irresistible in a way that left an imprint long after she was gone. Her skin, kissed by sunlight, seemed to glow with an effortless radiance. Dark hair cascaded in waves past her shoulders, softly framing her features. Her thick, dark lashes cast shadows over eyes that held far more than they ever revealed.

And that smile was a tether, pulling him toward something unknown, something inevitable.

She wasn't just the girl who captured his attention.

She was the one who held his gravity.

Dressed simply in a fitted top that hugged her slender frame and jeans that traced her stride's graceful lines, she was elegant in motion—unassuming, yet completely impossible to ignore. She carried herself with quiet confidence, a poise that suggested she didn't need the world's approval.

Jenna wasn't just romance. She was a force.

She was the counterweight to Derek's restlessness, the steady presence that grounded him when everything else felt like it was spiraling. She wasn't just meant to be his — she had already chosen him long before he understood what that meant.

And somewhere, deep in his bones, he knew —

Jenna was his future.

Meanwhile, in a van parked on San Marcos Pass below, an athletic black man wearing a snug sleeveless tee turned to a woman seated beside him. "Bartlett, that kid is setting her up. He will make his move — this will be the final home run."

"You think so, Johnson?" the ginger-haired woman replied, grinning as she sipped from a small steel thermos. "I predict he won't take her to home base. That young man treats her too well to be just after a fling."

Anna Bartlett, a seasoned intelligence agent, exuded an air of quiet confidence and razor-sharp intelligence. Her sleek, pulled-back auburn hair, styled in a practical yet elegant ponytail, framed a face marked by poise and determination. Her piercing gaze, accentuated by sharp, arched brows, suggested a mind constantly at work, assessing, strategizing, and always a step ahead of those around her. Her subtle smirk revealed a self-assured demeanor, hinting at her wit and ability to remain composed under pressure.

Agent Johnson chuckled. "What are you suggesting? Something beyond typical teenage hormones?"

"I think he loves her," Anna said, her tone playful yet earnest. Beneath the calm, calculating exterior lay a wealth of experience and perhaps an inner conflict from years in the intelligence world. Her piercing eyes seem to hold unspoken stories — victories, sacrifices, and maybe a trace of the personal cost of a life lived in the shadows.

"They're teenagers, Anna. Trust me, there's no such thing as true love at that age. It's all hormones — High School Chemistry 101. An expert can attest to this hormonal reality."

"Jason, not all teens let their hormones dictate how they treat their sweethearts. Believe it or not, I had a perfect gentleman who romanced me in high school, and we remained chaste until we got married."

"I'm not knocking chastity, just stating the facts," Jason replied, lingering on Anna's fit physique. "You were the exception. Virgins are great, but experience has its perks."

"Please, Agent Johnson! We may be monitoring them, but who is monitoring us?" Anna said, letting a moment of awkward silence linger. "Cat got your tongue?"

Jason's smile faded, and he glanced around nervously.

"I had you there!" Anna laughed, clearly enjoying the banter.

"Agent Bartlett, I have a better idea for eavesdropping on two high school sweethearts. How about I take you to lunch at a great place in Solvang? Let's kick off a Saturday you won't forget — my treat."

"You'll expense it to the CIA?" Anna teased, glancing at Jason's lean, muscular frame that stood out against his black fatigues and dark tan tank top, his deep brown skin absorbing the glow of the overhead lights. She looked down at her gray short-sleeved tee and dark tan fatigues, then quickly checked herself in a compact mirror.

"No, it's on me, not the company," Jason replied with a faint smirk.

Jason Johnson, a highly trained intelligence agent, embodied quiet strength and laser-focused determination. His sharp, penetrating gaze suggested a man who misses nothing, always observing and analyzing his surroundings precisely. His closely cropped hair and clean, no-nonsense appearance reinforced his practicality and disciplined approach to his work. There was a natural intensity about him, a sense of calm authority that commanded respect without needing words.

Dressed in a fitted tank top highlighting his lean, athletic build, Jason carried himself with an air of readiness as though prepared to spring into action at a moment's notice. His relaxed yet alert posture projected his confidence and adaptability, honed through years of rigorous training and field experience. The tension in his expression hinted at a man accustomed to high-stakes situations who thrived under pressure but carried the weight of his responsibilities with quiet resilience.

Beneath the surface, Jason's eyes revealed a more profound complexity. There was a hint of guardedness, a sign of someone who's seen the darker sides of his profession and was aware of the toll it can take. Yet, there was also a flicker of resolve, a steadfast commitment to his mission and those he protected.

Grinning back, Anna, who tried to mask her admiration for this man, realized she was near the best beaches on the West Coast, even if her skin was East Coast pale, and her slight freckles seemed to echo her reddish-brown hair. She tucked a strand of straight hair behind her ear and snapped the compact shut. "I need to catch some sun at the hotel pool this afternoon."

"Sounds like a plan. I've never seen you in a bikini."

"Who says I'll wear a bikini?"

Jason snickered. "I doubt the hotel allows skinny-dipping, but if you insist, I'll tell the pool guests we're from Sweden."

"You're hilarious. I have a one-piece suit. Are you finally buying? That's generous. Where do you propose we have lunch dressed like this?"

"Let's go back to the hotel and order room service," he suggested, flashing a slightly arrogant smirk as he rubbed a hand over his stubbled face. "Think I need to shave? Agent Kelly said she liked the unshaven look of a black dude. Many women prefer the softness of stubble."

"Dream on, Romeo."

Jason moved to the front of the van, peering up the hill with binoculars. "Looks like Romeo and Juliet are dancing."

"Why use binoculars when you get close-up shots on this high-resolution monitor?"

Back on the checkered picnic blanket, Derek and Jenna reclined, gazing from near the top of a mountain range over Santa Barbara and the Pacific coast. Derek gently took Jenna's hand in his. "You only find views this breathtaking in the Santa Ynez Mountains," he said, pouring her a glass of pink lemonade over ice.

"This hilltop is truly inspirational," Jenna exclaimed, her eyes sparkling as she investigated his expression. "And I love how the grass sways in the breeze, the vibrant poppies, the view of the Channel Islands — that song. And you. It's perfect."

Derek handed her a glass of frosty lemonade and chuckled. "What are you staring at?"

Jenna gazed at the glass, then up at him, moving her dark brown eyes between his forehead and deep blue eyes. "My mom calls it a widow's peak. Yours is so cute! It's prominently pointy!" She giggled. "You've got this amazing wavy thick brown hair with silver highlights that girls would die for, and your eyebrows and facial structure remind me of a wolf's — in a sexy way."

Derek laughed, feeling a blush creeping up his cheeks. "What? That's funny! Tell Julia I don't tint my hair or wear colored contacts. These are my real eyes and hair, Jenna. Also, mention that I confessed I was a wolf and bit you."

Jenna tossed her long, wavy, mahogany-brown hair with bronze highlights over her shoulder. "You could be a wolf."

They both laughed.

"Derek, you did seem mysterious when we first met. I remember thinking, who is this handsome guy? You looked so cute in those glasses. Julia is jealous, especially since you're with me and not her."

Derek's gaze drifted down the hill, spotting a van parked by the roadside. He turned up the volume on the boom box. "Jenna, she should be jealous of your gorgeous Indian-British hair. I seriously want to run my fingers through it." He lifted a strand of her hair, inhaling its scent. "It smells so good. Did you know your eyes match your hair? They're like two perfect cabochons of the clearest quartz."

Jenna's eyes lit up, her lower lip gently caught between her teeth. Although his flattery felt thin, it rolled off his tongue smoothly. "The perfect gentleman. You know my mom always gives credit to my British dad whenever someone compliments me in their presence?"

"Are you saying my complimenting you is a British thing I learned from my dad?"

"Well, isn't it?"

Just then, a song caught Jenna's attention. "Oh my! Derek, I love 'You Are the Sunshine of My Life.' Stevie Wonder is my all-time favorite. How did you know?"

The music from Derek's boom box filled the van's interior. Anna glanced at Jason as he surveyed her fit body, and when he caught her eye and winked, she turned back to the monitor.

Jason said, "Anna, you were thinking about how black men are gifted with 'genetics. I'm flattered, but this is pure Quantico lean mass. I started at the CIA as a skinny guy, and they doubted I could make the grade physically. Behold."

Anna turned to Jason, surprise written across her face. "How…? Do you presume to know my thoughts now? Please, Agent Johnson, that's rich."

"Did I read your mind? No. I overheard you say it to Sharon in the break room. There are eyes and ears everywhere!" he laughed, his gaze lingering on Anna's form-fitting slacks and tank top. "I was thinking about how redheads are gifted with genetics. I wish you would be flattered, but you're about to tell me it's pure Quantico lean mass."

Rolling her eyes, Anna smirked. "The views of Derek and Jenna appear as if invisible cameras are hovering around them. I'd give anything to know how this science works."

"It's classified," Agent Johnson replied. "That's all the CIA Director Conway said we need to know." He paused, noticing the blank stare on Anna's face, then exclaimed with laughter, "They're drones, Anna."

"Jason? They must be sophisticated drones not to get spotted. Those two lovebirds were lying on a blanket beside each other earlier, staring straight up at the camera as if they were looking right into it. They would surely have noticed it unless these 'drones' were microscopic. The side camera showed them talking, and right before they started making out, Jenna stared right through the camera as if it were invisible, behind blades of grass and flowers just a few feet away!"

"I'll let you in on a little secret. I overheard our CIA director say to Sharon Questar that they're called 'dark mirror drones.' Yes, they're microscopic. Questar rolled her eyes and reminded him not to talk about it."

"Jason, those so-called drones must be invisible to the eye!"

Both agents directed their attention to the monitors, where Derek and Jenna continued to engage with one another.

"Teens look so grown-up these days, don't they?" Agent Johnson remarked. "She's glad he took off his shirt. Look at that kid's physique; he must work out. He should apply to Quantico after graduation."

"Who's noticing?" Agent Bartlett replied with a knowing grin. "What creeps me out is how we can view this scene on Earth without any visible camera. Technology is light-years ahead of what I thought. Moreover, we are pinging a satellite and not the drones."

"Maybe a new high-powered satellite," Jason suggested.

Agent Bartlett stared at him. "No, the camera is close by; the blades of grass and flowers revealed its proximity at a horizontal angle. This is a side view, not an aerial view. They must have some miniature drone that's tiny enough to be invisible."

"You must have launched it," Agent Johnson shot back.

"I logged into the CIA over a secured satellite network and saw a vantage point from this van as it approached them," Bartlett explained.

"Maybe the drone theory is right. Perhaps it was deployed from a satellite or this tricked-out van, and a satellite controls it."

"Do you realize the technology involved in creating a tiny drone that is invisible to the naked eye, with precise navigation from a joystick or mouse? Can we launch it from a satellite or remotely from this vehicle? Your theory has holes, Jason."

Agent Johnson scratched his head. "No offense taken. Perhaps these two lovebirds just haven't noticed it?"

"Derek was looking right through me at times, and he would have noticed if the drone were large enough to spot. His blue eyes lit up momentarily as if he were gazing down toward the ocean."

"What do you mean his eyes lit up? What do you mean? I must have missed that. CIA Director Conway said you ask too many questions, Bartlett, and doing so will get you into trouble."

Agent Bartlett rolled her eyes, then fixed her gaze on Derek. "I ask too many questions? Then don't ask me what I meant by his eyes. Look at his eyes. His irises are luminous and deep blue, like when SEALs extracted him in Egypt during our interview at Langley."

Agent Johnson sat on a small mobile stool, studying Derek's eyes. "We need to get in closer." Scooting next to Agent Bartlett, he said, "Let me drive."

"Be my guest."

Maneuvering the joystick and tapping the keyboard, one of Derek's eyes filled the screen, revealing every detail of his iris.

"Don't get too close, Johnson; he'll see us."

"He won't. Trust me. Look, there's no re-action. I don't know if it's just a few feet away or zooming in, but it seems to have locked onto the target — his eye. His iris pulsates blue at this distance, yet his pupil is steady. Something is causing his irises to faintly glow in broad daylight."

Derek led Jenna in a slow dance to the music, gently twirling her. Standing behind her, he ran his fingers through a chain of seashells on her bracelet and whispered, "Jenna, is that a new dress? I love turquoise; it's my favorite color. Those white pearls with inset sapphires are stunning. My mother collects gemstones and teaches me all about them. Yours are stellar." Inhaling deeply, he added, "Did you make the shampoo from ingredients at Whole Foods? It smells so good."

"Derek, I love Whole Foods, but I found the ingredients for this shampoo at better prices on Amazon. Some were imported directly from India." Jenna returned his gaze, saying, "You know a lot for a high school boy, Derek. My mother gave me these graduated strands of pearls at the end of these white metal chains. She said it's a rare metal that's naturally pearl-white to match the pearls. I picked this turquoise summer dress because it goes so well with blue sapphires. I also chose blue sapphires because they match your beautiful eyes." Looking around, she continued, "I love this hill, the bright green grass swaying in the breeze, the vibrant poppies, the view of the Channel Islands, that song. And you. It's perfect."

Derek turned to her, drawing close. "I don't know about you, Jenna, but I feel like I'm in paradise."

She studied his face, starting from his widow's peak, moving down to his prominent nose and full lips, her gaze finally landing on his deep blue eyes. For a fleeting moment, an image of them making love under white satin sheets flooded her mind, their bodies floating above the bed in a stately room with cathedral ceilings and a view of stunning greenery. She glanced out the window, noticing two tiny parrots cozied together, and reflected on how they had never made love.

He surveyed her milky white skin, running his fingers under her seashell bracelet. With his other hand, he caressed her head, gently brushing her hair and leading her in a slow dance.

"Your thought was beautiful and illuminating," Derek whispered, kissing her forehead.

Smiling, Jenna feigned confusion. "What thought?"

Derek raised an eyebrow, his smile teasing.

Jenna's eyes widened, and she grinned, slowly shaking her head as a blush crept across her cheeks. "No…"

"Yes, Jenna." He leaned closer, whispering, "I feel the same way, but we must wait. My mom made me promise."

"Seriously, Derek, how did you know? Are you some mind reader?"

Derek shrugged. "I just sensed what you were thinking. It was beautiful."

Jenna's smile deepened, and she pondered, "How?"

Derek laughed. "You're right. Maybe I have an overly romantic imagination, and your thoughts are as innocent as your pure white

Egyptian cotton sheets and my mom's love-birds in a room overlooking paradise."

Jenna looked startled, studying his face. "You're pretty sure of yourself, aren't you? How did you know they were white? The birds? You've never even seen my bed sheets! My nanny insists that my bed is made after I get up."

Derek laughed. "How many boyfriends in this day and age can say they've never seen the sheets of their girlfriend's bed?"

Jenna chuckled. "Well, Derek, you better not mention they're satin and white, or my mom might not believe you sensed it."

In the van, Anna recalled her first high school love, Mike, and the kiss she would never forget. They had married, and he became a Navy SEAL. She smiled as she looked at the screen.

"That kid knows his moves," Jason exclaimed as he watched through binoculars.

Agent Bartlett buckled her seatbelt, smiling. "Why do you prefer binoculars over watching close-ups? Please do me a favor and lose the binoculars. They look creepy. I prefer these monitors; they make me feel more legit spying on these two. Let's get lunch. Your treat."

As Jason started the van and prepared to pull onto San Marcos Pass, he paused at the sound of Jenna's voice. They turned to view the screen.

Staring into Derek's eyes, Jenna squinted for a moment. "Derek, I don't know if it's my imagination, but your irises glow like there's a light behind them. It's breathtakingly beautiful, but…"

Suddenly, Derek looked down toward the van, his blue irises glowing like a wolf's eyes at night, even in daylight. Anna and Jason looked up the hill, and for a moment, Derek's eyes shone like two bright blue LED lights staring back at them. Anna gasped.

Agent Johnson slammed on the brakes and rushed to the monitor, zooming in. "Oh my God, Agent Bartlett, as Sharon Questar loves to say when viewing a home run, it's Christmas."

Agent Bartlett squatted beside him, staring in awe. "Yes, and Santa is looking right at us. I've never seen them glow this brightly, not in Langley. Jason, he's looking right at us. We're made."

"What?" Derek exclaimed, maintaining his smile as he continued to lead Jenna in their slow dance, forcing himself to look away from the van. "It's probably the sun reflecting off my eyes."

"You were facing away from the sun. Haven't you ever noticed?"

As they danced, Anna and Jason exchanged silent glances.

"Yes…" Derek finally replied. "Mom said not to worry about it, that it's likely genetic."

Jenna stared incredulously. "Genetic?"

"Jenna, trust me, Mom knows what she's talking about. She's a scientist, you know."

Derek twirled Jenna around, and they faced each other as they continued to dance across the grassy hilltop, weaving through patches of vibrant gold-yellow poppies. Reaching down, he picked one and raised it to her nose. As she inhaled its fragrance, she looked into his eyes, puzzled. His irises seemed to glow again like two neon blue Earths hovering over the whites of his eyes.

"Whoa, Derek, I'm getting some serious goosebumps. Your eyes are so awesome when they do that; they look like blue sapphires resting on fresh, virgin white snow. Each iris is like the blue Earth the astronauts saw out in space but floating on an ocean of white. It makes you look like one of those superheroes." Jenna smiled, continuing, "Are you a superhero, Derek Jones?"

Derek giggled. "Jenna, you're doing this. I've never felt this way about someone. I thought I would never feel the same after what happened in Egypt." He leaned closer and whispered, "You brought me back to sanity." Then he whispered into her ear, "I feel a burning sensation all over me, like a ravenous wolf that could devour his sweet young prey but loves her too much to harm a hair on her head."

Jenna gazed into his mesmerizing eyes, astonished. "You are a poet and a charmer. I almost see you transforming into a beautiful wolf. My mother says these endangered species are critical to the Earth's ecosystem and must be preserved at all costs. You better not take advantage of a girl with those incredible wolflike eyes. It's like you're casting a spell."

Derek gently rubbed the tip of his prominent nose against hers, his eyes surveying her face. "I'll tell you later, after our class field trip to Palomar Mountain and the Palomar Observatory."

"Tell me what?"

"Just things."

Agent Bartlett stared at Agent Johnson. "We need to order Dr. Rabinovich to run more tests. Something is happening, and it's escalating. This occurred in Egypt when the terrorists started dying. Although Derek was hooded, the camera captured radiation signatures, and a blue glow momentarily shone through the black cloth. They reacted to whatever was emanating from him with profuse ears and nose-bleeds. One of them vanished before the camera when he looked in his direction."

Jason grimaced and replied, "Insane video. Nobody vanishes into thin air. Labs at the company found nothing to explain the visuals, but I share your concerns. I think we're not in the 'need to know' loop, if you catch my drift. They know something, and we don't need to know. Is she in any danger? That is the question," Jason said, glancing up the hill again as Derek and Jenna danced faster, Derek executing a few cartwheels. "Wow, an acrobat. That kid did a few cartwheels."

"I can see it on the monitor," Anna replied, slightly annoyed at Jason's binoculars.

"I like these binoculars," Jason countered. "Don't hate on them."

Derek briefly shot an angry glance at the van down the hill before refocusing on Jenna as they danced.

Anna heard a faint voice, which sounded like Derek's in her mind, asking, "Who are you?" She instinctively thought in reply, "We are your friends. We're the good guys." The response echoed back, "You better be."

"I agree it was an insane video," Anna replied to Jason, her gaze darting nervously between the monitors. "Incidentally, I'm meeting with CIA Director Conway before he meets with NSA Director Questar. I don't know. We have orders not to take him into custody now but to monitor him. I hope no harm will come to her because he likes her."

"I would die for her, so just go," came another thought into Anna's mind.

There was a pause, followed by another thought: "Jason likes you."

Jason noticed Anna's sudden wonder as she stared at the monitors, puzzled. "Bartlett, are you okay? How did you schedule a meeting with Conway? Did he give you orders not to take Derek Jones into custody? Unbelievable. Who's in charge here?"

"He called me in, Johnson, with those orders. In answer to your question, I'm in charge. I'm flying to D.C. after we wrap it up."

"You're in charge?" Jason shook his head. "Why do my women always end up being on top? When were you going to tell me?"

"Excuse me? I was going to tell you if you even hinted at taking him into custody. Also, I was giving you a hard time, Jason. We're in charge. We're a team."

"Anna, I applaud your politically correct diplomacy, but it's clear who's in charge." Jason continued to eye her flirtatiously. "And that's cool."

"We need to go, Jason. Don't test my patience."

Sitting back on the picnic blanket, Derek glanced down the hill as the van drove away. Jenna slowly took Derek's hand. "What do you want to be when you grow up, Derek? What are your goals?"

Staring toward the Channel Islands, Derek thoughtfully replied, "Is saving the world and all life on it too ambitious?"

"Oh my God, that's such a sweet answer," Jenna replied ecstatically.

Derek chuckled. "But I'm dead serious. I mean it." He gently placed his hands on Jenna's upper arms and whispered, "Jenna, I saw Venaticora in a dream as another planet was smashing into it."

"You never told me about this dream of yours, Derek. Why do you call it Venaticora?"

Derek shook his head slowly. "I don't know, Jenna. It's weird how I knew that was the name of an Earth-like planet."

"About your wanting to save the world, maybe Venaticora is a metaphor for our world? I feel more passion in your voice than I usually hear when asking you a question. I feel it in my soul. It's as if we have some connection. Derek, my parents run a world relief organization. They've encouraged me to choose a school major that will help others. I've considered becoming a doctor or perhaps a lawyer to fight the corporations ruining this planet for greed. Not all corporations are bad, but some give the rest a bad name. Maybe I should become a biologist to help figure out how to save dying ecosystems. I must decide before graduating next year. Any thoughts about your major?"

"Jenna, I'm strongly leaning toward physics. The answer to humanity's future is colonization. Did you know my grandparents were physicists who worked on secret government projects? They said if they told me about these projects, they would have to kill me."

They both laughed.

Derek continued, "They said the only way we hope to colonize distant exoplanets is through faster-than-light travel, building stable wormholes, solar sails, and other technologies using exotic metals as light as foam but stronger than titanium. They believe any nation leading this effort must be morally and spiritually evolved. Otherwise, we could become a threat to other emerging civilizations that fear our barbaric governments, so our governments must change, starting with the United States and President Abigail Tubman. I'm thinking about applying to MIT next year, maybe Stanford."

Jenna paused thoughtfully. "President Tubman is a brave woman, and if any president could represent humanity before these civilizations and make humans appear worthy, it would be her. I still can't get the image of Air Force One from the cockpit of a fighter escort exploding in midair and killing President Wilson. I never thought about humans becoming like hostile ETs to other worlds. You know, Derek, I always wondered if peaceful civilizations are watching us, evaluating us, considering us primitive ETs, deciding if we are worthy of them, and waiting until we are ready to join them. Incidentally, my parents went to Stanford and recommended that university. They know people with degrees from both Stanford and MIT."

Derek paused again. "Both schools? Cool, two degrees. As I was about to point out, Jenna, we need an education to help us make this world a better place. Your parents sound awesome, like mine. So many people who go to Stanford, I hear, get into politics or high-level jobs at corporations. We need to focus on making a difference in the world. NASA would be a great place to work. I'll bet degrees from both institutions you mentioned will impress them."

Jenna sighed. "So many choices, so little time to decide."

Derek checked his watch. "Hey, Jenna, let's get back to the hotel. My parents want to meet for dinner at a great restaurant near Santa Barbara harbor, and I'm looking forward to meeting your parents and seeing their home in Montecito. We will hit it off. I can feel it."

"Sounds like a plan, Derek. Your eyes are back to normal, yet still beautiful sapphires on virgin white snow. My mom and dad can't wait to meet your dad. They've always wanted to meet the CEO of New Physics Corporation. Considering your mom's reputation in the scientific community, I suspect they will try convincing her to work with their organization to preserve endangered bird habitats."

Derek smiled, his joy infectious. "What are you smiling about, Jenna?"

"What are you smiling about, Derek?"

"I'm smiling because you're smiling…"

"And I'm smiling because you're smiling!"

They both laughed, and Derek added, "Avian habitats are a passion of my mom's, even though her primary scientific discipline is geophysics. Did you know birds are like canaries in coal mines? They die ahead of people. If birds die, life dies shortly after, which my mom calls an extinction-level event. Escaping our planetary habitat is our only hope. We need an escape route, just like coal miners build tunnels in coal mines. When the canaries start to drop, they flee through these tunnels. Humans must tunnel through spacetime to escape in an emergency. We are canaries in the cosmos and will perish unless we escape our terrestrial confines and go anywhere in the hospitable universe."

Meanwhile, Jason drove down the mountain highway, listening to Derek and Jenna's conversation. He glanced at Anna, who said, "He's right."

"I'm looking forward to that dinner conversation, Derek!" Jenna said, her excitement palpable.

"So am I. Don't underestimate my dad's deep dinner conversations. New Physics has a government contract to explore dark mirrors. This is top-secret, Jenna. Promise not to mention it to anyone, especially the words 'dark mirrors!' I'm not even sure Dad will bring it up."

"What do you mean by dark mirrors, Derek?"

"Dark mirrors were discovered in 1947 in Roswell, New Mexico. My dad was just ten years old. His dad, my grandpa Ray, told him about examining them with other physicists. Dark mirrors can tunnel through spacetime, creating stable openings that people can walk through, like walking in and out of your bedroom door. We found one in Egypt, in an undiscovered chamber beneath a major pyramid, before terrorists kidnapped me. It looked like a shiny ball bearing about an inch in diameter. It had no weight. It could float like a helium balloon and flatten into a giant, circular disc. The disc's surface was a mirror that suddenly turned into an opening."

"An opening? To where?"

"I have no idea. An Egyptian archaeologist named Zeyad Hassan entered the dark mirror and vanished. Jenna, I'm not supposed to talk about this to anyone. Promise me you won't mention any of this to anyone."

"Sure, Derek, cross my heart!" she promised.

"And hope to die?" Derek replied mischievously.

"Well, uh, no…" Jenna responded, her faint smile betraying her delight. "Whoa, terrorists kidnapped you?"

Derek's expression turned serious as he met her gaze. "Yes, Jenna, and they're all dead."

Anna and Jason exchanged nervous glances as they continued to monitor the situation, Jason's grip tightening on the steering wheel.

"Rick Jones has violated his top-secret security clearance by talking to Derek. Now she knows, and who knows whom she will tell? I say we turn around, take them both now, and get agents to bring in the Jones and Collins families," Jason declared.

"Are you out of your mind?" Anna retorted. "First off, you saw what happened to the terrorists in Egypt after they abducted Derek. Rick Jones explained the phenomenon Derek experienced there as part of a pattern he observed."

"What do you mean? A pattern? What the hell, Anna?" Jason demanded.

"Well, Jason, that's as far as your security clearance goes, so we'll leave it there. No,

Jason, we do not take them in," she said firmly. "To whom do you report?"

"Oh yeah, now the truth comes out. You ma — uh, ma'am. Are we still on a first-name basis?" Jason chuckled.

Anna shook her head, ruefully amused. "You're testing me, Jason, and yes, we're on a first-name basis now, but that's on thin ice because this is strictly company business. Listen carefully. I didn't say what I'm about to say. He also revealed information his grandfather Raymond Jones had told him."

Jason released an expletive. "Retired special agent Raymond Clarence Jones? CIA?"

"You didn't hear it from me. What did I say earlier in our discussion? Say it word for word. Agent Johnson, this is a test of your memory, so get it right."

"We have orders not to take Derek's dad, Rick Jones, Derek Jones, or Jenna Collins into custody now, but strictly monitor them. You're hoping that because he likes her, no harm, no foul. Right, Agent Bartlett?"

"Excellent memory. Do you have questions about these orders?"

"Uh… no, ma'am. Can I call you Anna again? And by the way, Anna, you're giving me orders, which is music to my ears."

Anna rolled her eyes, took her cell phone from her pocket, and impatiently held it to her face to unlock it. Her annoyed expression made it clear to Jason that the discussion was over.

"Derek," Jenna said softly, her smile gleaming, "you don't happen to have a Barbra Streisand song in that big box of yours?"

Derek's jaw dropped slightly. His mom had told him that Jenna's mother mentioned how much of a "huge Barbra Streisand fan" Jenna was, yet he had forgotten to download it in haste to prepare for their picnic. "Uh, shouldn't we leave so we're not late for dinner?"

Jenna studied the panicked look in his eyes. "I downloaded Mom's 1980 CD titled 'Woman in Love.'" She pulled her phone from her purse. "Can we dance to this song, Derek? Just one more dance before we leave. Please?"

As the song played, they danced. Staring into each other's eyes, they felt chills, not from the cool ocean breeze that made the poppies sway across the field.

"This song is awe-inspiring," Derek whispered into Jenna's ear.

"On clear nights, I would lie on the lawn, staring at the stars and listening to this song, wondering what it would be like to fall so deeply in love that I became untethered from time and space."

Derek smiled knowingly and whispered back, "Time and space are an illusion, Jenna, but love — that's real."

The restaurant overlooking the ocean was dimly lit when their waiter departed after taking their orders.

Rick Jones loosened his tie, raised his glass of red wine, and declared, "To the success of New Physics."

Rick Jones exuded a quiet charm and warmth, the kind of presence that attracted people without demanding attention. His slightly tousled dark hair, casual yet polished style, and simple denim shirt under a dark blazer gave him a relatable, approachable look. His expression was lighthearted — with a faint, knowing smile paired with eyes with a depth of experience and empathy. His demeanor suggested a man who valued humor, kindness, and connection, yet there was also a quiet resilience, hinting at someone who had weathered challenges with grace.

Rick's posture and expression reflected a steady and dependable man, the kind of father who would do anything to support his family.

His relationship with Derek was built on mutual respect and deep affection. There's a subtle pride in how he carried himself, as though he knew his role in shaping Derek into the person he is today.

Beneath Rick's calm exterior was a man of keen intelligence and wit. His slightly raised brow and relaxed expression suggested someone who enjoyed engaging in thoughtful conversations and had a knack for offering sage advice, often with a touch of humor to lighten the mood. He seemed like the kind of person who could diffuse tension with a clever remark while still providing profound insight.

Rick's close bond with Derek was rooted in shared values and open, meaningful communication history. He served not only as a father figure but also as a confidant and mentor, someone who understood Derek's struggles and ambitions on a level few others could. Their relationship was a cornerstone of Derek's emotional grounding, providing him with the strength and perspective needed to face the challenges in his life.

Brian Collins immediately raised his glass and replied, "To a profitable business partnership!"

Brian Collins had a composed and thoughtful demeanor, exuding the confidence and steadiness of a man who has gracefully lived through life's complexities. His neatly styled sandy-brown hair and stylish glasses framing his face gave him an air of intellectual sophistication. There was a quiet intensity in his gaze, as though he was always observing and analyzing the world around him, yet his soft expression suggested warmth and approachability.

Dressed in a tailored black suit, Brian's appearance reflected his attention to detail and a preference for understated elegance. His subtle smile conveyed a sense of calm and assurance, the hallmark of someone who served as a rock for those around him. Despite his composed exterior, a spark of humor and vitality was in his eyes, hinting at a playful and engaging personality beneath the professionalism.

As Jenna's father, Brian was a profoundly influential figure, providing her with the strength, wisdom, and moral compass that shaped her character. Their bond was mutual respect and trust, built on open communication and a shared sense of loyalty. Brian's demeanor suggested he was both a protector and an advisor, someone Jenna turned to for guidance when life felt uncertain.

Beneath his composed exterior was a man of great depth who has weathered personal and professional challenges with resilience. He carried a quiet strength that inspired those around him, making him a father figure, mentor, and confidant. His calm yet commanding presence made him a figure who naturally garnered respect from his family and anyone who entered his sphere.

Asha joined in, smiling, raising her red wine glass, and saying, "And might I add here is to the Collins World Relief efforts to create a global food distribution model."

Asha Jones exuded a gentle warmth and timeless grace that made her instantly endearing. Her soft, radiant features were complemented by her glowing complexion and expressive eyes that reflected kindness, empathy, and an unshakable sense of optimism. Her wavy, shoulder-length hair framed her face beautifully, with a hint of playfulness added by the bright red fresh flower adorning her hair. This small yet striking detail hinted at her joyful and vibrant personality.

Asha's relaxed and welcoming expression, with her slight, genuine smile, reflected her nurturing nature and deep bond with her son, Derek. Her presence radiated a calm strength, the kind of person who became the emotional anchor in any situation. She was approachable, suggesting that people naturally turned to her for comfort and advice.

Her understated elegance was a testament to her authenticity. Asha carried herself with quiet confidence, embodying a balance of inner strength and compassion. She played a pivotal role in Derek's life, grounding him with her wisdom and unconditional support. Her relationship with him was mutual admiration and respect, built on shared values and a deep emotional connection.

Beneath her gentle exterior was a woman of resilience and determination. Her kind eyes suggested someone who has faced challenges with grace, drawing from them the strength to guide and protect her loved ones. Asha was a loving mother and integral to Derek's foundation, shaping his character and inspiring his journey.

"Hear, hear!" Brian echoed in response to Asha, raising his drink.

Derek and Jenna lifted their virgin margaritas, and they all toasted and sipped their drinks.

"I appreciate your generous donation to Collins World Relief, Rick and Asha," Brian said. "Sustainable food distribution is key to moving fresh food to billions of starving people globally. Collins World Relief is developing internationally funded food distribution facilities modeled after currently functional mass distribution models like Amazon Fresh to get fresh food from the source to population centers and villages where the need is greatest. Food often rots on shipping docks or in inadequately cooled warehouses, never reaching starving individuals. A sustainable distribution chain is required so that food resources can solve world hunger."

"That is amazing!" Derek exclaimed. "I love how I can order fresh food online, and it shows up at my doorstep!"

Brian nodded at Derek, a broad smile on his face. "That's right. Internationally funded food distribution facilities will move fresh food from the source to population centers and villages worldwide where the need is greatest. Did you know the problem with world hunger is not a shortage of planetary resources, at least not in the foreseeable future? It's a distribution problem that Collins World Relief will solve."

"I've spoken with the board of directors at New Physics," Rick said. "They've unanimously agreed to donate one billion dollars to Collins World Relief."

Brian's mouth fell open, and his eyes sparkled with admiration. "Thank you from the bottom of my heart, Rick. Please thank the board of directors."

Rick nodded in acknowledgment.

"Mr. Collins, uh, I mean, Brian," Derek began hesitantly, "I read an article online that a high school friend shared on social media, stating that Collins Resorts International has expanded to space. The article claims it came from a source in the intelligence community who wishes to remain anonymous."

Everyone at the table exchanged bemused glances.

Jenna laughed. "Was that the article Timmy shared with Mrs. Strickland's science class? Timmy always shares articles from conspiracy sites."

Derek blushed since he had promoted that share.

"Derek," Brian said, leaning forward, "I haven't seen the article. What news organization?"

"Uh, I think it was All Not Fit to Print," Derek replied.

"Appropriate news organization name considering the content. Did the article give any details? Did we open a resort on Mars that even NASA doesn't know about? Perhaps astronauts could stay in one of our finest suites when they send a human-crewed mission there."

Everyone, including Derek, burst into laughter and replied, "Well, actually, the article claims it's called Earth Collins Resort, and it's, uh…" Derek hesitated.

Brian leaned in, taking a sip of his wine. "Yes, Derek?"

"It claims it's on the edge of our galaxy. I know it's a stupid article, and I should have ignored Timmy's share instead of sharing it further. Sorry, sir."

"No, Derek, don't be sorry. This is an example of the kind of news that floats around online. I gather you didn't believe it?"

"No, sir, of course not. I don't even know why I shared it to a wider audience."

"Because it was funny!" Brian exclaimed. "I would love to expand Collins Resorts International to a city outside our galaxy!"

"Dad," Jenna interjected, "Derek never mentioned a city outside our galaxy."

"Well, Jenna, I presume that if rumors of one of my resorts on the galaxy's edge are circulating, no pun intended, it would have to be in a city. Why would I build a resort in the middle of nowhere?"

Everyone laughed.

"Changing the topic from my new resort announced in All Not Fit to Print — an appropriate name — I'd love to hear about your work, Asha, with Derek and Jenna's science teacher, Elisa Strickland, on avian habitats."

"Thank you for asking, Brian. We're working with NASA on its life support systems for the Mars colony. NASA wants to construct an impressive aviary and greenhouse to study birds in otherworldly habitats while growing flora and fauna in Martian soil. Bird health in a human habitat can measure the health of plant and animal life in that habitat and help determine the long-term viability of humans living there. That's the basic explanation. We are exploring ways to transport birds to Mars, including cryostasis."

"What is cryostasis, Asha?" Jenna asked.

"It's a form of hibernation, also known as cryosleep. Transporting live birds in zero gravity for extended periods presents challenges. Creating a long-term habitat using what is known as torpor stasis, which occurs in nature among various species of animals, can allow humans and animals to travel to other planets. Torpor is a state in animals where they lower their metabolic rate and temperature, allowing them to hibernate for a long time. Birds, however, have unique anatomies. NASA contracted New Physics to adapt this technology for its Mars missions and transporting birds."

Asha looked at Rick sadly and continued, "Funding was cut to focus on their Dark Mirror Project."

Rick wiped his mouth and stared at Asha. "Sweetheart, please."

Asha sipped her wine defiantly while staring at Rick. "I'm sorry; I wasn't supposed to mention the project's name. It's just that the importance of the avian component has left me concerned about the shift in focus at our company. I was hoping that, as CEO, you could talk some sense to them. Don't get me wrong, Rick, I'm not blaming you."

"Dad, don't worry about secrecy. Grandma and Grandpa already told me about the Dark Mirror Project," Derek interjected.

Rick looked around the table with a look of surprise. "They what?"

Derek beamed with pride and answered, "Oh yeah, Dad. They sure did because they know I can be trusted."

"That's beside the point, Derek."

As Jenna looked at Derek with concern, Brian laughed and said, "Look, we're among family. We know about it, too."

"You know what, Brian?" Rick replied, annoyance creeping into his tone.

Brian chirped blithely, "Nothing deep — just the project name. Who doesn't know?"

"Who doesn't know? Nobody should know who doesn't have a top-secret security clearance. The existence of this project is highly classified on a need-to-know basis," Rick insisted.

Amara placed her hand on Brian's knee, looking at Rick with determination. "We all want what's best for this planet, Rick, and would never compromise a secret. Right, Derek and Jenna? Your secret is safe with us."

Derek and Jenna exchanged glances and said almost simultaneously, "Sure."

Rick thought without articulating, "Famous last words."

Asha dramatically placed her napkin beside her plate, looking sternly at Rick. "So why is this project, which is so secret, more important than revolutionizing ways to transport astronauts, scientists, and other sacred life forms to Mars?"

Rolling his eyes, Rick replied slowly, "If everyone at this table cares, please do not repeat anything discussed here." As everyone leaned forward in anticipation, Rick continued,

"Although I'm not at liberty to go into details, Derek and Jenna will soon discover the scope and grandeur of the project when they intern at New Physics."

"We get to intern at New Physics?" Derek exclaimed, excitement bubbling over.

"You both wanted summer internships for extra credit. Suffice to say, Asha, that the project will negate the need for cryostasis in transporting astronauts and, as you so eloquently put it, other life forms over vast distances."

"Now you've got my attention," Brian said, leaning closer.

"And mine," Asha added, placing her hand over Rick's.

"That's all any of you need to know," Rick said as the waiter approached, causing frustration among everyone at the table. "So, who's up for dessert and coffee?"

Celestial Canaries

 "*T*oday, our class theme is 'Celestial Canaries,'" Mrs. Strickland announced. "Can anyone guess why?"

Elisa Strickland was a teacher at Derek and Jenna's high school, and her vibrant energy and warmth made her both approachable and inspiring to her students. Her long, brown hair, casually styled with natural elegance, framed her face, illuminated by a genuine smile reflecting her passion for teaching and deep appreciation for knowledge. Her expressive hazel eyes held a spark of curiosity and a deep well of wisdom, hinting at her remarkable work as a scientist at the Vatican's renowned physics lab at the Vatican Observatory.

Elisa's demeanor was approachable yet confident. She was the kind of teacher who made even complex subjects like geophysics engaging and accessible. Her subtle makeup and minimal accessories, such as the elegant silver watch on her wrist, complemented her understated style, emphasizing her focus on substance over flash. She carried herself confidently, her gestures and expressions imbued with the patience and passion of someone enthusiastic about sharing knowledge and guiding others.

As a former researcher in a world-renowned lab, Elisa brought a wealth of expertise to her classroom, making her lessons profoundly insightful and captivating. Her teaching style was hands-on and thought-provoking, often blending rigorous scientific inquiry with the wonder of discovery. This combination resonated with Derek, whose intelligence and curiosity she recognized and respected. Elisa valued students who thought critically and challenged norms, and her relationship with Derek developed on mutual admiration for these traits.

Beneath her approachable exterior was a woman of great intellect and complexity. Elisa's transition from working on cutting-edge science at the Vatican to teaching high school students reflected a purposeful choice to inspire the next generation. She recognized Derek's immense potential and was one of his earliest mentors, encouraging him to push boundaries and embrace the natural world's mysteries. Her respect for Derek's intelligence was coupled with a quiet determination to guide him as he navigated his path, making her not just a teacher but a pivotal figure in his personal and intellectual development.

Derek took a sip of his strong coffee from his mom's favorite coffee shop, his eyes glued to the screen of his notebook computer. He was still reeling from a whirlwind weekend with Jenna in Santa Barbara, including the nerve-wracking experience of meeting her parents in Montecito. All he wanted was to zone out and escape.

Just then, a familiar voice cut through his thoughts like a shot of espresso. "Derek! Care to answer my question, or are you too busy texting Jenna?"

Derek looked up, annoyed. "I'm not texting Jenna, Mrs. Strickland. I did message her a minute ago, but I'm reading an excellent book."

Mrs. Strickland rolled her eyes and sauntered over to his desk. "You're living proof that sitting at the back of the class is a terrible strategy for dodging questions. And what's this?" She picked up his coffee cup, examined the logo, and suppressed a smile as laughter erupted around the room.

Derek locked eyes with unimpressed Mrs. Strickland's stare as she folded her arms.

"As I was saying, Professor Strickland, I'm engrossed in a fascinating book," he said with a hint of sarcasm.

"Professor?" she replied, raising an eyebrow. "I'm glad to see we've established that rapport. This book better be good." She extended her hand, and he reluctantly handed over his iPad. She glanced at the screen and read aloud, "Physics of the Impossible: A Scientific Exploration into the World of Phasers, Force Fields, Teleportation, and Time Travel, by Michio Kaku." Giggles spread throughout the room. "A brilliant physicist, but that's beside the point."

"Mrs. Strickland, before I got hooked on this book, I Googled a term you mentioned — 'geophysics' — to understand the class better and answer your question. It's so engaging that I distractedly tapped the Kindle icon and ended up where I left off," he explained, slightly defensive.

"Did I mention geophysics?" she shot back, laughter bubbling through the classroom as Derek's face turned crimson.

Mrs. Strickland stared him down as she gently placed the notepad back on his desk.

He glanced around, caught her gaze again, and said, "You're not wasting our time in this class. Our time is well spent."

"Correct. Now tell me why. Come to the chalkboard, Derek. Explain why this class is worthwhile," she commanded.

With slow, hesitant steps, Derek stood and went to the front. He caught Jenna's eye, her cheeks flushing, which only made him blush. The class erupted in jeers and whistles, then fell silent as he faced the chalkboard, staring into the blank space. "Why are we here?" he mused, his voice barely above a whisper.

"Derek? The class is facing the other way," Mrs. Strickland said, her impatience palpable.

Turning to face his classmates, his gaze locked onto Jenna's as if he were speaking only to her. "My mom is an ornithologist and a planetary geophysicist. For those who don't know, ornithology is the study of birds. She loves birds — she has two lovebirds occupying a room in our home. They listen to bird songs from hidden speakers all day. Sometimes, I swear they're singing back to the real birds outside. She calls it their nursery."

Derek paused, glancing at Mrs. Strickland, half-expecting her to interrupt.

"Your mother must play rainforest recordings," she said, her eyes gleaming with interest. "That way, they feel part of a community. Go on."

"My dad's a planetary geophysicist, too," Derek continued. "He studies the geology and geophysics of planets, tectonic movements, and groundwater flow — basically everything about planetary structures." He caught Jenna's dreamy stare and winked, suppressing a smile, and reacted to someone in the corner of his eye, raising his hand. "Jimmy, do you have a question?"

Jimmy Foster exuded an easygoing charm and a boy-next-door demeanor that made him instantly likable. His tousled, sandy blonde hair gave him a relaxed and approachable appearance, complementing his youthful, clean-cut features. His light, expressive eyes radiated warmth and curiosity, often betraying a playful sense of humor that made him the perfect counterpart to Derek's more intense personality.

Dressed casually yet neatly, Jimmy's style reflected his down-to-earth nature and preference for comfort over pretense. His slightly crooked smile suggested a mischievous streak, hinting at a personality that thrived on spontaneity and adventure. There was quiet confidence in him because he was comfortable in his skin and intensely loyal to those he cared about.

As Derek's best friend, Jimmy was not just a sidekick but a vital part of his life. Their bond was rooted in mutual respect, trust, and years of shared experiences. While Derek often took the lead, Jimmy provided balance with his lightheartedness and grounded perspective. He was the one who kept things in perspective when situations became tense, frequently using humor and quick wit to diffuse tension.

Beneath his laid-back demeanor, Jimmy was fiercely loyal and dependable. He was the friend who would drop everything to help Derek, regardless of the stakes. While he may not have shared Derek's larger-than-life ambitions, he stood as a steady, supportive presence, offering encouragement and grounding Derek when he needed it most. Their friendship was a testament to the power of opposites balancing each other out, with Jimmy bringing levity and heart to Derek's more serious journey.

Jimmy lowered his hand and said, "In English, please. What do planetary geology and birds have to do with the price of tea in China?"

Derek rolled his eyes. "If you haven't noticed, Jimmy, Earth is a terrestrial planet floating in a void. Birds are like canaries in a coal mine; they signal the health of our environment. If they die, we're next. If Earth can't support life, it becomes a lifeless rock drifting through space."

"Is that true?" Jimmy asked, skepticism leaking into his tone.

"It is," Derek replied, his confidence building. "Especially for fragile species like bees. We're all celestial canaries in the cosmos.

Unlike them, we have the potential to escape our terrestrial cage. But are we smart enough to do so?"

Mrs. Strickland shrugged. "Maybe, and maybe not. Some canaries are quite the escape artists."

Derek smirked. "My mom insisted I take this science elective because she says you are 'the best teacher on the planet,' and I assumed she meant this one."

Jimmy chimed in from the back, "Good one, bro!" and laughter erupted before quickly fading.

"You could teach at Yale, Harvard, or MIT," Derek continued, "yet you chose to teach this high school class. My mom appreciates your help with her research on the planetary geophysics of terrestrial bird habitats."

Mrs. Strickland smiled. "If you frame it that way, it suggests that birds could exist on other planets."

"They do," Derek replied, a playful glint in his eye. "Mom says so."

Mrs. Strickland surveyed the puzzled expressions of her students. "I would love to explore the possibilities of evolution on other habitable worlds, but that's a topic for another day. You may sit down, Derek."

As he returned to his seat, the room fell silent, eyes following him with a mix of admiration and curiosity. He exchanged glances with Jimmy and rolled his eyes, brushing against Jenna's outstretched hand. "Excuse me, my lady," he said with a grin, eliciting a wave of giggles.

"Class," Mrs. Strickland began, "I'm pleased your science elective is unusually lively for a Monday morning. Derek is correct in saying that we cannot escape our terrestrial confines. That's why understanding the science of Earth is so crucial — so no canaries or high school students drop."

Elisa folded her arms, her gaze sweeping across the classroom as she seized the moment to ignite their imaginations. The room fell into a hushed silence.

"As a teenager," she began, "I would lie beneath the stars and feel a profound emptiness. I imagined civilizations existing out there, looking back at me, and I felt sad knowing their light wouldn't reach me for billions of years."

The students listened intently, their eyes wide with wonder.

She continued, "I saw a photo album of light from ages past. It was as if I could see ancient civilizations — perhaps dinosaurs or even early humans — gazing up at the same stars I was."

She leaned closer, her voice dropping to a whisper, "But what if they were so far away that they looked into dark areas of the sky where our light hadn't arrived yet?"

Elisa's voice increased in volume, filling the room with excitement and energy. "Lying in the darkness, I realized the universe is teeming with intelligent beings, all pondering the same question: Are we alone? What if those dark areas are filled with civilizations looking back at us, wondering what we are doing now? What if, at this very moment, young minds in a classroom across the galaxy are discussing the same ideas?"

Her words hung in the air, captivating the students. "What if that door," she said, pointing to the classroom entrance, "led to a corridor across the galaxy? What if you could walk through it and instantly traverse a thousand light-years? The air could rush back and forth. Sound waves, cellular signals — everything could connect."

A boy raised his hand, excitement dancing in his eyes. "Mrs. Strickland, do you think there are teens with reptile blood? What color do you think it is?"

Laughter erupted once again.

Jenna raised her hand, and Elisa smiled and said, "Jenna, I'm guessing you're going to point out that we're way too primitive of a species to have access to such advanced physics?"

Jenna slowly lowered her hand and smiled at the boy who had just spoken. "Good-looking and primitive, yes. Neanderthal and driven by pure instinct. How did you know what I would say, Mrs. Strickland?"

The boy winked at Jenna, and she rolled her eyes. Other girls giggled.

Jenna continued, "Quite the contrary, Mrs. Strickland. The physics exists now." On saying that, Jenna covered her mouth and looked around.

Elisa smiled, laughed, and replied, "Interesting you say that, Jenna. At the PTA meeting, your dad, who is a physicist at New Physics Corporation, got into a discussion with me about the possibility of stable exotic event horizons in bidirectional wormholes. I contended that this is impossible, and he insisted that he had worked out the equations to show why negative matter makes bidirectional and stable exotic event horizons in wormholes possible."

As Jenna grimaced, Elisa's voice trailed off.

Elisa continued without missing a beat, "We politely ended our discussion by agreeing that humans would likely take thousands, if not millions of years, for their intelligence to evolve to a level where we could create stable exotic event horizons. To create such portals, for lack of a better word, these doorways would have to draw on energy from other dimensions or parallel universes, and only exotic matter with negative mass could make this possible. This matter is not known to exist. Lacking this matter, there isn't enough energy in our universe to create anything that would remain stable, with no mechanism for drawing energy from other universes. We agreed it's the stuff of science fiction."

Derek said, "When you say stable wormholes and negative mass, Mrs. Strickland, what does that mean to you? And what the heck is the difference between an event horizon and an exotic event horizon?"

"Derek, it's complicated. Exotic matter with negative mass could create a stable exotic event horizon, which certain exotic wormholes possess. Normally, black holes have one-way event horizons. You cross the event horizon, and you cannot return. You're spaghettified in the singularity. However, a stable wormhole with negative mass and an exotic event horizon is a theory derived from studying exotic matter found in lunar ore samples."

Jenna's voice immediately rang out. "My dad said the exotic event horizon to which you refer is a field of energy that theoretically blankets the wormhole's opening. He said that if the atmospheric pressure on either side of the opening is similar, you can pass through it without a space suit or vehicle. Otherwise, it would be best to have a suit or vehicle hull emitting a field of exotic energy that allows it to pass through the 'blanket.'"

Mrs. Strickland interjected, "The 'blanket' meaning an interdimensional membrane in physics that acts similarly to a membrane of a biological cell, preventing certain things like a vacuum from passing through it?"

Jenna replied, "Exactly. Imagine if you were going from an atmosphere on this planet to a vacuum in space. The opening would be like a hole in a spaceship, sucking you and air into space. The exotic event horizon, just a phrase they made up at New Physics to describe this bazaar physics, blankets the wormhole opening and prevents the displacement of the atmosphere to vacuum. Suppose you're wearing a suit or in a vehicle equipped with an exotic energy membrane, analogous to electrifying the outer shell of a suit or metallic vehicle hull. In that case, it can pierce the exotic event horizon and allow you to pass through the opening or, you know, the wormhole."

Jimmy's voice rang out. "Jenna, your dad is so far down a rabbit hole. Do you know how insane you sound?"

As giggles punctuated the classroom, Jenna rolled her eyes, crossed her arms, and leaned back in her chair. "Shut up, Jimmy!"

Derek steered the subject to the lunar ore samples mentioned by Mrs. Strickland. "If you mean dark mirror ore, my dad said that topic is out of bounds. And Jenna, I will pretend I didn't hear what you said."

Mrs. Strickland whispered as the class leaned forward to hear her, "I know there are many secrets, but we are all kindred spirits. Let's leave it at that. Let's say perhaps we're straying into the realm of science fiction to make our real point. Have you ever heard of spooky action at a distance?"

The students looked at one another and shrugged. Jenna raised her hand and said excitedly, "Yes! Albert Einstein postulated it. When there is an instant connection between particles that could be vast distances apart, it's as if they become one, and it doesn't matter how far apart. If these particles are light-years away, they can still interact instantly."

"That's faster than light," said Jimmy.

"That's right, Jimmy!" exclaimed Jenna. "My dad called it quantum entanglement. He said that someday, it might be possible to communicate instantly between vast distances like thirty light-years away. Two human colonies could talk to each other like they were talking here on Earth using cellphones."

"In real-time," said Elisa.

"Yeah, in real-time, Mrs. Strickland!" replied Jenna.

Elisa went to the chalkboard and drew a stick figure holding a phone and a doorway and another stick figure holding a phone on the opposite side of the doorway. Then, she drew a two-way arrow pointing at each stick figure through the doorway. "Suppose there was a stable exotic event horizon open between two people clear across the galaxy from one another, and the cellular signals passed through the doorway connecting the two. It wouldn't have to be a big doorway. It could be a microscopic opening just big enough to allow the signals to pass through and act similarly to a cellphone tower."

"That's brilliant," Derek said.

Elisa smiled at Derek. The class looked at each other in wonder.

"Derek, why is it brilliant?" Elisa asked.

"Easy. The signal doesn't have to travel clear across the galaxy. It passes instantly through folded space created by an exotic event horizon."

"Impressive, Derek. The son of a physicist."

Jimmy said, "Derek's dad is the CEO of New Physics Corporation, a government spook tank. Jenna's dad works with him."

"Jimmy, why do you keep calling it a spook tank?" Derek asked in a slightly annoyed voice.

"Because Dad said it was," Jimmy replied with a snicker.

Elisa laughed and said, "We have at least two dads of students in this class who are budding physicists."

Jimmy Foster raised his hand and said, "Three."

Elisa folded her arms. "Jimmy, so your dad is a physicist. Then why would he call New Physics a spook tank?"

"Last time I checked, Mrs. Strickland," replied Jimmy as he laughed and gave the student next to him a high-five, "New Physics is run by spooks in the CIA, NSA, and black ops." The class started to giggle.

"Shut up, Jimmy," said Derek. "You don't know what the…" Looking at Ms. Strickland's stern expression, he continued without taking his eyes off her, "Jimmy, you don't know what the fruit cake you're talking about."

Jimmy laughed. "Hey bro, chill out. We're supposed to be friends!"

Standing up while staring at Jimmy, Derek said, "I'll bet you don't know how the exotic event horizon works as described by Mrs. Strickland. Perhaps I should let you explain it to the class, especially you, Jimmy?"

Jimmy's face became somber, and he gave Derek a blank stare.

Derek approached the front of the class. "Mrs. Strickland, do you have a piece of paper and a black pen?"

"Why certainly, Derek," Elisa answered, giving Derek a blank sheet of paper and a black pen from her desk.

Placing the paper against the chalkboard, Derek took the pen and put a dot near the top of the sheet and another at the bottom. Holding the sheet to the class, he said, "What is the shortest distance between these two dots?"

The class stared at him quietly, with every-one looking around and shrugging.

Laughing, Derek answered his question with another question. "By drawing a straight line between the two dots?"

"Duh?" said Jimmy, causing laughter to erupt.

"Like this?" Derek slapped the page against the chalkboard and drew a straight line between the dots.

"Ya think?" repeated Jimmy.

"Jimmy, what if I did this?" Derek folded the sheet of paper until the two dots were on top of one another. Holding the folded sheet to the light from the window, he said, "See? The dots are completely lined up."

After looking around the silent classroom, Derek punched a hole with the pen's tip through the dots. Holding the folded page again so that light shined through the hole that intersected the two dots, Derek chuckled and said, "Zero distance. You walk right through it."

Elisa approached Derek, gently took the folded sheet with a hole through the dots, unfolded the paper, and said, "In a practical, real-life application, Derek, we created the first dot or 'Einstein-Rosen Bridge,' as Albert Einstein and Nathan Rosen postulated in 1935, the opening of the 'bridge' of Karl

Schwarzschild's famous wormhole theorem. How did you know where to draw the second dot?"

Derek looked at Elisa with a faint smile.

Elisa continued, "Derek, let's say the first dot is where we stand. The second dot is in the living room of an extraterrestrial family on a planet in the Andromeda Galaxy. How do you draw the second dot to a precision of an inch so that you arrive exactly in the right place?"

Derek whispered, "Genius. It's the question that drives us, as Trinity said in the movie The Matrix."

Elisa laughed. "Yes! The right question makes the right answer possible. The physics of passing through the wormhole is far more advanced than physicists in our civilization presently understand. From this point forward in our discussion, let's agree that the Einstein-Rosen Bridge is a metaphor based on a primitive construct because we are referring to a traversable wormhole that connects different points in our universe, and that connection must be precise. The question of how the exit to the wormhole forms in a precise distant location has confounded physicists."

Jimmy raised his hand and said excitedly, "I overheard my dad, one night at dinner, say the Schwarzschild Crater on the far side of the

Moon was given that name for a reason. When the man he was talking to asked if that NASA rumor was true, Dad said the crater had gravity anomalies. Dad also said the Schwarzschild Crater contained the mother lode of dark mirror ore. He said it's a new mineral discovered by NASA that contains negative mass that can hold a wormhole open indefinitely and violate all known laws of physics!"

Derek's eyes flashed with anger. "Jimmy, you called my dad a spook, yet your dad signed a nondisclosure agreement with my dad's company! Shut up! You're not supposed to talk about that!"

Jimmy replied, "About dark mirror ore?" and hunched his shoulders, sunk into his seat, and looked around at stares from students.

Elisa looked at the two boys intensely and slowly said, "Back to the subject at hand, boys. Derek, in a practical, real-life application, we created the first dot or opening of a 'bridge.' However, riddle me this with your best guess: How do we create the second dot at the desired destination, perhaps billions of light-years away, to create the other end of the opening? The destination cannot deviate; otherwise, we might arrive above the planet, below it, or any-where we do not want to arrive."

Derek thought carefully for a moment; his eyes lit up, and he replied, "You said it yourself, Mrs. Strickland! Spooky action at a distance!"

Elisa's face transformed into a big smile, and she said, "Just like your dad, Derek! You connected the dots! No pun intended. How does one use spooky action at a distance to identify the destination?"

Derek's face displayed an intensity of thought.

Jenna raised her hand and said, "Well, how do we even know where we want to go? We're sitting here blind. My dad, who works with Jimmy's dad, said it's like being in a big, huge castle that would take millions or even billions of years to explore. So, if we want to explore it through traversable wormholes, we must somehow see distant locations as they exist right now to lock in on the exact room of the castle where we want to enter through the wormhole."

"Jenna, you're onto something," said Derek.

Those in the classroom stared intently at him as he stared intently out the window.

After a few moments, his eyes lit up again. He replied, "Assuming one does not know the coordinates of the destination, the opening it-self could be used by a quantum computer to recursively scan and survey folded space while you sit there and watch, maybe on a screen attached to the quantum computer, until one targets a location and set of coordinates, based on what looks interesting, and then it transforms the opening into a bidirectional exotic event horizon. The negative matter used to create the opening would project itself through spooky action at a distance to the destination, thus creating the traversable opening."

Elisa looked at Derek with amazement. Sensing her approval, his pupils flashed glowing blue for a moment. Startled, Elisa said in almost a whisper, "Precisely. Your dad must have shared many secrets with you."

"Right, Derek, your dad is telling you things that you're not supposed to know!" boomed out Jimmy's voice in a tone of dismissal. Derek glared at Jimmy.

Mrs. Strickland told Derek, "Your dad is quite a genius in physics."

Derek blushed and said, "Ya, he is, but Dad didn't share secrets. Mrs. Strickland, my dad, says he met you at a physics conference. Do you know each other?"

Mrs. Strickland smiled warmly. "Derek, I've collaborated with your father at New

Physics Corporation back to my days in the Vatican physics lab, but let's keep our focus. You mentioned the quantum computer. We will explore the profound physics underlying a true quantum computer. Still, I want to leave you and the class with a thought-provoking question to ponder until we meet again."

The class leaned forward in rapt attention as Elisa paused thoughtfully.

She continued, "What if the mind operates like a quantum computer? What if the mind is a quantum computer?"

A gleaming smile spread across Derek's face as he unfolded the sheet of paper and pointed to the second dot, which had a hole in it. "If that were the case, then the mind could potentially pinpoint the location of the second dot to complete the bridge to a trillionth of an inch! You wouldn't need a mechanical quantum computer to scan the universe; your mind could do it instead!"

Elisa's eyes lit up with excitement, and they exchanged a knowing glance, a shared spark of inspiration igniting between them.

Jenna raised her hand as Derek intently watched her, and Elisa acknowledged her with a nod.

"Mrs. Strickland, can spooky action at a distance extend outside our known universe? I overheard my dad postulating that a wormhole could travel through multiverses and even clear to heaven."

Elisa looked startled and puzzled. She felt goosebumps pulsate over the back of her head. "You mean a wormhole to God? Well, Jenna, if God exists, which is a great mystery, then wouldn't God only allow the faithful to enter such a wormhole and heaven? Did you know that I worked at the Vatican in their physics lab before I got into teaching, and we pondered whether prayer passes through a portal in spacetime?"

Jenna's eyes sparkled with excitement as she exclaimed, "Absolutely! My dad is Catholic and loves discussing the intersection of physics and the divine with you. He's always pondering how to reconcile the laws of physics with the existence of God. He has this fascinating theory: if we assume that God exists and created the laws of physics much like a game programmer designs a virtual reality, then heaven could be a blind spot for those who don't believe."

Elisa rested her chin on her hand, gazing thoughtfully upward. "That's intriguing, Jenna. So, you're suggesting that even the most advanced extraterrestrial beings might remain oblivious to God's existence, convinced it's merely a myth?"

Jenna replied, "Exactly, Mrs. Strickland! Picture the most sophisticated life forms in the universe — despite their intelligence, they might never perceive God because He is shielded by an energy field that makes the dimension we call heaven invisible to them. My dad mentioned something exciting: extraterrestrials could visit our planet because human minds can bridge that barrier between God and our universe. There's a part of our brain that evolution might phase out, as it ties into belief in God. While evolution enhances survival instincts, faith can sometimes seem like an obstacle to pure Darwinian survival. We haven't yet evolved to the point where we view belief in God as a hindrance. However, as we progress toward becoming a space-faring species, we may activate that part of our brains that could eventually be lost."

Elisa's eyes teared up slightly, and she whispered, "A wise ancient Psalm says, 'out of the mouths of babes.'"

Whispering punctuated the silent classroom.

Mrs. Strickland continued, "Jenna, what a brilliant philosophical hypothesis. So, what your dad is hypothesizing is that God is a blind spot to those unwilling to embrace seemingly impossible concepts such as the existence of God. They have evolved to consider faith and prayer pointless, so some of the more enlightened hypothetical extraterrestrials view humans as their Einstein-Rosen Bridge, no, their traversable wormhole to the divine."

After a brief silence, Jimmy's voice rang out. "That explains why Dad says they're here, why they came."

"Seriously, Jimmy?" exclaimed Derek, shaking his head. Jimmy put his hand over his mouth momentarily and looked around.

The students looked at each other with puzzlement and wonder.

The bell rang.

As Derek returned to his desk to grab his backpack, Elisa reminded the class of their homework assignment on the board. "I will see all of you out in the high school main parking lot tomorrow at 9:00 a.m. sharp," she said, referring to the class field trip to Palomar Mountain and the Palomar Observatory. Write down the address of 35899 Canfield Road, Palomar Mountain. Put it into your mapping apps on your phones."

Filing out of Mrs. Strickland's class into the corridor, Jenna bumped into Derek. Placing his hands on her shoulders, he smiled and said, "Hey, Jenna, we keep running into each other."

Jenna grinned. "Why is that?"

After giving Jenna a light kiss, Derek continued, "My mom will pick us up after school. Are you packed for the field trip to Palomar to see what my parents call the 'Lunar Pearl,' and do you have your permission slip from your parents?"

"Lunar Pearl? I like the sound of it," Jenna exclaimed and continued, "Yes, they faxed it to my phone. I'm glad this long-distance thing will last until I finish school. Living with Aunt Thelma is tough, with her curfew and all. I get a sick and twisted thrill knowing she can't stand the thought of my staying at your house. My duffle bag and hiking boots are in my locker with my permission slip. I'm ready for the hiking trails and can't wait to see the observatory. As you put it, looking into the ocean of stars and this mysterious so-called Lunar Pearl will be awesome."

Derek curled his pinkie finger around Jenna's and looked at her intently. "I have something to show you through that telescope tomorrow night, Jenna, when it's aimed at the Lunar Pearl. It's a surprise — about tonight.

My parents are watching us like a hawk after Mom caught me kissing you the last time you stayed over. No more sneaking into my room at night to play video games, or she said you can't stay over."

"Come on, nothing happened, just a peck or two on the ears and neck. Well, okay, almost on the lips. Lasted all of two seconds."

"That was the problem, but a blissful two minutes seems like an eternity, I mean two seconds. That's major for adults. We're still kids, don't you know, so take this grown-up stuff seriously, Jenna. As mom said, 'Show them you two will sleep in the same house without gravitating to one bed.'"

"One bed, whoa, that sounds major. We were lying there playing video games on our laptops, Derek. We could be laying on the carpet in front of the television watching your dad's favorite golf tournament, but the comforter in your bedroom is cleaner and cushier."

"Nice spin, now try telling mom that, Jenna."

Jenna smiled, looked at the clock, and gently separated their fingers. "Got to run, Derek! See you after school."

In the locker room, Derek looked at the swimsuit, tank top, and knee-length shorts

Jenna had bought him. Then he found a cool Polo shirt Jenna had also tucked away in his gym bag. Always shy about undressing in front of others, he convinced his mom to get him a pass from physical education classes using his dad's clout as CEO of New Physics Corporation with the school board. Derek worked in their home gym, jogged, and got private physical education tutoring credits. He had quite a collection of fashionable workout clothes and shoes, yet he dressed very plainly for school with oversized everything.

Jenna finally convinced him to showcase his impressive lean and muscular physique to the football team to end bullying at school. Although naturally muscular, his build was obscured by the oversized long-sleeved shirt hanging halfway down his thighs. The players on the football team relentlessly picked on him, labeling him a nerd because of his glasses and turning his high school experience into a nightmare. They taunted him mercilessly, claiming he only received private physical education tutoring because he was "a total weakling."

"Derek!" Jenna's voice echoed in his mind as he felt her gentle hand brush against his cheek, sending a wave of warmth through him. The sensation was comforting. "When you enter the locker room for swimming class today, you must undress confidently in front of everyone and hold their gaze as if you own the place! Do you understand?”

Derek laughed. “Yes, ma’am.”

“That’s the spirit. Think of me as you do it for motivation.”

Derek chuckled. “Oh, Jenna, you’re good. Nothing is stopping me now!”

Jenna kissed him on the cheek, smiled, and walked away.

Derek’s thoughts returned to reality as he faced the meanest, most muscular boy on the football team.

“Dude, why are you here,” the boy said as he looked down at Derek. “You’re shorter than I thought. You must be under six feet.”

“Swimming,” Derek answered confidently, thinking of Jenna.

“Really. You’re going to sport that wimpy body that you’ve been hiding from the girls out there in that pool? You’ve never done that!” The boy laughed hysterically and looked at other football players entering the locker room. “Derek here is going swimming with us! We’ll get to see his wimpy excuse for a body.”

The boys looked at each other and laughed, then looked Derek up and down.

Derek could hear Jenna's voice clearly in his mind. "When you go into the locker room today for swimming class, you will undress in front of them and stare them down like you own them! Understand?"

Staring up at the boy, Derek said intently, "You want to see it?"

The boy looked around the locker room at the other boys, snickered, and said, "See what."

Derek rolled his eyes and stared down at the boy.

"Ha, you mean to see that wimpy body. That's funny. You're afraid to remove that stupid oversized shirt you're hiding under. We can expect to see nothing. You're one of those pretty little boys that looks pathetic without being covered from head to toe, aren't you?"

Derek stared intently at the boy, his blue eyes slightly phosphorus as he felt a surge of adrenaline. The other boys in the locker room at a distance couldn't see the glow in Derek's eyes, but the boy he stared at, only a foot away, looked vaguely disturbed as he tried to hide a sense of fear.

The boy watched as Derek removed his glasses and tucked them into his gym bag. With a challenging gaze, Derek unbuttoned his shirt, and once the last button was undone, he leaned in close, pulled his arms out of the sleeves, and let the shirt drop to the floor. "Dude!" came a startled voice from the locker room. The boy's eyes roamed over Derek's lean physique before he met his gaze and said, "Uh, all right then. Wanna join the team?"

"I'm too skinny," Derek replied, sarcasm lacing his words.

"No way, man! You're like a lean fighting machine!" chimed in another boy. "What will it take to get you on our team? We'll teach you how to play football."

A subtle wave of colorful phosphorescence, almost imperceptible, coursed over Derek's body as he felt empowered in response to their enthusiasm. "Jenna was right!" he thought. Confusion flickered across the faces of the boys as they exchanged glances, silently questioning whether anyone else had witnessed what just happened. Then, shaking their heads in disbelief, they dismissed it.

Derek quickly slipped into his swimsuit, a grin spreading across his face as he said, "Don't just stand there — let's go swimming!" With a sense of accomplishment from taking Jenna's advice, he strode confidently toward the showers. Meanwhile, the boys exchanged eager glances, their competitive spirit evident as they rushed to change into their swimsuits.

Lunar Pearl

Mount Palomar Observatory at sunset was breathtaking. The full Moon shined clearly in the deep azure blue skies above the dome. A buzz was in the air this summer night as the students looked forward to the weekend.

"Lunar Pearl," whispered Derek to Jenna, motioning his head toward the Moon, "is more than you think."

Jenna looked at Derek with questioning eyes. Derek pointed to the Moon. "Do you know its pearl white glow is masking the kaleidoscope of its true mineral composition? Meteorites hit the lunar surface over time, punching deep craters and creating dazzling mineral deposits. Iron-bearing minerals such as pyroxene, olivine, and ilmenite. That last mineral is essential to eventual Moon bases, as ilmenite provides iron and titanium for building lunar structures and even oxygen extraction. And there's a whole lot of volcanic glass."

Staring into Derek's eyes, she replied, "Cool. You always know so much about space."

"My mom is like the encyclopedia of space and anything planetary. She knows everything there is to know about the subject. She said there is one discipline that makes understanding space and planetary sciences possible, that will drive our future to the stars and their habitable worlds."

"What is that, Derek?"

"Math."

Jenna looked stunned. "Wow. Seriously? I thought math was just a boring subject."

"Not when you know it is like…" Derek paused, struggled for words, then continued, "like a cryptographic key unlocking the universe. Jenna, think of the universe as a door to cool places. My mom always said that mathematics is the key to unlocking that door."

Jenna stared into Derek's eyes and replied, "Are you sure those cool eyes are not the key to unlocking infinite doors I could spend forever exploring?"

A smile and blush slowly swept over Derek's face, and he nervously laughed, not knowing what to say to Jenna's flattering question. "You mean, like a retinal scanner opens doors for authorized users?"

Jenna laughed. "You're funny."

Mrs. Strickland spoke. "Class, the observatory tour is starting. Follow me inside, where we'll take roll call."

After the roll call, Mrs. Strickland raised her voice over the conversations throughout the room. "Class, now for the surprise. By special arrangement, someone very close to me, Brian and Amara Collins, have arranged for our class to view the cosmos through the 200-inch Hale Telescope. Normally, this is not part of the tour, so please do not touch anything unless instructed. Follow me."

Derek smiled at Jenna. "Your mom and dad got us in? That is so awesome. But then you already knew about the Lunar Pearl…"

Jenna smiled. "My dad is a major contributor and made our viewing a condition. My mom said the figure was eight digits. And no, he didn't mention anything about a Lunar Pearl."

"No way, Jenna, he made an eight-digit contribution? That is so cool! I did some research. Did you know that in 1934, the Hale mirror was manufactured by Corning Glass Works in New York with 20 tons of borosilicate glass? Named Pyrex, its low expansion properties prevented it from changing shape, preventing distortion of the stars. Get this, Jenna; they can image exoplanets using just a 1.5-meter portion of the Hale Telescope."

"Derek, will they show us the new exoplanets they discovered?"

Derek gleamed at Jenna.

"What, Derek? What's that look?" asked Jenna as she studied his expression, then whispered, "Is it the Lunar Pearl?"

"You'll see."

"Class, your attention, please!" said Mrs. Strickland excitedly. "The people who made this special event possible, Brian and Amara Collins." Mrs. Strickland stepped back as Jenna's parents came through the door, accompanied by Rick Jones, Derek's dad. Derek smiled at Jenna, and her jaw dropped. She thought they were home in Montecito, ninety miles north.

"Oh my God, Derek, you didn't tell me!" she said, smiling. "What's your dad doing here?"

"You'll see," Derek replied gleefully.

"My name is Brian Collins," began Jenna's dad as he leaned toward the microphone. "This is my lovely wife, Amara, and my friend and colleague from New Physics Corporation, Rick Jones."

Mrs. Strickland began clapping, and the students followed, spontaneously engaging in applause and whistles.

"It's a full moon, and we're running slightly behind schedule, so let's cut to the chase," Brian continued. "Anyone. Why do you think we're at the prestigious Mount Palomar Observatory after sunset on the night of the Supermoon? Before anyone posts a guess, allow me to explain what a Supermoon is for anyone who does not know. The Supermoon is a full moon at its closest point in the sky while passing Earth on its elliptical orbit. It looks bigger and brighter in the sky, if you haven't noticed. This phenomenon has a technical name, but we won't go into that. What the heck, it's the perigee-syzygy of the Earth-Moon-Sun system. There, I said it and confused everyone."

The class broke out in laughter, followed by a peaceful silence.

"What's so special about a Supermoon on Mount Palomar at this observatory? Well, believe it or not, the 200-inch Hale Telescope is rarely pointed at the Moon. The full moon is over 50,000 times brighter than the brightest stars. I'm told the total power collected is only 0.02 watts, but Hale's highly sensitive imaging systems still require special precautions. Then there's Earth's atmosphere, the telescope's detraction limit, preventing the viewing of detail necessary for our viewing enjoyment. Special filters might allow us to zoom in to about two kilometers. At that resolution, we can see any equipment we left during the Apollo missions.

It needs to be tighter, and that's where Rick Jones comes in. The New Physics Corporation is working on a project that partly involves surveying the Moon. It's not a big part, but it's also not classified to the extent we can't show Mrs. Strickland's students — my lovely daughter Jenna, who is amongst them — to see Rick's handiwork."

Brian glanced at Jenna and winked at her as she gleamed proudly back at him. He then glanced at Derek.

Brian continued. "And, may I add, her handsome young friend Derek Jones is Rick Jones's son. Derek has expressed a special interest in the Moon." Looking around at the students who looked at him mesmerized, Brian smiled. "This is going to be very cool. For the first time in what I gather is a long time, we will point the Hale Telescope at the Moon after engineers at New Physics Corporation have retrofitted it with classified, shall we say, filters to allow viewing of the surface up to one meter. Impossible, a few scientists here have insisted. We shall see about that. We will view the LEM base and rover tracks closely. If Jenna and Derek would please step to the front, they will take the first look, and then each of you will have a turn." Brian motioned his head toward the front of the crowd, and Derek took Jenna's hand and walked toward him.

"Why do they get to go first," asked Jimmy Foster, whose voice rang out from the back.

Brian smiled, "Because I'm Jenna's dad, and I say so. Is that good enough?"

The students laughed, and Jimmy grinned with a faint smile and shrugged. "Whatever, sir."

"Great attitude; I may have a place for you in our organization," Brian said with a laugh. "If you all will wait here, great non-alcoholic drinks and snacks exist. We'll be right back."

Derek and Jenna looked with wonder as they followed Jenna's parents and Derek's dad to the telescope. As they entered the dome with the 200-inch Hale Telescope, Derek stopped abruptly. Before him stood Anna Bartlett and Jason Johnson. Agent Bartlett approached him and extended her hand, which Derek grasped as he smiled.

"It's good to see you again, Derek," she said with a friendly smile.

"Agent Bartlett! What are you doing here?" Derek replied excitedly, with a big smile.

"Again, you can call me Anna. This is agent Jason Johnson," she replied, nodding to her partner as he approached Derek. They shook hands, and Derek nodded.

"You can call me Jason," replied Agent Johnson.

"Derek and Jenna, if you'll step this way." Brian pulled back two office chairs in front of an oversized monitor. "This high-definition monitor will allow you to observe the lunar surface." Brian lowered his voice and continued in a whisper, "What you're about to see is Project Lunar Pearl."

As Derek surveyed the large wafer-thin screen, his eyes lit up, and his jaw dropped. He looked at Brian, and Brian smiled. Jenna looked at Derek's expression with puzzlement.

"Yes, that is the last Apollo landing site. At least the one on this side," Brian continued.

Jenna exclaimed, "No way."

Derek studied the image. "This is so clear. This can't be real."

"It's genuine, thanks to proprietary equipment from New Physics retrofitted to the Hale Telescope."

"This isn't right," said Derek slowly as he squinted at the screen.

"Care to zoom in closer to get a little more detail?" Brian asked, grinning knowingly.

Derek exchanged glances with Jenna with a perplexed look. Jenna looked at the screen, looked at Derek, and her lips were motioning the word, "What?"

"Derek, I said we could zoom in to one meter, less than one meter, to be precise." Brian's eyes motioned for Derek to look at a device resembling a mouse and a video game joystick to the keyboard's right.

Derek slowly rolled the chair to the keyboard. Not taking his eyes off the screen, he slowly took hold of the peripheral, looked at Brian, and then back at the screen. Instinctively, he manipulated the device, and the screen zoomed in and moved toward the ladder of the Lunar Module. Derek continued to zoom in to see how close he could get. "Why is the lunar rover here? All Apollo missions left the surface."

"All known missions," Brian replied.

"Observatories would have seen it by now," Derek said in a halting voice while zooming.

"Not if it was invisible," replied Brian with a faint smile. "Let's not get ahead of ourselves."

"Whoa!" Derek exclaimed as the ladder steps filled the screen. Then his jaw dropped. "Where is the plaque?" he said slowly.

"There was no plaque on the Lunar Module for Apollo 18," Brian replied, studying Derek's expression.

Jenna looked puzzled and said, "Dad, Apollo 18 was canceled. There's no Apollo 18."

Brian interrupted his daughter and said, "Jenna, Apollo 18 was classified. They wouldn't fund it, so the Pentagon and NASA militarized it. That technology is not ours. There's a lot you don't know, darling, that you need to know now."

"Why, Dad? Why do I need to know?" replied Jenna. "Don't get me wrong, I want to know everything. Irina Spalko said, 'I want to know everything' in Indiana Jones and the Kingdom of the Crystal Skull and look at what happened to her."

Looking at Derek and then back at Jenna with a somber expression, Brian's head slightly moved from side to side, and he scratched the back of his head. He replied to his daughter, "Because you are our daughter, there is a lot you and your mother need to talk about. Trust me. You need to know. Derek needs to know. Now, time waits for no one, so if you'll trust me and pay attention, we must get on with this."

Derek studied Brian's eyes, which were now welling up with tears. Brian wiped the tears away and said, "Derek, this is the landing site. Why do you think the Lunar Module is still there?"

Gasping, Derek replied, "Oh my God, you're right. It shouldn't even be there. You said it's invisible. Do you mean as in cloaked? Are they…" Derek stopped in mid-sentence and exchanged nervous glances with Jenna.

Brian placed his hand on Derek's shoulder. "It should, that is, it should be there. If you zoom out and pan around, you'll notice one set of tracks from a Lunar Rover moving away from the Lunar Module. Follow those tracks.

Derek did as Brian asked, spotted the tracks, and followed them. The tracks ended abruptly. Derek looked up at Brian. "What happened?"

"As the Rover rolled away from the LM, the astronaut's camera picked up a tiny metallic sphere ahead, hovering a few feet above the ground. As they moved forward, the sphere maintained its distance. At the point where the tracks end, the sphere unfurled."

"Unfurled?"

"Opened up into a flat disc that looked like a mirror."

"Opened up? What does that mean?" asked Derek, again exchanging glances with Jenna, who now stood apprehensively beside her chair with her arms folded as she studied her dad's facial expressions.

"It means the sphere, the size of a ball bearing, flattened and transformed into an exotic event horizon. To make a long story short, we call it a dark mirror. Your dad told you about a Dark Mirror Project because of your interest in the Apollo missions. You've got quite an impressive collection of models, autographed photos of every astronaut, except maybe for those on the Apollo 18 and 19 missions."

"Apollo 19?" replied Derek, wide-eyed and rubbing his hand nervously against his neck. Derek's blue eyes began to phosphoresce faintly and seemed to glow slightly as emotion and anxiety overtook him.

Brian continued, studying Derek's eyes and exchanging glances with Agent Bartlett, "I'd like you to meet one of those astronauts who landed a Lunar Module on the far side of the Moon for the Apollo 19 mission."

Brian looked up as Carter Smith approached. A gray-haired man in his 70s, Carter Smith embodied the ideal combination of discipline, intelligence, and charisma, a man who has earned his place as both an astronaut and a

Navy SEAL. His neatly trimmed silver hair and clean-shaven face reflected his precision and professionalism. At the same time, his bright, clear eyes radiated warmth and curiosity, suggesting a genuine passion for exploration and discovery. He carried himself with relaxed confidence from years of navigating high-stakes environments with a calm and steady hand.

Carter's appearance immediately conveyed his status as a seasoned professional. His approachable smile and affable demeanor made him easy to trust. At the same time, his sharp intellect and unwavering focus reminded those around him that he was not just a team player but a leader. Whether in the lab at New Physics Corporation or on high-stakes missions, Carter exuded a sense of calm authority that inspired those working alongside him.

Carter's dual background as an astronaut and Navy SEAL gave him a unique edge, making him equally adept at solving complex scientific challenges and handling high-pressure, tactical situations. His work on the Dark Mirror Project alongside Rick Jones reflected his deep commitment to pushing the boundaries of human knowledge and capability. His ability to bridge the gap between his roles' physical and intellectual demands made him an invaluable asset to the team.

Despite his impressive resume, Carter was grounded and approachable. He shared a close camaraderie with Rick, built on mutual respect and a sense of purpose. Carter's role as a mentor or collaborator to Derek adds another dimension to his character, as his wisdom and experience offer a guiding light to the younger generation.

Carter approached Derek and extended his hand, which Derek shook without hesitation.

"You look confused," Carter said to Derek, "and I don't blame you. First, you learn there was an Apollo 18 mission. The Lunar Module, which you see at a very high resolution, is 'cloaked' like in some science fiction movies to evade detection from observatories on Earth. You find out the astronauts of that mission never returned, and now you find out there's an Apollo 19 mission."

Carter looked at Brian, who nodded, and Carter continued. "Our mission was to look further at the Moon's far side. The video of the sphere ahead of the Lunar Rover on the Apollo 18 mission didn't end with those tracks. It showed the Rover approaching what looked like a mirror that seemed to unfurl from the small metallic sphere ahead of the Rover. At first, we could see the reflection of the Rover in this mirror, but suddenly, it went dark."

After an awkward silence, Derek said, "Then what?"

Carter continued, "Then, there was what appeared to be a structure inside the exotic event horizon, where the mirror transformed into an opening. The mission Commander decided to drive into the opening."

After another awkward silence, Derek said, "And?"

Carter rubbed the back of his head and continued, "There must have been a force field, with some physicists on the project calling it a dimensional membrane, for lack of a better phrase, which contained the atmosphere inside the structure. The Rover passed effortlessly into the opening, which, as I said, we've come to call an exotic event horizon, and remarkable footage of an underground structure was transmitted for over thirty minutes before transmissions abruptly ceased."

Derek asked with impatience, "Then what happened?"

Carter paused and replied, "During the thirty minutes before we lost transmission, the astronauts got out of the Rover. They must have known there was an atmosphere for reasons we cannot explain. They took off their helmets, breathed, and looked around. Then they walked away. We lost transmission."

Carter continued, "Apollo 19 was launched a year later, and I was the Lunar Module Pilot. While in orbit, I observed strange anomalies on the far side, which we thought might be connected. We thought there was a connection between these anomalies on both sides. Navy SEALs were chosen for the mission to train as astronauts because there was a concern that intelligent life was potentially involved, and we had no idea if it was hostile or friendly. I was one of the SEALs. Commander Arthur Wilson was the other SEAL in charge of the mission."

Derek laughed nervously and replied, "You don't mean President Arthur Wilson?"

Carter looked down sadly and replied, "Arthur was my best friend. We trained together as Navy SEALs and, of course, as astronauts. Arthur's recent assassination was especially rough, but we're in good hands with President Abigail Tubman. I have met her and have the utmost confidence in her leadership capabilities. As a black woman, she certainly will blaze a trail on many fronts. Sorry to digress into politics."

During the silence, Carter reflected on Arthur Wilson and Abigail Tubman.

Carter recalled how Arthur's sharp features and intense expression were complemented by a subtle charisma, making him a natural leader among his peers. As part of the Apollo 19 mission alongside Carter Smith, Arthur's pioneering spirit and scientific brilliance came to the forefront. His double PhDs in physics from MIT and Stanford add an unmatched level of expertise to his role, making him both the brains and the brawn of any mission. In this era of his life, Arthur represented the ideal of a man who balances intelligence, strength, and courage, willing to push the boundaries of human exploration.

As President of the United States in 2033, Arthur's full white beard and composed expression added to his gravitas, making him a leader who inspired trust and confidence. His manner was one of calm authority, the kind of presence that reassured a nation even in times of crisis. Arthur's background in physics and his achievements in space exploration lend a unique perspective to his presidency, deeply rooted in scientific understanding and a vision for humanity's future.

Despite his achievements, Arthur remains grounded, his leadership shaped by the lessons learned in the harsh vacuum of space and the grueling battles of political life. His assassination in the explosion of Air Force One was a tragic end to a remarkable life, cutting short a presidency that was as ambitious and forward-thinking as his storied career. His legacy, however, lives on in the people he inspired — including Carter Smith — and the changes he set into motion, including the rise of his Vice President, Abigail Tubman.

President Abigail Tubman was a radiant and commanding presence, embodying elegance, intelligence, and an unshakable sense of purpose. At 62, she was the epitome of grace and poise, her flawless complexion and confident demeanor reflecting the strength and wisdom of a life spent breaking barriers. Her warm, expressive eyes seemed to carry the weight of history while radiating a hopeful, forward-looking spirit that inspired everyone around her.

Abigail's style was sophisticated and signature, with her signature white blazer and form-fitting knee-length skirt highlighting her polished and professional appearance. Every detail of her outfit — crisp, tailored, and graceful — underscored her position as a trailblazer who effortlessly balanced power and charm. Her whole figure, which President Arthur Wilson once jokingly referred to as "eye candy" in conversations with his close friend Carter Smith, complimented her commanding presence, exuding confidence and authenticity.

As a former law school graduate from New York State, Abigail's sharp intellect and passion for justice have been the foundation of her leadership. Her steady rise in politics, combined with her ability to connect with people on a deeply personal level and breaking through the so-called "bulletproof glass ceiling" as the most popular black woman around the world, made her an exceptional leader in the wake of President Wilson's tragic assassination. Abigail's unique ability to navigate personal and political complexities allowed her to lead with a balance of empathy and resolve, which Arthur deeply admired.

Her friendships with Arthur and Carter, cultivated through years of shared values and mutual respect, were a testament to her authenticity. The camaraderie she shared with Arthur, often highlighted during their gatherings at the Round Robin on Pennsylvania Avenue, revealed her ability to form meaningful connections even amidst the pressures of political life. These bonds reinforced her humanity and reminded her of the personal relationships that often influence the course of history.

Sitting sideways on the sofa's edge, as Arthur would often describe, Abigail embodied approachability and dignity. Her relaxed yet intentional posture spoke to her innate ability to balance warmth with authority. She was a leader who commanded respect for her position and the genuine care and determination she brought to her role.

Carter's memories were punctuated with Derek's voice.

"No, that's okay," Derek replied. "I like her too. I learned in my history class that she has quite a fantastic ancestral line."

Brian looked at his watch. "Derek, there is a reason for showing you the truth. We have some good news for you, and it's appropriate, your dad tells you. We thought of telling you about it at dinner in Montecito. Still, we decided to wait until you saw the remnant of a highly classified mission, Apollo 18, and met the one still living astronaut of Apollo 19."

"Sir," said Derek, clearing his throat. "Where are the Apollo 18 astronauts?"

Brian paused somberly and replied, "We don't know. We lost contact with them in that underground structure and have not heard from them since. They are assumed missing in action and very likely dead, to put it bluntly."

Rick Jones approached his son, who was quietly standing with his mom, Asha, after observing him. Placing his hand on Derek's shoulder, Asha came, leaned down, and hugged him. She said, "We love you, Derek, and I wish there were a better way to have acclimated you to what is happening."

"Derek," Rick began, "I need you and Jenna to work as interns at New Physics Corporation. We believe you were being used as a hostage to obtain enough ransom to fund whatever they're up to. The powers you manifested, observed by the CIA, are from your mother's side, from a dormant gene that she believes is only activated under certain circumstances. The government believes you can help us by harnessing your abilities."

"Where does this gene come from?" Derek asked. Then he blurted out, "Am I Pentillion?"

Everyone looked at each other, trying not to react.

"Instead of asking you where you got this thought, Derek, there is much I must tell you, but now is neither the time nor place," Asha replied.

"Why is Jenna involved?" Derek asked, looking at her with concern.

Amara locked eyes with Derek, gently holding his shoulders, and replied, "Jenna is your friend, to put it in simple terms to which you can relate. Your mom says separating you from her since you're so closely bonded through friendship could adversely affect your abilities. First and foremost, Derek, we want you and Jenna to remain together. We've seen how close you two are. Secondly, the government wants you to focus on your summer internship at New Physics and feels Jenna could be a good influence. Does that make sense?"

"Sure, Amara, I'm glad she will be interning with me. Did you know we get extra credits for work related to our area of interest when we go to college?"

Amara smiled and looked at Rick.

"No, I had no idea," replied Rick, looking at his watch. "That's great. Always good to kill two birds with one stone." Looking at Asha, Rick continued, "Or should I say, it's always good to feed two birds with one hand."

Rick looked at Asha again, and she smiled approvingly.

Chapter 2 Darkness on the Far Side

"The moon hangs alien, heavy, like a lock on a door; the door is tightly shut."

— Yevgeny Zamyatin

Dark Mirror Abduction

*P*resident Abigail Tubman thrashed in her bed, caught in the unrelenting grip of the same dream that had haunted her for weeks. The world around her faded, and she was once again drawn into the vivid and unsettling replay:

Air Force One glided over the Atlantic Ocean at 43,000 feet, the deep hum of its engines reverberating through her subconscious. On a screen in her living room in Silver Creek, San Jose, Abigail sat cross-legged on her plush sofa, her fingers nervously tracing the seam of her white blazer. Across the virtual divide, President Arthur Wilson smiled at her from his office aboard the aircraft, his presence as warm and steady as ever.

"Abigail, it's Arthur," he began, his sharp eyes betraying a flicker of unease beneath his familiar calm.

Her lips curved into a soft smile, and the tension in her chest subsided for a fleeting moment. She studied him carefully, as she always did — his silver hair, a testament to decades of service and wisdom, framed his face, which seemed a perfect balance of intellect and kindness. His emerald tie, a signature piece of his wardrobe, glinted under the soft light of his office.

"You look tired, Arthur," she said warmly, though her tone carried a note of concern.

"And you, Abigail, look as stunning as ever," he replied, his eyes alight with admiration. "Moffett Field's preparing for my arrival, I hear. I hope you've got Maggie working her magic in the kitchen."

"She wouldn't have it any other way," Abigail teased, her laugh a quiet ripple of warmth. "Dinner will be unforgettable."

But even as they exchanged lighthearted banter, Abigail noticed something off. Arthur's gaze darted briefly toward the door of his office. A shadow flickered. The lines of his face hardened, and his smile faltered.

"Arthur?" Abigail asked, her voice tinged with worry.

Then she saw it — the doorway behind him seemed to shimmer, bending reality. Figures emerged, their military uniforms oddly alien, and their skin glistened with reptilian scales. Abigail's pulse quickened as one of them tossed a cylindrical object into the room.

Arthur turned back to the screen, his expression ghostly pale. "Abigail…"

The screen dissolved into static, and Abigail's gasp shattered the silence of her dream.

"No!" she cried, bolting upright in her bed. Her chest heaved as she clutched the covers, trying to calm her racing heart. The clock beside her read 1:11 a.m. The absence of her husband's familiar snoring deepened the ache in her chest. "He's gone," she whispered to herself, the memory of his death in Pakistan a fresh wound that refused to heal.

Wrapped in her oversized cotton robe, Abigail went to the kitchen. Maggie, her lifelong friend and confidante, stood across the island, her face etched with concern.

"These dreams again?" Maggie asked softly, sliding a steaming mug of tea toward her.

Abigail nodded, her gaze distant. "I keep seeing Arthur — on Air Force One. The moment it…" She trailed off, her voice cracking.

Maggie leaned closer, her brow furrowed. "What happened, Abby? What did you see?"

Abigail's eyes darted to the window, where the lights of Silicon Valley twinkled like stars. "Walk with me," she said suddenly. "The moon's full tonight. The air might clear my head."

The cool breeze brushed against their robes as they stepped onto the patio. The vast lawn stretched before them, bathed in moonlight. A Secret Service agent nearby fixed his gaze on a peculiar lighted object moving across the sky.

"Everything all right?" Abigail asked, her tone unusually calm.

The agent hesitated. "Yes, ma'am. But that light… it's getting brighter."

Abigail and Maggie exchanged a glance before continuing down the lawn. The wind carried a faint hum, barely audible at first but growing louder. Abigail tilted her head upward, her breath hitching as the stars seemed to vanish one by one, replaced by a vast, glimmering metallic expanse.

"Madam President, you need to get inside!" a Secret Service officer shouted, panic thick in his voice.

Before Abigail could respond, she froze. The officers surrounding her stood rigid, their faces locked in expressions of shock. Even Maggie stumbled, clinging to Abigail's arm as tears filled her eyes.

A small, glowing sphere descended from the colossal object above. It hovered just feet from the ground, shimmering as it flattened into a mirrored disc. Abigail and Maggie stared at their reflections, their wide eyes filled with fear before the image dissolved into darkness.

From the void stepped a figure — a striking woman with flowing braids adorned in a gown that shimmered like a living constellation. Her skin glowed with a warm, golden tan, and her eyes sparkled with mischief.

"Madam President," the woman said, her voice melodic yet commanding. "I am Empress Rastri of Dragos. I bring tidings from across the galaxy."

Abigail's voice was steady, though her heart raced. "What do you want with us?"

Empress Rastri laughed, a sound both musical and unsettling. "Oh, we'll get to that. But first, a little spectacle for your people's social media, no?" She gestured toward the stunned onlookers, their phones raised to capture the surreal scene.

As Abigail stood rooted in place, the Empress leaned closer, her smile fading. "Your moon holds secrets, Madam President. And soon, the balance of your world will shift."

The Empress's words hung in the air like a shroud, their weight sinking into Abigail's chest as the metallic ceiling above began to retreat, the stars slowly returning to the sky.

Abigail's voice trembled as she whispered to Maggie, "This changes everything."

Dome Fly-by

Classified Mission Name: Apollo 19 Dome Fly-by

Mission type: Crewed lunar landing.

Date: Thursday, December 4, 1975.

Mission status: Top-secret.

Operator: NASA, Department of Defense.

"Quite a beautiful sight in the lunar noon sun," Arthur Wilson said, his voice steady but tinged with awe. The vast expanse of the Moon's far side stretched endlessly before them, bathed in a harsh, unfiltered light that seemed to erase every shadow. "If this mission officially existed, I'd send these photos straight to Walter Cronkite. Can you imagine this on the Evening News?" He glanced at Carter Smith, his tone both reverent and laced with irony.

"Still hard to believe people call this the 'dark side,'" Carter replied, his brow furrowing as he adjusted his visor. The lunar surface below, dotted with towering craters and jagged terrain, reflected sunlight with an almost other-worldly brilliance. "If only they could see this side in broad daylight. It's… humbling."

Mick O'Rourke, seated slightly behind them in the cramped command module, let out a low whistle. "Humbling doesn't even begin to cover it," he said, his voice cracking slightly. "'Here, men from Earth first set foot upon the Moon in July 1969 A.D. We came in peace for all mankind.' It gives me goosebumps every time. That plaque — they left it as a promise. And now here we are, fulfilling it in ways they never imagined."

The Apollo 19 crew was flying low over the far side of the Moon, skimming the surface at NASA's behest to photograph the massive Lobachevsky crater. The mission, officially titled "Apollo 19 Dome Fly-by," had a straightforward cover story: to study lunar volcanic domes. But every man on board knew there was more to it.

"Volcanic domes," Mick muttered skeptically as he peered at the camera feed. "Arthur, why is the mission's name classified? These things don't look volcanic to me."

Arthur didn't answer immediately, his eyes narrowing as he studied the domes below. The structures were unnaturally symmetrical, their smooth, reflective surfaces glinting sharply in the sunlight. "They don't look volcanic to me, either," he finally admitted, his voice low.

"And classified names are never for something simple, Mick."

Carter leaned forward, his body tense. "Arthur, are we sure —" He stopped abruptly, his breath hitching as something shimmered on the horizon. A faint light, barely distinguishable from the lunar surface at first, grew brighter. He rubbed the back of his neck and glanced nervously at Arthur. "Do you see that?"

Before anyone could answer, the object broke free from the horizon. It was a perfect sphere, about three meters in diameter, with a surface as smooth and reflective as a liquid mirror. It moved toward them with a slow, deliberate grace, as though it were examining the Apollo 19 module in return.

Carter's voice trembled as he reported, "Mission Control, we have an unidentified flying object. It's spherical, approximately three meters in diameter. The surface is reflective — like polished liquid metal."

The cameras captured every detail. At first, the sphere reflected the stark gray of the Moon's surface, but its mirrored surface began to ripple as it drew closer. Colors began to emerge — deep ruby red, sapphire blue, and vivid emerald green lights danced across its surface, pulsing as though alive. Then, as if the sphere were a window, the colors shifted to reveal a breathtaking view of stars and galaxies. It was as though they were peering through the lens of a cosmic telescope.

"It's showing us the universe," Arthur whispered, his voice cracking under the moment's weight. "My God, it's showing us everything."

The sphere hovered near the window, spinning lazily before drifting away. The astronauts barely had time to process what they'd seen when the sphere accelerated and vanished in the distance. In its place, hundreds of smaller objects appeared — tiny, reflective spheres like fireflies, drifting in random motion across the expanse of space.

"This… this isn't possible," Arthur murmured, his hands trembling as he reached for the camera controls. "They're like fireflies on a summer night. So many of them."

Then, something even stranger unfolded. Farther away, one of the larger spheres began to transform. Its surface expanded and stretched, flattening into a perfect mirrored disc. The edges shimmered faintly as the center turned dark, a void seemingly carved out of space. As a sleek, elongated craft emerged from the disc, the crew watched in stunned silence. Its surface glimmered with the same liquid-metal quality as the sphere, except it had a metallic gold hue, its shape unmistakably engineered — fluid, aerodynamic, and impossibly advanced.

They saw them through the cockpit's transparent bubble. Silhouetted figures moved within the craft, their upper torsos visible as they operated controls. One figure grasped what looked like a steering column, its movements deliberate and calculated.

"Oh my God," Carter breathed, his voice trembling. "Are those… people?"

The craft moved across their field of view with graceful speed, its polished surface reflecting the stark lunar landscape below. Just as it was about to disappear beyond the edge of the window and was facing away from the Apollo 19 Eagle, the English word "StarCar" was emblazoned on the rear of the craft, which was reminiscent of an automobile on Earth. One of the figures turned around and stared out the back window. It was brief — a flash of recognition, an expression of surprise, as though the occupant, a youthful man with stunningly blue luminescent eyes, hadn't expected to be seen.

"Arthur, did you see that?" Carter exclaimed, gripping the console tightly, his face pale. "The occupant is human! The word 'StarCar' is in the English language!"

Arthur's hands shook as he wiped tears from the corner of his eyes. "I saw it," he said quietly, his voice thick with emotion. "NASA, did you see that?" He reached instinctively for the communications console.

Static filled the cabin.

Carter's voice was tight with tension. "We're in a blackout."

The three men sat silently, staring out the window as the StarCar raced away and disappeared on the lunar horizon. Tiny spheres continued their slow, random drift, like stars scattered across a velvet sky. The emptiness of the Moon's far side suddenly felt alive, charged with the presence of something vast and incomprehensible.

Arthur finally broke the silence, his voice barely audible. "If this mission doesn't officially exist, then neither does what we've just seen."

Mick, still staring at the void beyond, shook his head slowly. "We exist, Arthur. But I don't think we're writing the story anymore."

Event Horizon Mirror

"**M**irrored exotic event horizon," murmured CIA Special Agent Anna Bartlett as she flipped through pages of a three-hole-punched binder.

"Excuse me?" said Major Carter Smith, former Apollo 19 astronaut, as his memories of the dome fly-by abruptly halted on hearing Anna's voice.

Looking at Carter, Agent Bartlett replied, "That got your attention."

"That was secondary, Agent Bartlett," replied Carter. "It's all there."

The glass pitcher of iced water, covered with beads of condensed water, was the primary focus of Major Carter Smith's stare. Removing his wire-frame spectacles, the 70-year-old retired astronaut and Navy SEAL stared at the pitcher, took a breath on each lens, and wiped off the fog with a clean white handkerchief.

Anna Bartlett smiled politely as she looked over the conference room table and surveyed his indigo-blue silk cardigan sweater with a black collar. An embroidered NASA patch was on one side of the cardigan, and on the opposite side was a NASA Wings badge with a navy-blue background, embroidered and framed in white thread, with the name CARTER SMITH below the white extended wings of an Eagle. The NASA emblem replaced the eagle's body between the wings.

"Don't you want to take that off?" Agent Bartlett grinned.

"Take off what?"

"The NASA sweater. You're sweating."

"May I have a glass of water, Agent Bartlett?" he asked deliberately as he slowly put on his now cleaned wire-frame glasses and removed the sweater.

"Why, of course, that's what it's there for, Major Smith," replied Agent Bartlett as she laid the binder on the conference room table, stood, and quickly brushed down her snug, form-fitting knee-length black business skirt. Taking the pitcher, she bent slightly and poured iced water into a sparkling clear glass. Major Smith couldn't help but glance at her solid athletic figure and form-fitting business skirt. The white blouse was unbuttoned at the top. She caught his glance, smiled politely yet scolded, and slowly slid the tray over the conference table. Quickly moving his gaze away from her skirt, he nodded, took a few gulps from the glass, finished half of it, and smiled.

"It's hot out there, and I see you're hot too," Carter Smith said. "Thanks, Agent Bartlett." Then he backtracked. "I mean, I see you're not wearing a sweater, so you must be hot; uh, I meant to say that my body burns hotter than most in high temperate climates; uh, what I meant to say is…"

"You're welcome," she interrupted with a polite smile. "Tell me about how hot it is outside! The air-conditioning is kicking in full blast, but I think the ambient heat from the runway had its lingering effects. The weather is chilly in D.C. Walking down to the tarmac from that air-conditioned Air Force jet was like being in a scorching inferno. Entering this Air Force facility felt like paradise, like jumping into an iced cold pool." Pausing, Agent Bartlett poured herself a glass of water, slowly sipped it, and continued, looking intently at Major Smith over the conference room table. "Enough with the small talk, Major Smith."

Glancing up at a camera in the corner of the conference room, Major Smith smiled and surveyed agent Bartlett's deep green eyes, glancing at her earrings with teardrop emeralds and straight, thick auburn hair parted slightly to the right, pulled back severely with a wavy ponytail flowing over her left shoulder. Then he smiled and took another sip of water.

"I must say, Agent Bartlett, I feel old sitting across from you. I'm reminded of my lovely daughter."

"How is Rebecca?" Agent Bartlett asked, breaking her stare into Major Smith's spectacled brown eyes, then glancing at his military-cut black and silver hair, thick black eyebrows, and his pale but very youngish-looking complexion for a 70-year-old man.

"She's doing very well, thank you. She just passed the bar exam."

Agent Bartlett leaned forward and said approvingly, "Congratulations."

Major Smith smiled and replied, "Thank you. I know you want to get to the point. Starting a bit earlier from the mirrored exotic event horizon reference you mentioned, we found a manufactured object similar to an earlier discovery in 1947 at Area 51 in Nevada from the wreckage of a UFO that crashed in Roswell, New Mexico. The object we found on our Apollo 19 mission was returned to Earth in secrecy by Apollo 19, a classified crewed mission to the Moon, through a mirrored exotic event horizon."

"A mirrored exotic event horizon," replied Agent Bartlett in a bemused tone. "I've done my homework, and wormholes do not have exotic event horizons."

"The wormhole I'm talking about is no ordinary one, like you might read about in a physics book, Agent Bartlett," continued Carter in a matter-of-fact tone. "Apollo 19 astronauts, myself one of them, and my crew mate Commander Arthur Wilson, made a secret landing on the far side of the Moon to study unusual and massive dome-like structures in craters. During our mission, we photographed the domes in a fly-by of the far side and then landed the Lunar Module to investigate these anomalies."

"President Wilson's passing was very tragic," agent Bartlett responded.

"Yes, it was," replied Carter, bowing his head. "He was not just my crew mate, but my best friend. We were assigned to training as Navy SEALs back in the seventies before Apollo 19. It's funny how envious I was of his chiseled, almost perfect athletic physique, strength, and ability to maneuver in situations I struggled to master. We grew old, and he became President of the United States. Arthur was still very handsome, bald yet so stately with that pure white beard and mustache." Major Smith downed the remaining water. "I'm digressing. Sorry about that."

"No need to apologize," said Agent Bartlett. "I was floored when I saw a photo of him as a Navy SEAL on a combat mission. I thought, what a looker."

Major Smith laughed as he looked around the conference room. Then he looked into Agent Bartlett's eyes and said, "' When I look at the moon, I do not see a hostile, empty world. I see the radiant body where man has taken his first steps into a frontier that will never end. Do you know who said this, Agent Bartlett?"

Agent Bartlett looked puzzled at the quote and said, "No, not off the top of my head. Who?"

"David Scott, Commander, Apollo 15."

Agent Bartlett leaned forward, clasping her hands before her on the conference table, and looked at him questioningly.

Smiling and giving Agent Bartlett a piercing stare, Major Smith continued, "That haunting quote came to mind for some reason. Here's another quote. 'The moon hangs alien, heavy, like a lock on a door; the door is tightly shut.' Science fiction author Yevgeny Zamyatin, who was George Orwell's inspiration, made this observation." Major Smith leaned forward and whispered, "We found the key, Agent Bartlett, and the door is ajar."

Agent Bartlett felt goosebumps pulse over her body as she gave Major Smith a startled look.

"Continuing my last train of thought, Agent Bartlett. I started appreciating women when Martha came into my life, and we married. Arthur and I talked about women peripherally, and I remember commiserating with him at a bar over drinks. I regrettably recall commenting that I was lucky to get his 'table scraps.' We were crude in the day, but we both evolved into gentlemen. At least, I think so."

"How much did the Department of Defense reveal to you about the scope and grandeur of your mission?" asked Agent Bartlett.

As Major Smith suspected, military personnel sat in an adjacent conference room and watched the interview on a large monitor.

Glancing at the camera, Major Smith replied, "The Department of Defense was placed in charge of NASA missions after Apollo 17, as I'm sure many civilians suspect. Subsequent missions were classified as top-secret, on a 'need to know' basis, and launched from a secret site in Russia. The technology was said to be based on extraterrestrial vehicles found in previous Apollo missions. Originally a J-class mission using the Extended Lunar Module retrofitted with hardware using physics that is classified, capable of a three-day stay minimum on the Moon, and carrying the lunar rover, Apollo 19 was launched in Russia at a similar launch facility as Cape Canaveral, Florida."

Anna replied, "What was your mission?"

"To evolve into gentlemen, ma'am?" replied Major Smith with a slight smile.

"Why recruit Navy SEALs as astronauts," Agent Bartlett said, without reacting to Major Carter's answer, then leaned forward, keenly staring at Carter Smith while grasping her hands. "Why is the military involved?"

Carter glanced at her diamond wedding band. "You're married, agent Bartlett? I heard you were single," Carter said. "Sorry to sound nosey. I should have just answered your question."

"No, you're right; I am single, widowed, to be precise. My husband Mike Bartlett, a brother of yours, died on a mission in Afghanistan after being abducted by the Taliban. He was held in the mountains, in a cave system, and never found except for our wedding band that was mysteriously returned to the base."

"I am so sorry, my apologies for bringing it up, Agent Bartlett. I lost a friend that way in a gunfight with barbarians on the far side. Mick

O'Rourke, Apollo 19's Command Module Pilot. A sniper took him out."

"No apology is needed. I am so sorry."
Pausing thoughtfully, Agent Bartlett said,
"What do you mean on the far side?"

Major Smith lowered his head to collect his
thoughts and replied, "Did I say that? I meant
in a remote area of Afghanistan, of course. You
surely have done the research."

"Indeed, I have. I'm sorry for your friend.
Mick O'Rourke sounds familiar. I wonder if
my husband and he knew one another. My husband worked at NASA around the time Mick
was on the Moon. I had no idea at the time that
Mike was involved in Apollo 19, as it was top
secret. No matter. As you were saying, Major
Smith?"

"You know what's blowing my mind,
Agent Bartlett?"

"What's that?"

"Mick died around the same time as Mike.
His wedding band was returned to the base."

"I always wondered who returned his wedding band," said Agent Barnett, looking shaken
momentarily, then regaining her composure.

"Such a long way to return a wedding
band," Major Smith said in almost a whisper.

"You mean from the far side of Afghanistan," replied Agent Bartlett as she searched Major Smith's eyes. "Well, yes, they told me Mike's body was never found. Where do you think it is? He needs a proper burial at Arlington cemetery."

Major Smith immediately looked away, then at the camera. "I wish that I could tell you. I'm sorry."

Anna immediately flashed back to the knock on the door she received, seeing Mike's ring gently placed into her hand, grasping the ring, and collapsing onto the floor before the Navy SEALS and crying hysterically. Her eyes glazed over, and then she regained her composure.

Carter reached over, took the glass pitcher of iced water, poured himself another glass, and raised the pitcher to Anna. After she shook her head politely, Carter sipped it and continued. "The Apollo 19 mission was focused on the Lobachevsky lunar crater landing site on the Moon's far side. We arrived during daylight hours, and the theater was quite a site."

"The theater? You speak like a military man," replied Agent Bartlett as she twirled her wedding ring. "Continue."

"I was a Navy SEAL, Agent Bartlett, and trained as an astronaut for this mission. To continue, a satellite placed some miles above the lunar surface transmitted all communication between NASA and us since direct communication is impossible on the far side. However, sometimes our communications were blacked out, and we couldn't communicate with NASA."

"Tell me about the domes, Carter. May I call you Carter?"

"Absolutely. May I call you Anna?"

"Sure."

"Ah, the domes, Anna, the domes." Carter lifted his glasses and brushed away a small tear in his eye. "They haunt me to this day. Unusual sparkling glassy domes initially thought as land features, appearing like lunar volcanic domes with obsidian surfaces, were the tops of massive buried transparent geodesic domes."

"As in artificial or natural geologic phenomenon, Carter?"

"I'm sorry if I'm about to sound rude. Did you hear what I just said, Anna? As in manufactured domes with exposed curved sides extruding 10 meters above the massive crater floor, constructed of thick glass-like materials."

Anna felt goosebumps and an icy chill simultaneously. She had a flashback of Mike tossing and turning in bed, repeatedly saying, "Oh my God, glass domes. No!" When he woke and sat up, his pajamas blotched in sweat. Mike always told Anna he didn't remember saying that and sometimes experienced a heart arrhythmia episode so severe that Anna would call 911. He would be taken to the emergency room.

"Mike talked in his sleep while working for NASA. He referred to 'glass domes.' Constructed?" asked Anna as her voice faintly trembled.

Carter paused, giving her a spooky stare. Anna began to feel goosebumps pulsate over her entire body once again. For a moment, she thought, "I'm going to be sick," and felt disoriented, but she quickly righted herself, taking a few deep breaths, sipping water, and taking a bite out of a small piece of ice. She heard a faint motor sound and knew a camera was zooming in on her.

"Are you all right, Anna?" Carter asked.

"I'm fine, Carter. Please continue."

"That's right, Anna. After landing nearby, Arthur and I filmed each other walking on the sloped surfaces of these dome extrusions. We also photographed the inside of the structures through the glass. Other high-resolution camera footage was taken by positioning the cameras on the domes, aimed downwards toward the interior structures when the sun was at an angle where the insides were illuminated."

"Those must have been expansive domes. Where is this footage?"

"The Department of Defense, of course. The footage revealed military vehicles and about a dozen humanoid figures in military uniform that I didn't recognize."

"Were these humanoid figures human or otherwise?"

Carter gulped down the last of his water, stared at Agent Bartlett, then looked up and directly toward the camera. Agent Bartlett couldn't resist slightly rolling her eyes, realizing he knew their interview was under observation.

"Both," Carter replied. "I'll never forget exclaiming, 'Mission Control! My God, there are soldiers down there!' And I was referring to humans and, shall we say, other humanoids." Carter fought back tears, and Anna quickly wiped a tear away that welled up in her eye.

"Tell me about the spheres, Carter."

"In my periphery, I noticed a swarm of tiny mirrored spheres the size of ball bearings hovering next to my helmet."

"Ball bearings? Estimate their size."

"Half an inch, give or take. They were slightly different sizes. Some were so tiny their presence was only betrayed by glints of reflecting light. They were so reflective and perfectly smooth. I could see my reflection in them. I stared straight ahead, keeping my periphery sight of tiny objects hovering around my helmet like insects. Some of the spheres remained motionless and appeared to float weightless without any interference from lunar gravity. And so, I turned, facing one of them, reached up, and touched it. The object moved slightly to my touch. I can only describe the effect as how a weightless helium balloon floating in the air might feel, as it might move by the touch of a finger from inertia. It didn't seem to react to my touch intelligently. The Moon has low gravity, but nothing floats without dropping from gravity. These objects were odd in that if I touched them, inertia would cause them to keep moving, whereas these objects moved slightly and stopped abruptly."

"You took one of these objects, I understand."

"Yes. Reaching up and firmly taking the object into my hand, I examined it. Interrupted by a voice, I quickly placed the object into a pocket of my space suit."

"What happened next?"

"A transmission of another astronaut that sounded vaguely like Mick, only I wasn't sure because there was static interference," exclaimed Carter. "He said,' Aim your camera to the north! Hurry!' and so I did."

Carter paused.

Agent Bartlett said impatiently, "And?"

"I slowly moved the camera angle up, away from the military vehicles and soldiers on the floor of the stadium-sized dome interior, to the horizon. A light approached from the horizon. As it hovered closer, the shape of a sphere about three meters in diameter with a mirrored finish became visible. I could see my reflection on its mirrored surface. I exclaimed, 'Mission Control, we have a bogie approaching from the north horizon! Oh my God!' My heart rate kept climbing on seeing it, and I wondered if I would have a heart attack. A woman's voice, barely understandable through high static, said, 'Carter, your heart rate is too high; you must relax using the techniques you learned.' So, I used the technique my psychologist, Dr. Rabinovich, taught me. I was certain it was her voice over the microphone."

Anna leaned forward and said, "Alexandria Rabinovich? Describe this object."

"Yes, Dr. Alex, as some called her. As I
continued filming the sphere, as it drew closer,
I could see its mirrored surface, which looked
like liquid metal. Deep ruby red, sapphire blue
and emerald green lights flashed. Then the
sphere started reflecting sparkling points of
light as if from inside of it, pulsating in gem-
like emerald green, and like a lens, it came into
focus, followed by the image of stars and galaxies."

"You mean, like peering through a telescope at distant celestial objects?"

"Yes, Anna! Suddenly, I heard a voice
cracking with static on our audio channel. I
asked, "Mick, is that you?" He said, "This is a
transmission from NASA. When you see the
inside of the NASA hangar to your north, move
toward it and enter it. You must do so immediately." Carter continued in almost a whisper, "I
was thinking this cannot be happening."

Carter's glasses started to fog up; he removed them and wiped them slowly with his
handkerchief.

"What did you do then?"

"Arthur and I looked at each other with
astonishment as the three-meter sphere flattened into a circular vertical wall, about 6 meters in diameter, with a mirrored finish. The
edges of the surface were so thin. I walked to

the edge and looked sideways at this flat disc to gauge its thickness, and the disc disappeared. Only something nanometers thin or less could vanish when viewed from a side angle. I remember exclaiming in a forced whisper, my voice starting to freeze from fear, 'It has no depth.'" I placed my hand on the thin edge of the disc and immediately withdrew it because I would swear it would start to breach the outer membrane like butter, like the razor-sharp blade of a knife. It's like it was so thin it could have decapitated my fingers. It was very fortunate I barely grazed it with my suit glove, or it would have caused my suit to depressurize.

Agent Bartlett stared intently into Carter's eyes searchingly, trying to detect whether he was truthful or lying.

Carter continued. "The mirrored finish changed into what appeared like a massive circular movie screen, with the bottom part of the circle extruding into the lunar surface so there was a flat area from the lunar surface to a paved surface, showing the familiar image of the inside of a large aircraft hangar at NASA on Earth. Men in NASA work suits were moving about their business. I could even hear the distant sounds of birds chirping and a breeze through my external mic. I recall us exchanging glances and asking Arthur that I wondered how the sphere was orienting itself to the surface of both worlds. I felt a tug from higher gravity just behind the exotic event horizon. We were in shock, and I thought, 'It's 1975, for God's sake. This technology doesn't exist! How is there no explosive decompression? What is preventing it? Then he walked into my view."

"Who walked into your view, Carter?"

Carter fought back tears, and his voice stammered. "Mick O'Rourke."

Carter bowed his head, began to cry, and immediately raised his head and took a deep breath, and a forced calm abruptly took over.

"Carter, this makes no sense. Mike O'Rourke was the mission's Command Module Pilot. He was in orbit around the Moon in the Command Module. Perhaps it was someone who looked like him?"

"No, it was Mick. It was Mick. Slowly walking toward the hangar in disbelief, we instinctively put our fingers through the opening to feel if there was a force field, for lack of a better phrase. Then we walked into the hangar, and Mick greeted us. We stood there in shock and disbelief, staring at each other and our surroundings, and as we gazed around at the massive hangar, Arthur pointed back toward the exotic event horizon, then pointed at Mick."

"Again, how did you 'enter' the hanger from the surface of the Moon?" asked Anna.

"We walked through the exotic event horizon based on our debriefing."

"Exotic event horizon? You keep using that terminology. I need clarification. I know it's a wormhole that violates known laws of physics."

Carter leaned back, stared at the ceiling, and replied, "Well, that is what I've heard it called. I've heard it also called 'spooky action at a distance.' Each particle on the surface of this exotic matter, perhaps some form of dark matter, is connected by a micro wormhole to a particle on the surface of exotic matter in a distance, in this case, in the hangar. Space becomes folded on the surface. This wormhole must be imbued with artificial intelligence to prevent explosive decompression between the Earth and Moon's surface."

Carter stood up, walked to a whiteboard, and picked up a blue marker. Drawing two dots on each side of the whiteboard, he asked, "What is the shortest point of distance between these two dots?"

Anna laughed. "I know the answer to that one! The shortest point is zero."

Carter laughed. "This is how we walked from the Moon's surface into the NASA hangar on Earth."

Anna rolled her eyes and folded her arms.

"Anna, all particles on the surface of the two exotic event horizons connect to form a larger wormhole. In the array of particles that form the origin and destination, each particle's proverbial 'front' faces the wormhole's opening, and the 'back' of each same particle faces the exit. As I digress, upon stepping through the exotic event horizon and entering the hangar, there was a glow around our suits as if some force field, for lack of a better term, was enveloping us through the passage. The theory is that some form of quantum intelligence is imbued in exotic matter in these so-called 'dark mirrors,' forming the exotic event horizons."

Anna interrupted Carter and said, "Dark mirrors?"

"That is their government designation. That's the only way I can explain how there was no explosive decompression when the exotic event horizon opened for us. On entering, we suddenly felt Earth's gravity kick in. We both temporarily lost balance as we adjusted to the sudden feeling of increased weight on our bodies from Earth's gravity. Turning slowly, I looked back to see the Moon's surface and dome through a circular mirrored surface like the one I entered. The vision was surreal, and I have dreamt about it for decades. The opening we stepped through collapsed into a tiny inch sphere that hovered above the hangar's concrete floor. A man in a white lab coat approached it as the sphere moved into an open metal container, seemingly driven by some form of intelligence, and he then closed the container. Others in lab coats, office attire, and military uniforms converged on us. The man in the lab coat said, 'Please come this way for a debriefing.' We followed him to a large conference room."

"What did Mick have to say?"

"He was gone. I later ran into him in a bar, and he told me how he claimed he got back to Earth."

"And?"

"He claims to have crawled through a smaller exotic event horizon that passed through the wall of the Eagle, opened inside the compartment, saw the hangar and crawled into it, and emerged on the concrete floor of the hanger where we emerged. The Eagle orbited the Moon until it crashed."

"Carter, please excuse me for a moment," Anna replied, standing abruptly and walking out of the conference room.

Walking down the corridor, Agent Bartlett entered another conference room with military personnel, including Five-star Generals. CIA Director Arlin Conway stood and motioned her to take an empty seat.

"We owe you an apology, Agent Bartlett," Arlin Conway began. "I felt you best hear it from Major Smith so that he would sense genuine surprise in your reaction. Rest assured, you will be fully debriefed on the program known as Project Dark Mirror. You are now reassigned to the CIA office in Los Angeles, California, where you will be debriefed at a government contractor company, New Physics Corporation. I will be in that debriefing and answer any questions you have — undoubtedly, you will have many."

Wiping tears, Anna replied, "Mike was there."

The room was silent.

Anna continued, "Where is Mike?"

Surveying the men and women in military uniform sitting around the large conference table, Agent Bartlett looked up at the screen. Carter Smith stared into space, slowly sipping water.

Anna asked, "Am I done interviewing Major Smith, Director Conway?"

"Not at all, Agent Bartlett, not at all," replied the CIA Director in a deliberately calm tone. "You're just getting started. Major Smith will be working with you at New Physics. However, before your assignment at New Physics, someone wants to debrief you further in the conference room directly to your left when you walk out the door."

"Thank you, Director Conway." Anna paused and continued, "Mike is still alive. I know it." She was met by silence. The response gave her goosebumps.

"Down the hall, Agent Barlett," said Director Conway. "You know the conference room."

Anna walked out of the conference room, down the corridor, and entered another conference room. It was dimly lit, and a video of a spacecraft that Anna immediately recognized as Apollo played on the wall-sized, high-resolution flat panel monitor. In front of the screen at the end of the conference table, a woman was sitting in a chair facing the video with her back to the door, her golden-blonde hair falling slightly behind the top of the ergonomic chair.

"I gather you recognize that spacecraft, Agent Bartlett?" the woman asked, picking up a remote control and hitting pause.

"It's Apollo. I display a model in my office from Mike's collection."

"My condolences for your loss, Agent Bartlett," the woman said. "I wanted to stop by and tell you what a fine man he was. He died on the far side with honor."

"You mean on the far side of Afghanistan," Anna quipped.

The woman pivoted around in her chair, facing Anna. "Mike was a good man, our finest. The specifics of his death are on a need-to-know basis and at the highest classified level."

"He was with a SEAL team on the far side when he died," Anna said quietly and resolutely, "wasn't he? Not on the far side of Afghanistan. Let's cut the b.s. and say it was on the far side of the Moon. Did they go back the same way, through the exotic event horizon? Did they join military personnel inside the dome area?"

The woman stared at Anna silently. An eerie silence engulfed the conference room for a few very long moments.

"Yes, Mike was a good man," Anna proudly continued. "Without a shadow of doubt, he still is. I am shocked and honored to finally meet you, Director Questar."

"Please, Anna — may I call you Anna?"

"Why, of course? May I call you Sharon?"

Sharon smiled and said, "Absolutely." Motioning to a chair near where Anna stood, Sharon continued, "Please, Anna, sit down. I have something to show you that is highly relevant to your understanding of dark mirrors or, as some call them, mirrored exotic event horizons."

Sharon Questar exuded an air of authority and intelligence, perfectly befitting her role as a high-ranking intelligence director in the United States government. Her sharp, angular features conveyed a no-nonsense demeanor, while her piercing eyes reflected a mind always working several steps ahead. Her golden-blonde hair was styled neatly, complementing her polished appearance and professional confidence.

Her poised expression suggested a woman who thrived under pressure, unshaken by the chaos around her. Yet, there's a certain warmth to her gaze, a hint of empathy that balanced her otherwise formidable presence. Dressed impeccably in a tailored suit, Sharon's appearance spoke volumes about her meticulous nature and unwavering commitment to her role. Carrying herself with a natural elegance, her commanding presence set her apart from others in the intelligence community. She radiated a sense of control and decisiveness in a high-stakes meeting or overseeing a critical mission.

Beneath her composed exterior was a sharp intellect and a deep understanding of the complexities of global and political dynamics.

Anna sat down and replied, "That was quite a revelation from Carter Smith. Especially since I've spent countless sleepless nights wondering what happened to Mike."

"Well, Major Smith has top-secret information, such as his mention of the mirrored exotic event horizons, also called dark mirrors. Let me ask you, Anna, what is your understanding of how the Apollo missions got to the Moon?"

Anna paused thoughtfully and replied, "I don't think I follow you, Sharon."

"The Eagle and Command Module or CM containing the astronauts transported them from launch to orbit around the Moon and returned them to Earth. Would you agree this statement is correct, Anna?"

"Yes, that is correct."

Looking at her laptop, Sharon continued. "The CM was about 11 feet tall, by almost 13 feet in diameter, and weighed about 12,250 pounds." Sharon paused thoughtfully. "The CM was atop a Service Module or SM, with a propulsion engine and RCS with propellants, including a fuel cell power generation system containing liquid hydrogen and liquid oxygen reactants. The module was almost 25 feet by almost 13 feet. The lunar flight version weighed about 51,000 pounds."

Anna almost laughed after thinking she could have Googled that information herself.

Sharon looked up at Anna with a haunted expression and glassy eyes. "Anna, several hundred miles from Earth, the Apollo 18 CM shutdown."

"Shutdown?"

"The engines failed."

"And then?"

"Nothing. The astronauts could not restart the engines. There was a massive failure. All hope was lost."

"Sharon, please don't tell me the conspiracy nuts were right, and the rest was done in a Hollywood studio?"

"No, Anna, the Apollo missions up to the top-secret Apollo 19, preceded by the follow-up Apollo 18, went by the numbers."

"Then did they perish in Apollo 18?" Anna replied with bewilderment.

"The mission was a success. Well, sort of. Apollo 18 made it to the Moon; the astronauts walked on it and drove a lunar rover to an internal government audience of enthusiastic supporters, but they never returned home." Sharon swept her hair behind her ear.

"Then they did die?"

"We don't know. The rover drove through a mirrored exotic event horizon that Major Smith told you about." Sharon leaned back in her chair and studied Anna's confused expression.

Anna finally replied thoughtfully, "A dark mirror? To where?"

"Good question, Anna. According to NASA's top-secret reports, they drove into the mirrored exotic event horizon or dark mirror into what appeared like an underground lunar structure. They could see the inside of this structure through the exotic event horizon directly in front of the rover, and they chose to drive forward. Then it closed. You are about to see a highly classified video showing the astronauts driving the lunar rover into the dark mirror."

"Who took this video?" Anna interrupted, looking increasingly perplexed.

"In the instance of the astronauts driving the lunar rover into the dark mirror on the lunar surface, the video was taken from the Lunar Module. You will be debriefed further at New

Physics Corporation on additional video and data transmitted to NASA." Sharon pressed the play button.

Anna and Sharon watched the video of the rover moving across the lunar soil, and suddenly, a glint of light appeared ahead. It sparkled.

"What is that?" exclaimed Anna.

"It's a mirrored sphere, too tiny to see, but NASA thinks it caught the sun's reflection."

The glint of sparkling light suddenly expanded into a large mirrored disc, and the rover stopped. The disc went dark momentarily, then revealed an internal structure. After a few moments, the rover moved into the opening as bluish light pulsated across its outer hull at the line of demarcation for its entry.

"How did they know to drive into it?" asked Anna.

"We have been asking that very question, Anna, without coming to a plausible conclusion," Sharon replied, pausing the video after the rover was inside the structure and continuing, "This remarkable footage was transmitted for over thirty minutes before transmissions abruptly ended, and the dark mirror collapsed into a tiny metallic sphere that hovered over the lunar surface."

"That is unbelievable, to say the least," Anna said and raised her hand to her head.

"Are you all right, Anna?" Sharon asked with concern.

"I felt a sensation of dizziness, but it has subsided. I could use a glass of water."

"Let's take a walk to the coffee machine. There's also a water cooler there. Then we can talk."

Chapter 3 Quasi-Human

"To see a world in a grain of sand and a heaven in a wildflower, hold infinity in the palm of your hand and eternity in an hour."

— William Blake

Project Hush

"**M**adam President, Abby, we are ready to proceed with Project Hush, which we will also refer to as Operation Hush," said Sharon Questar, Director of the NSA, as she sat on a sofa in the Oval Office across from President Abigail Tubman.

Abigail Tubman sat on a sofa across from Sharon Questar, a coffee table separating them. Leaning forward and adjusting her white skirt, Abigail lifted a silver teapot and asked, "More tea, Sharon?"

"No thanks, Abby," Sharon said with a smile.

"It's steeped with my favorite organic peppermint grown on The White House grounds."

"It's delicious," Sharon replied, her voice wholehearted.

Abigail poured herself a cup, lifted and inhaled the rising steam with a blissful look, and sat up straight while staring intensely at Sharon. An elegant African American woman, Abigail's flowing shoulder-length black hair, form-fitting signature business skirt, and all-white blazer projected her understated look with sparse jewelry consisting of only a pearl necklace and matching earrings, a diamond wedding band, and an eternally optimistic smile. Sharon regretted telling the President something that would compromise the glowing smile that always brought light into her dark, covert world at the National Security Agency.

After taking a sip of tea, Abigail looked intently at Sharon. "Let's end the suspense, Sharon. You were going to tell me about Project Hush. That somber look on your face tells me the reason for this project is not good."

"Indeed, it's not, Abby." Leaning forward, Sharon continued, "Let's cut to the chase. There is an assassination plot against you, and our best intelligence agencies designed Hush to expose it."

Abigail sipped her tea in silence while staring into Sharon's eyes.

Nervously running her fingers through her straight shoulder-length blonde hair with golden highlights, Sharon continued, "Try Vice President Niles Milan and CIA Director Arlin Conway."

Abigail almost dropped her steaming tea but held on to the porcelain cup without spilling a drop as it sloshed dangerously to the gold edge.

"Continue," Abigail said with a slightly quivering voice.

"Well, where to begin? There are two components of Hush. One, President Wilson, who was believed assassinated when his body disintegrated in the fiery crash of Air Force One from sabotage, is still alive."

Abigail gasped, and her hand trembled as she lowered the teacup to the table. "Continue," she said, her voice quivering more.

"Vice President Milan and CIA Director Conway are plotting to assassinate you by having a CIA psychologist, Dr. Alexandria Rabinovich, use mind control through a combination of drugs and hypnosis to program a minor child; well, I promised my teen son not to call teens children. The boy is a high school student in Los Angeles, California, who is seventeen years of age, whose name is Derek Jones, who is slated for conditioning through drugs and hypnosis to follow CIA kill orders. Those kill orders will include assassinating the President of the United States."

Abigail squinted and shook her head. "Does the child know?"

Sharon shook her head and replied, "Of course not. Children are angels that are easily beguiled."

Abigail responded haltingly, "Oh. My. God. This is unbelievable. First, how could a teen get past the Secret Service to commit such a dastardly deed? Secondly, how can our own Central Intelligence Agency train teens to do their dirty work?"

"This is no ordinary teen. This teen is the grandson of retired CIA agents Ray and Caroline Jones, the latter a physicist whose knowledge of quantum physics was used for special black operations assignments reporting to CIA Director Arlin Conway. Indeed, Caroline Jones's IQ has been measured. Are you ready? 320."

Abigail put her head back and looked at Sharon in disbelief, paused thoughtfully, and said, "Have you heard the famous quote by Frederick Douglass from the Life and Times of Frederick Douglass in 1892? It said, 'Knowledge unfits a child to be a slave.'"

Sharon paused thoughtfully and said, "Theoretically, there is no upper limit to an IQ score, and as regards Derek Jones, a child of any IQ should never become enslaved or exploited. Derek's grandmother, Carolyn Jones, was tested five times because we considered the IQ result impossible each time. This ordinary woman is beautiful and healthy for her age, socially active in high society and the arts, and loves reading children's stories at elementary schools. Kids love her. Ray and Caroline Jones have been invited to Arlin Conway's estate for dinner and social events. Their relationship appears to be purely cordial. Here is where it gets interesting. Caroline Jones has DNA unlike anything scientists have seen. While analyzing samples of her DNA as part of the hiring process at the CIA, anomalies in her samples resulted in those samples getting forwarded to genetics labs worldwide that work with the CIA. It's like other anomalous DNA samples on file at the Pentagon."

"Sharon, when you say anomalous DNA, surely you don't mean the DNA is not human?"

"Why do you ask that question, Abby?"

"Well, in working to gain access to records about Roswell and the UFO phenomenon, perhaps to satisfy my morbid curiosity and because I'm told that's what past Presidents have done, I ran across information there are 'anomalous' DNA samples of humans on file in government archives. So far, I have never got much farther."

Sharon leaned back, looked thoughtfully, and replied, "Perhaps it's because that is past your pay grade, Madam President." Pausing to gauge Abigail's expressionless reaction, she continued, "Human, yes, but a better way of stating this DNA's nature is that it's quasi-human. It's like an entirely different species of human, far more advanced. It changes."

"Changes?"

Sharon paused as if trying to find words to elaborate on her comment. "Abby, you know the rules. My bad for approaching that line in the sand. Taking a few steps back, let me avoid straying off the reservation with our discussion. I'm not a geneticist and don't completely understand everything I've read. However, it suffices to say that this DNA could help solve many problems humans face, such as genetic diseases and cancers and yes, even aging. To get back to the issue, Derek Jones has this unique DNA and has expressed an extraordinarily high level of intelligence. His IQ requires clearance above my level."

Abigail whispered with a faint smile, "Even your level? That is indeed rich. That's absurd, Sharon. I thought you had access to, well, everything. I'll be glad to log in and tell you."

"Not everything. And you don't have access to it either, Madam President. That's how far down the rabbit hole it hides. As I was going to say, it's high enough to be classified and available to people higher than you or myself, so it might exceed Caroline Jones's clearance level, considering my clearance level can access her file and IQ. Usually, high IQs, even in the realm of the Einsteins of this world, are problematic and impact social behavior, so I'm told. Yet, Derek Jones is perfectly socially adjusted for his age, and I could, as a guest on Jimmy Fallon, state Carolyn's IQ as I sat next to her, and the audience might laugh hysterically. A movie script with this plot would get tossed into the circular bin. To cut to the chase, the NSA believes the CIA Director and Vice President have gained access to top-secret files on Derek Jones that have a level of clearance above even my grade, which is very troubling. In that even I cannot access these records, that even you, Madam President, cannot access."

Abigail stared at Sharon as her mind filled with thoughts, questions, and concerns. After a long pause, she said, "My own Vice President has access to information that I don't?" Pausing again, she continued, "I gather they think Derek Jones is capable of getting past the Secret Service to perform the deed they brainwashed him to perform."

"Not brainwashed to perform, Abigail, but about to be brainwashed to perform."

"Then you can stop them before they ruin this young man's life and end mine and who knows how many other Americans."

"It's not that easy, I'm afraid. Unless we let them think they have succeeded, we cannot discover how deep the rabbit hole goes in the CIA or what else is down there. And if the CIA Director and Vice President are plotting, for lack of a better phrase, coup d'etat."

"A takeover of the United States government?"

"Abby, we need to know what we're up against. The CIA psychologist Dr. Rabinovich is planning to administer CIA mind control drugs and hypnosis and give Derek a code phrase to activate his behavior when spoken. Derek will be instructed to do exactly what Arlin Conway orders him to do after Arlin Conway states that phrase. Dr. Rabinovich has agreed to work with the NSA to lead Arlin Conway and his cohorts into a trap. It involves giving Derek Jones the code phrase but then giving him another code phrase that anyone can state, which will deactivate the first code phrase. When Arlin Conway uses the first code phrase, he will give Derek Jones specific orders. This is critical because we can later have Derek tell us these orders. Then, a special agent will state the second code phrase, causing Derek not to carry out Arlin Conway's orders. However, Derek will also be instructed, on hearing the second code phrase, to pretend he is going to carry out these orders while using his advanced intellect to thwart Arlin Conway's plans and expose the assassination plot. At that point, we will contact Derek Jones and enlist his help. Derek Jones will become a double agent, but he will belong to the NSA and become our operative."

"Careful, Sharon, this is a teenage boy you're talking about. He belongs to God and nobody else."

Sharon nodded.

Abigail continued, "How do you know Derek will cooperate with you?"

"We don't, but based on Derek's profile, I believe he will, and I'm willing to stake my life on it."

Remember Egypt

Returning home from school, Derek ran through the front door to the kitchen.

"Debriefing" was written on a yellow Post-it note on the refrigerator. Staring at the note for a moment, Derek opened the fridge.

After quickly eating a small container of strawberry yogurt, Derek ran upstairs and walked down the hall to his room. Hearing birds singing as he passed a room, he opened the door to the room his mother Asha affectionately called "the nursery" and stared at the Jones family's African lovebirds, Ajit and Nita. They immediately went silent and stared at him as birds around them continued to sing.

"Hello there, Ajit and Nita. You sing so pretty! Why stop on my account?" Derek walked around the room as Ajit and Nita's eyes followed him. "Where are those birds? Your mommy says they come from hidden speakers, but I've never found them."

Ajit chirped loudly.

"Oh, so you won't tell me where they are? That figures! What about you, Nita?"

Silence.

"Derek, if birds fall and become extinct, so will humans," he could hear a memory of his mother's voice echo in his mind.

Birds' songs sounded as if they were in the room from around the room. The lovebirds started chirping at them again as if they were in the room. The invisible birds seemed to chirp back from places unseen.

"They're hidden speakers," his mother's voice echoed through Derek's memory. "Birds are sentient beings, social creatures like humans. In essence, they are quasi-human. They need to know others are present and they are not alone. They must interact with other birds."

Immersed in a euphony of exotic bird calls, the lovebirds seemed to be interacting with them vocally.

"Where are those speakers?" pondered Derek aloud, feeling confused again. "Every time I come in here, I ask the same question, Ajit and Nita. You and your mommy are keeping secrets from me. My mom says you're like their son and daughter, and I'm your brother. Surely, you can let your brother in on your little secret."

Ajit chirped loudly again, and Derek laughed. "Ajit, I don't speak birdie, so if you decided to let me in on your secret, it's still a secret."

Remembering his new running shoes were in the closet, Derek stripped down to his underwear in preparation for working out in the gym downstairs. Staring into the mirror at his underwear-clad body, he whispered, "Hmm, Jenna is right; my efforts are paying off." The birds sang louder, interrupting his self-attention. Looking up at the mirror, he stared at them as one preened the other affectionately and smiled. "You two are so in love. No wonder you're called lovebirds."

Then he heard a whisper in his mind. "Derek, your mother is sending us to Paradiso. Remember, we will not miss your wedding!"

Derek stared questioningly in the mirror at the birds as they stared intently at him. At that moment, the chilliness pulsated over his body, and he caught a faint, colorful luminescence from head to underwear at the corner of his eye. Instinctively staring into his own eyes in the mirror, Derek was startled to see his pupils turn into slits. The colors of the room suddenly became more vivid.

"This is so cool. What's happening to me?"

Turning to Ajit and Nita, they stared mesmerized into Derek's eyes.

"Did you… uh, did you say that in my mind?"

They stared at him in silence. A cacophony of bird songs filled the room, and the colors appeared clearer and more vivid than ever. Derek instinctively turned to the mirror and was startled to see a metallic luminescence encompassing every rainbow color pulsating over his body.

"Am I dreaming? I must be dreaming. This is so weird. What's happening to me?"

Then he heard a whisper in his mind. "Derek, we will miss you, but we promise not to miss your wedding!"

"What wedding?"

"Yours and Jenna's, of course."

"We're not getting married. Who are you?"

"I think you know."

Derek walked closer to Ajit and Nita while looking at them suspiciously, and instinctively, they suspiciously looked back and defensively hopped to the farthest corner of the cage. Laughing, Derek said, "Am I losing my mind?" Derek was startled by the loud chirp of a bird from behind him. Turning around, he saw a vibrantly colored songbird sitting on his mother's antique armoire. "How did you get there?" At that moment, the bird turned and flew away, vanishing before it could get far.

Seeing a blue glint of light in the corner of his eye, he walked back to the mirror. His blue irises were illuminated. Remembering why he came into Ajit and Nita's bedroom, he went to the closet and grabbed a pair of new sneakers that his mom had bought him. Walking before the mirror again, his eyes and body appeared normal. Looking around, the room seemed dull compared to its earlier vibrant colors.

After returning to his bedroom, showering, and putting on his workout shorts and tank, Derek looked closely at his eyes in the bathroom mirror, shrugged, and sprinted downstairs.

Derek's aunt met him at the bottom of the stairs and said, "Derek, there is someone very important from the government who wants to see you. Her name is Agent Anna Bartlett. She is here to take you to the debriefing."

"Is that what that cryptic note meant?" replied Derek.

"That was more for me, to remind you," his aunt replied.

Entering the living room, Derek said with a questioning voice, as he recognized the woman, "Agent Anna Bartlett?"

"How are you holding up, Derek?" she replied.

"I'll leave you two alone," said Derek's aunt.

Derek stared at Agent Bartlett with a puzzled expression.

Looking him over, she smiled. "I find this encouraging."

"What?"

"You are keeping fit, Derek. You have looked great since your nine-month ordeal. You are the same age as my son. Getting him interested in physical activities as a software gamer junkie — that was quite a feat. Yet here you are, writing video games at seventeen, and you regularly workout and jog a few miles daily."

"How do you know I jog every day?"

"Do you think we're not keeping a close eye on you, Derek, after what happened to you?"

"You guys know how to remain invisible, just like in the movies."

Agent Bartlett laughed. "Why, Derek, don't you know that is our claim to fame? To make a long story short as to why I'm here, I'm taking over the investigation. The CIA believes you were abducted by the same terrorist organization that held government employees for ransom in Egypt."

"I still don't remember anything," replied Derek with a note of desperation and trembling.

"Derek, it is imperative you remember. I have a car waiting outside. Your father's company has agreed to allow us to use his company's facilities for what we call a debriefing, where we want you to meet a psychologist who is an expert in memory recall."

"I can't," Derek protested.

"You want to find your abductors, and doing so could save other lives. Your entire family agrees. We believe their abductions are tied to your abduction in Egypt."

Derek looked toward the dining room, and his aunt stood there. Staring intently at him, she nodded.

"All right, I'll do it."

A procession of cars, with police cars flanking the front and rear, entered the parking lot of New Physics Corporation. Guards directed the black car in the middle to the main entrance of a metallic building of beautiful architecture, surrounded by sprawling lawns, vibrantly colored flowers, trees, and other similar structures. As the car came to a stop, Derek noticed a beautiful butterfly landed on a flower.

He stared at it, mesmerized, thinking how amazing this creature looked.

"Remember Egypt," Agent Bartlett responded to Derek's question about how he could help the CIA.

Entering a large conference room, Agent Bartlett introduced Derek to an attractive and well-dressed woman wearing large glasses. "Derek, this is Dr. Alexandria Rabinovich."

Dr. Rabinovich extended her hand to Derek, smiled as she surveyed his tank-top-clad physique, and said, "Nice to meet you, Derek. You can call me Alex."

Derek slowly extended his hand, nodded, gently grasped her hand, let go, and studied her beautiful, full, cherubic face with thick, curly brown hair pulled back.

"Derek, I've never seen irises so deeply sapphire blue!" Dr. Rabinovich exclaimed with a smile. She turned and walked to the end of the conference room table as Derek studied her vertical braid behind her head and slender body in a form-fitting skirt. She sat and nodded to the chair adjacent to the end of the conference room table. Derek approached her and sat down.

Down the corridor, another conference room was filled with CIA personnel. The CIA

Director, Arlin Conway, stood before the group. He said, "Secretary of State Roland Nichols has alerted Vice President Niles Milan of the existence of a Pentagon special ops team, developed to keep the Vice President and CIA Director, yours truly, and all of you, under surveillance." Arlin Conway paused as top CIA officials gathered before him. They looked stunned, and a few whispered to each other.

"Under whose supervision, sir?" asked a voice from the back of the conference room.

Arlin Conway looked intently at the group and raised one eyebrow. "Under the President's supervision."

A silence filled the room.

"I know," continued the CIA Director, "this came to me as a complete shock. I always considered collaboration with The White House as a team effort."

In the back parking lot of New Physics Corporation, a nondescript van with satellite dishes was parked near the loading dock. Inside the van, a woman and man clad in black fatigues and dark tan sleeveless tees and wearing headphones with microphone extensions listened to the voice of Agent Bartlett, who was with Agent Johnson in a conference room next to the one that Derek and Dr. Rabinovich occupied.

"You have the go to begin Operation Hush, Agent Darson," ordered Agent Bartlett as she nervously stared at Agent Johnson.

Agent Darson, catching the other agent checking her out, rolled her eyes and gave him the middle finger as she replied, "Got it, Bartlett, we're going." She immediately scooted to a computer keyboard and monitor and quickly began typing.

Arlin Conway looked puzzled at a blank overhead projector screen in the conference room where all the CIA officials sat and picked up his cell phone. "We have no video or audio," he said in a low voice with annoyance.

As Derek stared intently at Dr. Rabinovich, she gently tapped his muscular shoulder, looking over his thin but muscular arms. "Nice workout shirt," she said with a smile. "It always helps to have short sleeves, or better, no sleeves for an injection. I promise I'm very good at this. It won't hurt at all."

Derek looked away, closed his eyes, and whispered, "Why do they always say that?"

"Because it's usually true?" she replied, giving him an injection.

Derek grinned sheepishly. "Guess you're right. I didn't feel anything. What is this for again, Dr. Rabinovich?"

"It helps subjects to relax and increases their suggestibility," she replied. "For you to remember Egypt, you need this first."

Agent Bartlett and her partner, Agent Jason Johnson, watched a monitor displaying a close-up of the increasingly annoyed CIA Director.

"I better go stand in front of the door in case CIA Director Conway decides to interrupt the session."

Agent Johnson replied, "He knows entering the conference room while Derek is hypnotized is against medical protocol and could ruin everything. Look at his expression. I know that expression. That control freak demands complete control, and we've taken that control away from him." Motioning upwards, he continued, "What if someone is watching us?" Then he leaned forward and whispered, "If this goes sideways, we are screwed, Anna."

"Get a grip," replied Agent Bartlett, "The NSA has swept this room. There's an old saying, 'Don't play with the NSA.' This room might as well be on Mars." Smiling at Agent Johnson, who was looking at her wide-eyed, she continued, "Everything is under control. Trust me." She then grabbed a pair of video goggles, walked out, stood in front of the door to the conference room where Derek and Dr. Rabinovich were, put on the goggles, adjusted her earbuds, and listened as she looked at Derek while Dr. Rabinovich hypnotized him.

Moving the camera to Dr. Rabinovich, Agent Johnson said into the microphone on her earbud, "Dr. Rabinovich, Operation Hush is fully operational."

Nodding to the camera, Dr. Rabinovich asked Derek, "How do you feel?"

Derek said nothing, giving her a vacant stare. The drug began to cause his mind to drift, and listening to Dr. Rabinovich's voice as she soothingly spoke to him, he went into a hypnotic trance.

Derek could see inside the large room filled with Egyptian artifacts, where his father examined Egyptian relics. It was a sea of gold, Derek vividly recalled. "I can't believe this was here all along," said Derek in a deadpan voice, as he repeated his dad Rick Jones' voice echoing audibly in Derek's memory. His eyes remaining closed, Derek repeated his dad's words to Dr. Rabinovich in a lower tone voice that bordered on a whisper, "I can't believe this was here all along." Under Derek's eyelids, his eyes pulsated rapidly. Derek continued to vocalize his recollections as he saw them. The memories were suddenly flooding back.

Zeyad Hassan of Egyptian Antiquities stared in disbelief at something. Rick Jones said, "What is it, Zeyad?"

"How did this get here?" exclaimed Zeyad.

On a dusty surface lay a tiny orb, no bigger than a ball bearing, with a mirrored surface. Derek walked up to the orb.

"Don't touch it," Zeyad warned Derek.

"What is it?" asked Derek as he stared at the orb intently.

Zeyad whispered something to a young Egyptian woman in the chamber in Egyptian Arabic, and she replied. Then, she began taking photos of the object. Zeyad put on a glove. Carefully placing his thumb and forefinger on each side of the tiny orb, he lifted it.

"This can't be," Zeyad whispered in astonishment.

"What?" Rick replied.

"There's no weight. None whatsoever. This… this is impossible. It is lighter than a balloon. It doesn't even feel like the weight of tissue paper. It is lighter than air itself." Zeyad widened his thumb and forefinger. The object remained stationary in space, floating several feet above the ground before him.

"No, this can't be real," said Derek loudly, his eyes closed but gyrating back and forth under his eyelids. His eyelids suddenly displayed a faint glow under the surface. Agents Bartlett and Johnson looked at each other as they watched him on the monitor, now zoomed in on Derek's face.

Derek was silent.

"What do you see, Derek?" asked Dr. Rabinovich.

Derek watched as Dr. Hassan took the object between his fingers and placed it in the palm of his hand. Suddenly, he gasped with alarm, and his hand drooped.

"What is it?" asked Derek with alarm.

"It's suddenly heavy, like tungsten! Wait. Now, it doesn't weigh anything again." Dr. Hassan let go of the sphere, and it floated again.

"The object. It's flat now. No, this isn't real." said Derek. Dr. Rabinovich studied his facial expression as he squinted with an expression of fear. "No, it's a mirror. It's a shiny dark mirror."

"Derek, you said it was a shiny orb, like a ball bearing, maybe an inch in diameter?"

"Yes. It became flat and dark, then expanded. It is still circular but flat, a few feet tall, vertical, and floating. It looks black with a mirror finish. I can see myself in it. There's movement in it. Something is behind the mirror."

"This is the same object we found at Area 51," said Zeyad as he walked around the flat disc and inspected the area behind it. "It was 1947. How did it get here?"

As Rick and Zeyad exchanged puzzled, wide-eyed glances, the vertical, flat, mirrored object expanded in diameter until its circular edges extended into the chamber's floor and ceiling.

"There's something inside. It's another chamber," said Zeyad. "This could explain everything."

"No!" exclaimed Derek. "Dr. Hassan, where are you going? Dad, stop him! Something moved in there! Don't go!"

"Derek, where is who going," replied Dr. Rabinovich.

"Dr. Hassan has walked into the exotic event horizon," Derek slowly whispered with a trembling voice.

"Exotic event horizon? What does that mean?" asked Dr. Rabinovich.

Agent Bartlett immediately picked up her cellphone and quickly dialed a number. "You better get down here," she said.

"Who are you?" exclaimed Derek. Several men who looked Middle Eastern entered the chamber wearing gas masks. There was a hissing sound and a strange smell.

On awakening, it was pitch dark. Derek realized a hood was on his head because he could see pinpoints of light through the black fabric. Feeling the sting of a syringe, Derek went in and out of consciousness. Thus began his nine-month incarceration by militants whose sole objective was to extract one billion dollars from Rick Jones and the United States government funding the expedition.

Derek opened his eyes and stared at Dr. Rabinovich. She was startled. Derek's pupils were vertically slitted like reptile eyes. "They said they wanted one billion dollars but were after something far greater. Something far more deadly they planned on turning over to a hostile faction of the Reptilian Empire."

"The Reptilian Empire?" exclaimed Dr. Rabinovich, shaking her head and marveling at his slitted pupils. "What were they after, Derek?"

"Me."

Then he described a beautiful, thin woman wearing a burka or veil who entered Derek's prison cell daily.

"She fed me, gave me water, and everything. She had amazing strength," Derek said as Dr. Rabinovich took notes.

Derek continued, describing her extraordinary strength as she effortlessly lifted him, bathed him, brushed his teeth, combed his hair, and sang him to sleep in an unrecognizable language. Her voice and the song's beauty were beyond anything he had ever heard. Derek felt deep compassion emanating from her. She would never answer his question, "Who are you?"

Finally, on the last day of his captivity, when he asked the question again, he asked, "Please, who are you?"

She answered, "Someone who knows that greatness is your destiny."

Hooded men forcibly walked Derek into a large room in the prison. On his knees, his head covered with a hood, Derek faced a video camera.

Derek remembered his aunt in the United States, who later described holding his mother as they wept and watched the live broadcast. "This is a CNN exclusive report broadcast live from Egypt. This live video feed is being transmitted live worldwide." Holding a sword, one of the hooded men gave a speech in Aramaic, translated into English. Derek could feel the cold blade of the sword barely touching the back of his neck with a sharp yet gentle caress, like a razor's edge. The man holding the sword faintly whispered something into his ear in Aramaic.

Thinking he was imagining what might be happening externally, Derek described how he imagined Navy SEALs outside preparing to battle his terrorist captors. Derek could see one SEAL on the prison rooftop above the room where he was held captive, which he described as looking through the nuclear-green tint of night-vision goggles. The SEAL attached a small video drive to a cable near a tiny satellite communications device, then machine-gunned all other communications equipment around him. The live broadcast was abruptly terminated, blacking out stunned viewers worldwide. Hearing machine gun fire, Derek's captors looked up at the ceiling.

"How do you know all this, Derek?" asked Dr. Rabinovich. "How did you know these were Navy SEALs? How did you know your captors looked up at the ceiling? Did they remove your hood?"

"That's just it. I don't know how I knew. Something was covering my head. I could enter their heads. I had some kind of x-ray vision, but even more creepy, I could see through their eyes!"

Derek continued his narrative. Locating the room that was the source of the live satellite broadcast and wearing gas masks, the SEALs blasted open the steel door with explosives and threw gas canisters into the room. Entering the room, as the gas cleared, they could see Derek wearing a hood and kneeling in front of cameras, with a sword lying next to him. The gas came no closer to Derek's body than a few inches, forming what appeared like an envelope of clear air surrounding him.

The bodies of his captors were on the floor. One SEAL shook his head, glaring at the other. The other SEAL took their pulses. "They're dead. Don't look at me like that, man. Look, the boy is still alive. See? I used non-lethal canisters."

The other SEAL picked up a canister, read it, and replied, "Look, the boy's not coughing. The gas is not touching him. That's just weird, man."

Derek went silent. Dr. Rabinovich continued. "Derek, what do you remember next?"

"It's a blank. The next thing I remember is lying in a bed. I could hear beeping. I looked up, and a soldier with a weapon on his shoulder walked by me. Then, he walked out of the room and closed the door. Suddenly, that woman who cared for me stood beside my bed in a gown that sparkled like a clear midnight sky. She looked down at me and placed her warm hand on my head. Her hand felt warm and comforting on my forehead."

"Then?"

"I found myself sitting in a large room with polished metal panels, being interviewed by agent Anna Bartlett. She said we were at CIA headquarters in Langley, Virginia." Derek looked at Agent Bartlett over the table and said, "The bodies were autopsied at Walter Reed National Military Medical Center. The coroner's examination revealed massive brain hemorrhaging from microwave radiation as the cause of death. Am I right?"

Agent Bartlett stared at Derek, refusing to acknowledge he was correct.

"Dr. Rabinovich, she knew I was right."

"Derek, what happened between Egypt and Langley?"

"I don't know. I must have blacked out after realizing they were going to behead me."

"Then how could you claim to know details about autopsies, Derek?"

"What do you mean?"

"You just said it, Derek."

"No, I didn't."

Dr. Rabinovich shook her head slowly and furiously wrote down more notes.

"After I got home, months later, I kept having these flashbacks and nightmares, seeing them through my hood, as if I had some x-ray vision. I remember being so angry at them. I started repeating in my mind, 'Make them dead.' Then, the sound of a machine gun caused them to look up at the ceiling." Derek paused, and a tear ran down his cheek. "I remembered seeing a ghostly image of the woman in the burka and veil standing near me," Derek continued as Dr. Rabinovich took notes. "She said, 'This must not happen. You are destined for greatness. You know what you must do.' And I did it."

"You said she was wearing a beautiful robe that looked like it was covered with stars, Derek."

"No, she did, at Langley, but she wore a burka in Egypt."

"Are you sure she was the same woman?"

"Yes, Dr. Rabinovich."

"Then what happened?"

"All these emotions felt like they were suffocating me. I felt pressure in my head like it was going to burst. All the men around me grabbed their heads and began to scream. I felt no pity. They deserved it. Some pulled off their hoods. The whites of their eyes had red veins. Then…"

Derek started to weep and reached out his hands toward Dr. Rabinovich.

She squeezed his hands tightly and said, "It's all right. You can tell me."

"The veins in their eyes broke open. Blood began streaming from their eyes and noses! And from their ears! I looked up at the ceiling from where the machine gun fire originated. I saw a man in a military uniform standing on the rooftop above my head. I mean, the ceiling was semi-transparent. I heard the faint mechanical sound of a camera lens. Please don't ask me how I know, but that sound was because the camera continued to record the room. The SEAL attached a video flash drive to the optical cable on the rooftop. The camera recorded everything, didn't it." Derek's voice changed in tone, and he continued. "CIA and experts have been analyzing this classified footage since and don't know what to make of it," he quipped in a deadpan voice as if he was repeating something he heard.

Agent Johnson and several other observers in military uniform, whom Agent Bartlett called to the conference room where they were viewing Dr. Rabinovich's session, looked at each other in disbelief as they watched Dr. Rabinovich and Derek on the monitor.

CIA Director Arlin Conway stormed down the hall toward Agent Bartlett, his expression dark with frustration. She stood rigidly in front of the conference room where Dr. Rabinovich and Derek were waiting. Stopping inches from her, he shoved her video glasses up to her forehead and locked eyes with her.

"What's going on, Agent Bartlett?" he demanded. "We've lost the audio feed. I want that video and sound restored before Dr. Rabinovich starts the session with Derek Jones."

"No feed?" Agent Bartlett asked with a feigned surprised expression. "Why didn't you say something? The session is almost over."

Arlin Conway rolled his eyes in disbelief, put his head back in indignation, and said calmly, "What do you mean the session is almost over? Tell me someone was taping that session."

"You were taping it," Agent Bartlett replied.

"Except I have no video or audio feed. I have a blank screen. Are you saying I was taping a blank screen? What about you? Agent Johnson, you weren't taping it?"

"No," Agent Bartlett replied. "Multiple taping of mind control sessions is against company protocol."

"Against protocol?" Arlin Conway replied incredulously and grabbed the door handle, giggling at it. "Why is this door locked?"

Agent Bartlett gently touched Arlin Conway's shoulder and said quietly, "Security precautions. If you interrupt now, it will interfere with the hypnosis, and you will not have full and unquestioned control of Derek Jones. If you interrupt now and give him a critical order later, he may not carry out the order without hesitation."

Arlin Conway looked at his shoulder where agent Bartlett's hand rested, then angrily at her. Agent Bartlett lowered her hand slowly.

"My apologies, CIA Director Conway, I just used hand lotion. If you find I smeared any lotion on your expensive Armani blazer, I will personally deliver it to the CIA dry cleaners and pay for it out of my departmental budget. I doubt it will leave a permanent stain. It's organic."

"Organic?" Arlin Conway asked in a hoarse whisper, then pressed his lips together, shook his head slightly while lowering it, looked at her hands as she rubbed them together, turned away, and stormed down the hall.

Agent Bartlett suppressed laughter, pushed her hair behind her ear, adjusted her earpieces, and placed the video goggles back over her eyes.

Glancing briefly at the monitor, Dr. Rabinovich said, "Derek, when you hear the word combination 'Fox Trots' spoken to you by CIA Director Arlin Conway or NSA Director Sharon Questar, you will follow their orders without hesitation. However, when you hear the words 'Fox Stops' spoken to you by anyone, you will stop carrying out these orders and follow their orders instead." Dr. Rabinovich stopped, looked away, and whispered into her earbud microphone, "What am I doing, Agents Bartlett and Johnson? A seventeen-year-old teenager programmed like a piece of military hardware?"

"Dr. Rabinovich," replied Agent Johnson, "that seventeen-year-old teen has an IQ measuring genius and has paranormal abilities the government must harness for the greater good. How do you think he neutralized a dozen or more terrorists while bound and blindfolded?"

Dr. Rabinovich nodded, turned to Derek, and continued, "While I count to three, you will wake up. One. Two." She watched as Derek slowly opened his eyes. "Three."

She was mesmerized by his deep blue irises staring at her with a faint phosphorescence, subtly pulsating like slowly moving water. Staring at him intently and hearing the faint sound of an adjusting camera lens, she heard agent Bartlett's voice in her earbud.

"Dr. Rabinovich, what's going on with his eyes?"

"I don't know. Perhaps an after-effect from the hypnosis."

Our Baby from the Stars

"Our baby from the stars," said Salena Chandra as she watched through the front window. The CIA drove up, and Agent Bartlett escorted Derek to the front door.

Derek walked through the front door to face Salena and Amrit Chandra, his aunt and uncle. Salena walked up to him, hugged him, and looked into his eyes, gently lifting his eyelids. She and Amrit exchanged knowing glances. The sapphire phosphorescent glow in Derek's deep blue eyes was fading.

"I knew they would bring it out, Derek. It was only a matter of time."

"Bring what out, Aunt Salena," Derek replied.

Salena motioned to the living room. He followed her and Amrit. "Sit down, Derek. We have something to tell you." She looks at Amrit.

"Your dreams, Derek," Amrit began, "we said they were just dreams. We believe they are memories. Let us tell you about your true childhood. It begins in India."

Derek listened as his aunt and uncle began.

Amrit and Salena Chandra were a young married couple who were childless and living in poverty in a village. They asked God for a baby. Salena could not get pregnant after trying for years.

Salena Chandra was a vision of elegance and compassion, a woman whose warmth and resilience illuminated every aspect of her demeanor. Her expressive eyes, large and soulful, seemed to hold the wisdom of countless lifetimes, while her radiant smile carried a quiet strength that immediately put those around her at ease. Adorned in vibrant traditional Indian attire, Salena's presence exuded a rich cultural heritage, and her carefully chosen jewelry — delicate yet intricate — added a touch of regal grace to her appearance.

Her belief that Derek Jones was a divine gift was etched into how she looked at him, her affection and pride for him as clear as the stars on a cloudless night. Salena's unshakable faith and profound love for Derek stemmed from the moment she first saw the tiny spaceship land — a surreal event that she interpreted as a sign from God. She often told Derek, "You didn't just fall into my life; you were sent," her voice filled with conviction and tenderness. This deep-seated belief fueled her unwavering commitment to raising Derek as her own, shielding him from the mysteries and dangers of his otherworldly origins.

Salena's connection to Derek was more than familial. It was spiritual. She considered him her destiny, a purpose bestowed upon her during a time of uncertainty in her life. With her husband, she raised him in a home filled with love, teaching him the values of kindness, courage, and faith. Her nurturing nature and fierce protectiveness shaped Derek into the young man he is, grounding him even as he uncovered the extraordinary truth of his heritage.

While Salena was deeply spiritual, she was also pragmatic and intelligent, traits that helped her navigate the complexities of raising a child with origins far beyond Earth. Her quiet strength and enduring hope served as an anchor for Derek, especially as the secrets of his past surfaced. Despite the extraordinary circumstances of his arrival, Salena has always sought to provide him with a sense of normalcy, a balance between his remarkable destiny and his human upbringing.

Salena was not only Derek's aunt but also a symbol of unconditional love and faith. She views the divine in the extraordinary and the extraordinary in the mundane, her belief in Derek's purpose unwavering even as the universe around them becomes increasingly uncertain.

Amrit Chandra was a man of quiet dignity and unwavering strength, the kind of presence that commanded respect without demanding it. His sharp, intelligent eyes, framed by thin glasses, reflected a lifetime of introspection and a profound sense of responsibility. With his neatly combed silver hair and impeccable style — whether in a tailored suit or a more casual blazer and shirt — Amrit embodied both wisdom and grace.

Amrit's calm demeanor and steady nature made him the perfect partner for his wife, Salena, in the extraordinary task of raising Derek Jones. While Salena's faith and nurturing spirit guided much of their parenting, Amrit's practical and analytical mind ensured Derek grew up with a balance of love and discipline. He was the one who quietly marveled at the scientific and cosmic mystery of Derek's arrival on Earth, often spending long nights pondering the mechanics of the dark mirror and the technology that had brought the infant to their doorstep.

Amrit's bond with Derek was built on a foundation of mentorship. He viewed Derek not just as a child to be loved and protected but also as a being of immense potential who may hold the key to bridging worlds. He was always a guiding hand in Derek's life, teaching him the value of logic, perseverance, and quiet resilience. His deep affection balanced his occasional sternness, and his subtle sense of humor often lightened the weight of the secrets they carry.

Though Amrit was deeply grounded, he had an air of mystery. He held many thoughts close to his chest, not out of secrecy but of a profound understanding that some truths are best revealed in their own time. His calm exterior belied the immense courage and adaptability he displayed when he and Salena decided to take in Derek, a decision that forever changed their lives.

Amrit considered Derek not just a nephew but a gift, one he believed they were chosen to protect. His belief in this divine purpose, tempered by his logical nature, created an intriguing duality in his character. While Salena openly celebrated Derek's miraculous arrival, Amrit pondered why and how his curiosity and sense of duty intertwined to shape his role as Derek's steadfast guardian.

Amrit continued, "One night, we stood outside our tiny dwelling in complete darkness. We gazed in complete awe at a crystal-clear canopy of stars. Salena looked into my eyes. For the first time, I could see hope."

As they gazed upward, Amrit recounted Salina's voice.

"Amrit, this is the night."

"What do you mean?"

"Our son."

Amrit looked at her, a question struggling to burst from his lips.

They observed a glowing point of light appearing in the sky as if out of nowhere. As it quickly approached, it was spherical in shape and bright blue. Slowing down, it hovered over a nearby hill and then slowly descended behind the hill.

They walked quickly up and over the hill, stopping abruptly at the top. On the other side of the slope below, a glowing sphere at rest on the ground illuminated the surrounding vegetation with a bluish light approximately five feet in diameter. They cautiously walked down the hill toward the object, and upon reaching it, a cow looked at them.

"I could tell by the look on her face that our child was in the orb," Amrit recalled.

Derek's eyes grew wide with anticipation at what his aunt and uncle told him.

Walking cautiously around the orb, Amrit said to Salena, "Get back, let me look."

Salena smiled. "There is nothing to fear, Amrit."

The glowing object was silent.

"Don't touch it, Salena!" Amrit cautioned her as she held her hand inches from its translucent surface.

"It looks like a blue sapphire stone," Salena whispered in awe, her hand within inches of its surface.

"No, don't!" Amrit said with a quivering voice as Salena rested her hand on the top of the glowing sphere. They exchanged awestruck glances.

The moment her hand touched the sphere, a reflection of her hand appeared inches below its translucent surface, followed by a musical echo. Salena stared at the sphere as her hand rested on it. Amrit gazed wide-eyed at his wife.

"Don't be afraid, Amrit, it is telling me something."

"What is it telling you?" whispered Amrit.

"Do you love this child? It asks me if we shall promise to love and cherish this child." As she looked at the sphere intently, Salena said, "Yes, I do."

"What is it telling you now?" whispered Amrit.

"It is thinking."

Salena slowly lifted her hand from the sphere. Amrit and Salena's gaze locked on the sphere's top half. Slowly rising into the air, the top half levitated several feet above the sphere. Their attention was fixed upon the inside of the sphere by the sound of a crying baby.

Reaching into the sphere, Salena lifted the baby to her bosom as Amrit stared in disbelief. Salena smiled joyfully and said to Amrit, "It is a boy."

Carrying the child over the hill and home, they tried to feed it, but the baby refused to eat. Recognizing that the baby needed nourishment and Salena could not breastfeed, they prepared to journey to a neighboring city where they would ask a Red Cross outpost for help.

As they were about to depart, a caravan of four-wheel drive vehicles approached from the distance. The cars stopped before their tiny house, and a British man and an Indian woman approached them.

After introducing themselves as Rick and Asha Jones, Salena introduced herself and her husband. Rick and Asha stared at the baby.

After a long pause, Rick said to Chandra, "Thank you for rescuing our baby."

Salena recalled her heart sinking at those last two words — "Our baby."

Salena's eyes began to tear up, and she kissed the baby. Asha looked at the two of them with compassion. She seemed to understand the bond Salena had with the baby.

"We are so happy our son's aunt and uncle rescued him. Derek will be your nephew for eternity, Salena and Amrit."

Salena wept, her tears falling on the baby's face.

The Joneses then told them the truth about where Derek was from.

Salena and Amrit sat in stunned silence, their breaths shallow as they tried to absorb the surreal tale that had just unfolded before them. Asha Jones, regal even in her simple earthbound attire, clasped her hands tightly together, her knuckles pale. Her dark eyes glistened with emotion, and her calm voice carried the weight of years of loss and longing.

"You must understand," Asha began, her tone heavy with urgency and sorrow. "We didn't send Derek away because we wanted to. We sent him because we had no choice." She paused, her gaze flicking between Salena and

Amrit, her expression a mix of gratitude and pain. "It was the only way to ensure his survival."

Salena leaned forward, her hands clasped together, the compassion in her eyes shining through. "Asha, please. Start from the beginning. We want to understand everything."

Asha took a deep breath, her elegant posture stiffening as if bracing herself to relive the memories. "We lived on a planet called Ethosa, hundreds of light-years from here," she began. "Our family… we were part of Ethosa's royal lineage. But Ethosa wasn't ruled by a monarchy in the traditional sense. It was… democratic, though deeply tied to traditions and the ceremonial leadership of our family. Think of it as how the British monarchy operates alongside Parliament."

Her voice faltered slightly, and she blinked back tears before continuing. "Our family served as the custodians of Ethosa's culture, history, and unity for generations. But all that changed when… they came."

"Who?" Amrit asked gently, his brow furrowed.

Asha's lips tightened. "A faction from within our government. They had grown corrupt, hungry for power. They staged a coup, a swift and brutal takeover. Ethosa's military fractured — some were loyal to us, some falling to the rebels. It wasn't long before they came for us. They wanted to wipe out our bloodline to cement their rule."

Salena gasped, her hand flying to her mouth. "And Derek?"

Asha's face softened, a mix of maternal pride and anguish washing over her. "Derek was just a baby. Innocent and full of life. My husband and I… we couldn't let him be caught in the chaos. We couldn't risk him falling into their hands. They would have used him as a pawn or worse…"

She paused, her voice catching in her throat. After a moment, she continued. "We had one chance. Our scientists had developed a means of escape — through a dark mirror. These have existed for billions of years, but we haven't used dark mirrors as escape routes.

Amrit asked, "What is a dark mirror?"

Salena replied, "It's a kind of portal, a passage between points in space. We used it to send Derek to Earth, hoping he'd land safely."

"Why Earth?" Amrit asked, his analytical mind searching for logic amidst the extraordinary.

Asha offered a small, bittersweet smile. "Because it's hidden in plain sight, and because

Earth has been a vacation destination for Ethosans since your Middle Ages, and especially as your technology made exponential advancements in your early twentieth century. Ethosa's scholars had long known about Earth, a planet teeming with life and yet primitive compared to many others in the galaxy. As your civilization advanced, it was a place where Derek could grow up away from our enemies and be safe. We chose India because it was rich in culture and spirit, where we believed a soul like his could thrive."

Salena reached out, her hand gently covering Asha's. "And you planned to retrieve him?"

"Yes," Asha replied, her voice wavering slightly. "The mirror was supposed to open again, and we intended to rescue him. But the coup unfolded more quickly than we expected. We had to go into hiding, always fleeing. With each passing day, with every moment we couldn't reach him… it broke us."

Tears streamed down her face now, unchecked, and Salena's heart ached as she watched the mother's anguish. "We never stopped trying. We finally found a way to Earth… Ironically, shortly after we sent Derek to Earth and came here shortly thereafter to join him, the rebellion was crushed, and Ethosa is now a peaceful world again. We decided to start a life here.”

Amrit, his voice low and thoughtful, finally spoke. “We found him in that pod, Asha. It was intact, perfectly preserved. We always wondered… we always felt he wasn’t like any other child. And now we know why.”

Asha’s tearful eyes met his. “You saved him,” she said, her voice filled with gratitude. “You were willing to give him a life. I will never be able to thank you enough for that.”

Salena shook her head, her own eyes misty. “We didn’t save him, Asha. He saved us. God sent him to us, of that I’m certain. Derek’s arrival was our greatest joy, our greatest blessing. Whatever his origins, he felt like our son in every way that matters.”

Asha smiled through her tears, nodding. “And for that, I will forever be in your debt.”

The weight of Asha’s story settles heavily around them. Finally, Salena spoke, her voice trembling with emotion. “He’s meant for something extraordinary.”

Asha’s gaze softened. “He’s stronger than we ever could have imagined. And he will need that strength for what lies ahead. Ethosa’s story isn’t over, and neither is Derek’s.”

The three sat together, bound now by their shared love for a boy whose destiny was far greater than they could comprehend. As they prepared for the journey, the future stretched out before them, uncertain and full of promise.

"Our baby from the stars is now your nephew," Asha concluded.

At one moment, as Salena started to cry and expressed her belief that God had sent the baby to her and Amrit in response to their prayers, Asha gently reminded her, "Salena, you and Amrit will always be Derek's aunt and uncle. You saved our child. The transport pod was linked to Derek; it would only open for those with good intentions toward him. You are now bonded with Derek for life as part of his family. We see you both as our siblings and his aunt and uncle. Would you like to live with us in America and help us raise Derek?"

Looking at each other, Salena and Amrit began to weep and nod. "Yes," exclaimed Salena. "God did answer our prayers."

"Then pack the things you wish to bring, and let us go," replied Asha as she exchanged loving glances with her husband, Rick. "Leave what you cannot carry, and we will send someone to retrieve it and bring it to your new home in America."

"Where did you say we are going?" asked Amrit.

"To the United States!" replied Rick.

Salena paused from recounting a memory that seemed as fresh as if it were yesterday.

Derek stared at her, then looked at Amrit. "Then what happened?"

"Our life together began," replied Salena as she wiped a tear from her eye. "We've loved you ever since. You are our baby from the stars. You are the pride and joy of your parents, whom we helped reunite you with."

Amrit nodded. They all coalesced together in an affectionate huddle.

Chapter 4 Project Dark Mirror

"There is force in the universe, which, if we permit it, will flow through us and produce miraculous results."

— Mahatma Gandhi

Dark Mirror Telescope

*I*t was sunset at the Mount Palomar Observatory. The "Dark Mirror Telescope," called after the 200-inch Hale Telescope retrofit with a dark mirror, was about to go online, and anticipation was building in the control center.

"Is the Dark Mirror in position?" Brian Collins asked, trying to contain his excitement.

"Yes, Mr. Collins, all systems go," replied Ira Rothbard, a young technician, in front of a large high-definition monitor.

The teenage son of Silicon Valley technology billionaire Jonathan and his mother, Marilyn Rothbard, Ira Rothbard carried an enigmatic charm that belied the complexity of his life story. His bright blue eyes, full of warmth and curiosity, seemed to hold secrets he had to yet uncover. With a radiant smile and a soft, approachable demeanor, Ira's presence was effortlessly magnetic. Yet, beneath his cheerful exterior was a labyrinth of unanswered questions and hidden truths.

"Ira, you are now at the center of the universe where the action is," Brian said as he studied the technician staring at the monitor.

"What can be more rewarding than what we are about to witness."

"Indeed, Mr. Collins," replied Ira with a knowing grin as he looked at Brian out of the corner of his eye and then back at the monitor.

Ira continued, "I had to walk away from this and gather my thoughts. One tends to keep thinking about the ramifications of what one is about to see. Brian, I was deeply moved when I first saw V111 closeup." Ira whispered before raising his voice to a normal volume, turning in his chair, and staring Brian directly in the eyes, startling Brian with a glint of iridescent blue. "I cried."

Brian looked searchingly into Ira's eyes and grinned. "Seriously? So did I."

The tone in Ira's voice and the glint of blue iridescence in his eyes caused waves of goosebumps to pulse over Brian's body, and he instinctively folded his arms and rubbed his biceps.

Ira smiled faintly as if suppressing the deepest of emotions. "My heart was racing. It was like a hundred-shot Americana at Starbucks in one of those big steel tumblers."

The goosebumps increased exponentially, and Brian's voice trembled. "I would like to treat you to that Americana, with perhaps fewer shots for your health's sake, and hear about your education and experience. We are very fortunate to have someone with your education onboard."

Ira smiled and replied, "Thank you, Brian; when you're ready to stop by again after our demonstration, let me know, and we can do that. I'm a Starbucks junkie, and I like to talk about myself."

Ira Rothbard was not just the teenage son of billionaires Jonathan and Marilyn Rothbard; he was a young man wrapped in an aura of enigmatic charm, a quality that concealed the layers of complexity woven into his life story. With bright blue eyes that sparkled with warmth and curiosity, Ira seemed to hold secrets beyond his grasp. His radiant smile and approachable demeanor made him magnetic, drawing people in effortlessly. Yet, beneath that cheerful exterior lay a labyrinth of unanswered questions and hidden truths waiting to be discovered.

As a child, Ira had survived a catastrophic StarCar accident that he believed had taken the lives of his birth parents. The tragedy haunted him, leaving him with fragmented memories of that fateful day. In his dreams, he often encountered a luminous figure of otherworldly beauty and grace who seemed to watch over him, offering comfort he couldn't quite understand. Unbeknownst to Ira, the truth was far more profound than he could imagine. His adoptive parents, Jonathan and Marilyn, were his biological parents, returned to him through the intervention of an extraterrestrial being named Seraphina. They had been granted a second chance to raise him, under the bittersweet promise that one day they would reveal the truth of their bond.

Jonathan Rothbard, a visionary billionaire, industrialist, and Brian Collins's close friend, was deeply involved in the mysterious Dark Mirror Project, collaborating with the NSA and its formidable director, Sharon Questar. Ira's life was intricately linked to the project's shadowy objectives in ways he could not yet comprehend. His unique psychic ability to control dark mirrors was not just a gift but a key to the project's success and, ultimately, the galaxy's survival.

Ira's feelings for Derek ran deeper than friendship, rooted in a love he knew would never be fully reciprocated. Derek, ever loyal and compassionate, saw Ira as a brother in every sense but blood, their connection steadfast despite their unspoken complexities. With quiet grace, Ira channeled his affection into unwavering loyalty, mirroring their bond.

Despite the extraordinary circumstances that surrounded him, Ira remained grounded. A sense of humor and enduring kindness counterbalanced his inner struggles. His journey was one of self-discovery, courage, and the realization that love, in all its forms, was the most potent force in the universe. As he healed and prepared for the next chapter of his life, Ira began to embrace the duality of his existence, drawing strength from the knowledge that even across timelines, his soul was destined to fight for what was right.

Brian smiled. "Who isn't, and who doesn't? I like Peet's myself. Starbucks is great. I would also like to talk about myself, but I want to hear about you since you burned the midnight oil to keep the Dark Mirror Project on track. I can't believe you're twenty-three. You have that wise beyond his years look about you. Nobody mentioned that. Not that it's a problem. It's cool that someone your age is that smart, and if there's wisdom, that's a bonus."

Taking a deep breath and nervously smiling, Brian slowly pulled up a chair beside Ira, sat down, stretched, placed his hand on Ira's shoulder, and said, "Let us start the grand tour. I wouldn't miss that for the world."

Ira started clicking the keyboard at lightning speed, so Brian leaned back in his chair and looked up at Amara, who smiled at him benevolently. Ira began. "The telescope is aimed at the exoplanet Venaticora 111, or V111 abbreviated, that orbits the star Chara, also known as Beta Canum Venaticorum, a Sun-like star about 26 light-years away in the constellation Canes Venatici. V111 is a world like Earth, except it is 3.5 times Earth's size, with only 80% gravity due to its lesser density, which we theorize is due to massive subterranean caverns, a less dense geological composition, and a far less dense core. On a flyby with the Dark Mirror, V111 has a rather impressive kaleidoscope of exotic and lush desert landscapes, canyons, and electrifying sapphire neon-blue dunes stretching for thousands of miles with surface openings to what appears to be a network of underground caverns and other natural wonders that rival Earth's most scenic national parks. It's simply amazing, Mr. Collins. Care to peek?"

A smile filled Brian Collins' face, and his pulse began racing. Amara instinctively walked behind him and started massaging his shoulders. Brian placed his hand gently on hers. "That feels good, Amara; how did you know I need this right now? What the … This is like, wow, are you serious?"

"Deep breath, darling," said Amara's voice soothingly. Looking at Ira, she said, "Should we postpone this?"

Brian quickly said, "What, dear, no, let's continue. I'm fine."

"Take a look for yourself." Ira wheeled his chair aside, and Brian wheeled his chair up to the large, high-resolution, flat-panel screen.

"What am I looking at right now? What is this?" Brian looked at the technician, whose eyes beamed with delight.

"A city."

Brian laughed and stared at Ira with glazed eyes. "Are you serious? You must have aimed the Dark Mirror at Italy." Brian leaned forward, and his smile turned to puzzlement as he studied the image.

"A city like one in Italy, Mr. Collins, perhaps?" Ira queried.

"It's so different. This is better than Star Wars, you know, that planet Naboo, I believe it was called. There are canals; it has an Italy sort of look, but it…" Suddenly, Brian felt a dizzy spell, overwhelmed by the ramifications of what he was seeing, and Amara grabbed his shoulders as he swayed in the chair for a moment. "I'm all right, Amara," Brian said as he steadied himself.

"Amazing, Mr. Collins?" Ira asked.

Brian shook his head slowly in awe and dismay. "More than amazing. This… this can't be real."

Wheeling up to the console alongside Brian, Ira gently placed his hand on Brian's visibly shaking hand. Brian's hand held the mouse, but Ira's hand moved it while Brian pressed some keys with his other hand.

"What is your name, son?" asked Brian in a slightly disoriented voice. Amara and Ira exchanged nervous glances, wondering why Brian had forgotten Ira's name.

"Ira Rothbard."

Brian shook his head as he smiled. "Sorry, you already told me your name, Ira. Not of the Rothbard family? I mean, the family that owns the Rothbard Corporation?"

"Wow, Mr. Collins, you know of my family?"

"Ira, you can call me Brian." Awkwardly laughing, Brian continued, "You have called me Brian! Yes, I do know them. Your dad and I play golf when I'm in Martha's Vineyard. How old are you, Ira, if I may ask?"

"I'm twenty-three. Is that a problem?"

"Silly me, I knew that. Not at all. Proceed." Brian wheeled his chair back and motioned for Ira to take over.

Ira smiled and said, "Okie dokie. You'll notice we are now looking at an area of V111 with giant blue dunes. Did I mention it is also known as Ethosa by the civilization there? The analysis concludes these dunes are comprised of a blue form of jadeite. Notice that the dunes appear to have massive openings, all facing in the same direction. My guess is that these openings lead to subterranean areas of the planet. In a mountainous region in the middle of these dunes are large structures at higher altitudes built into what has a composition of granite, only this granite-like rock is a cool blue, similar in color to the blue jadeite dunes. If you zoom in on these structures…"

Ira paused, looked intently at the screen with another glint of iridescent blue in his eyes as Brian leaned slightly forward and briefly studied his eyes, then looked again at the screen. The view quickly zoomed to the rooftop level. "At least to me, they look similar in architecture to monasteries in Tibet. In this courtyard, some people look human-like, wearing blue robes and facing an open view of the dunes. They are stationary, and I'm guessing they're engaged in meditation. When I was in

Tibet with my dad, we visited a monastery, and meditation was a major thing."

Brian suddenly felt dizzy again, and his heart began racing. He pushed his hand against his chest. "I can't…" Brian couldn't continue the sentence, so he opened his blazer and patted the inside as his breathing became irregular. "I can't find my Cardizem. I carry it just in case. It controls these rare episodes."

"What is wrong, Brian?" asked Ira with concern, placing his hand on Brian's shoulder.

"I was afraid this would happen," Brian replied. "I used to have panic attacks, and these panic attacks trigger atrial fibrillation episodes. It feels like I'm having a heart attack, but my cardiologist assures me that it will pass. If I could just find that damn Cardizem." Brian spun his chair away from the screen as if not to see the monitor and wiped perspiration from his forehead. "I wanted this all my life. To find the truth of what's out there. Now, it's staring at me, and I can't handle it. I must turn away. I'm embarrassed to admit that I feel fear. My heart rate is increasing."

As Amara dug through her purse, Ira stood up and massaged Brian's shoulders. In a soothing voice, he replied, "Don't feel bad, Brian. My dad gets panic attacks and feels like he's going to have a heart attack. I discovered that he calms down by massaging his neck a certain way, and his heart rate returns to normal — like I shall teach Amara to do."

Brian slowly rolled his head around in circles, responding to Ira's massage. "That feels great."

"Direct your thoughts to someone you love."

Amara found the medication bottle Brian needed, poured a pill into her hand, and grabbed a bottle of water on the desk. Brian swallowed the pill with the water. Amara watched in wonder as Ira's eyes started to become iridescently vivid blue and was glad Brian could not see the fantastic sight.

"Brian," Ira replied quietly. "Close your eyes and think of her. Oh, the thought of her is so beautiful, isn't it."

Brian smiled ecstatically and said quietly. "When I met Amara, she was so dedicated to science."

"You're from Italy, aren't you, Brian?" asked Ira.

"Yes, Ira, I lived in Italy for many years. My hometown is Cambridge, Massachusetts."

"I graduated from MIT at Cambridge," Ira replied.

"Best school on the planet. What major?"

"Ph.D. in Physics and Astrophysical Sciences."

"Impressive, Ira. When do you graduate?"

"I graduated early with a PhD in Physics and Astrophysical Sciences," replied Ira.

"At twenty-three?" Brian took a deep breath, lowered his head, and then laughed as Ira continued to massage his neck. "I apologize for you having to see this. Thank you. Let me guess: Are you also a certified massage therapist? You are perfect."

Ira laughed and replied, "Until now, I wondered if that field would have been more emotionally rewarding. Just kidding. I deeply love the field in which I majored."

"Love it? Now that's dedication," Brian replied with a laugh. "Awesome."

"Brian," said Ira as he looked at Amara and nodded, "you need to go home with your wife, discuss what you've seen, and rest. May we continue this tomorrow?"

Brian nodded. "I'm suddenly so tired. Thank you, Ira."

Later that night, wearing his pajamas and slippers, Brian sipped a martini on the bedroom patio at his home in Montecito, California.

Deep in thought, he stared at the moonlit coast, with the shadow of the Channel Islands across the water. Looking up at the Moon, Brian smiled at the memory of Amara taking him there in her StarCar. Amara approached him from behind, affectionately placed her arms around him, her face against his shoulder, and looked up at the Moon.

Brian turned to her, they embraced, and they kissed.

"Amara," Brian said quietly in almost a whisper, "Part of me kept saying this can't be real. I can't believe it. I almost went into shock. I felt cold, my heart was racing, I had that old feeling of a panic attack coming on, and I was short of breath. For a moment, I thought I would pass out. How is that possible? Why did this trigger that reaction? I'm a scientist. We are supposed to be detached from our work, not emotional."

Amara looked up at Brian and searched his eyes. "You are in denial, my darling. We are like primitives who lived in the forest all our lives. We bravely ventured out into a clearing. We saw the Moon and stars for the very first time. It terrifies us. It triggers an irrational primal fear. Brian, you know we are not alone. You were so calm that day. We flew in my StarCar to the Moon and touched down on the surface. I opened the top, and only its force field separated us from the thin lunar atmosphere. I was in awe at your serenity, and your kiss enchanted me and placed me under your spell forever."

Brian's eyes became tearful as he smiled at Amara. "That was because I was in a dream with the Princess I had always longed for. I found true love for the first time; science no longer mattered, and you were all I could ever see again. Everything else was like a dreamscape. I never really made a connection with reality. It was like, this can't be real, and that's okay. If this is a dream, please, God, don't let me ever wake up. Today, Amara, I finally realized this was not a dream, and I couldn't handle the truth. I woke up and discovered the dream was reality. May I ask you to do something for me, my love?"

"Anything, Brian," Amara replied.

Brian squeezed Amara's hands and continued, "Will you sit next to me tomorrow when Ira gives me the grand tour of V111 and hold my hand? You are my connection to what's out there. I know in my heart that if you're there, it will be like on the lunar surface in your StarCar. If we do this, I will connect to the reality of what is out there. I will finally be free to face this scientific reality on my own. I need you to hold my hand and take me there."

Amara snuggled up to Brian's chest as he cradled her head, running his hands through her shiny, dark brown flowing hair. She looked up at him. He studied her flawless face, deep brown irises floating on satin white sheets, beautiful eyebrows, and full lips. "You are so beautiful," he whispered. "Take me there."

Leading him by the hand and motioning to the patio door to the bedroom, the warm air hitting them as it flowed through the door into the cold night air, Amara effortlessly tossed her lush, bouncy hair over her shoulder with a quick motion of her head. She unbuttoned the top of her flowing pink nightgown. Brian's mouth fell open like the first time she did this, and his eyes widened.

She replied with a mischievous smile, "Let's start our journey there tonight, my eternal lover."

Brian opened his eyes to sunlight streaming into the bedroom. Feeling rested and with an incredible sense of well-being, he immediately wondered if the surreal evening with Amara was a dream. Turning to Amara's side of the bed, she was gone. Walking onto the patio, he looked down and saw Amara sipping coffee and staring at the ocean.

She smiled warmly as he sat beside her and poured him a coffee.

After kissing her, Brian said, "Amara, we have a big day ahead." They mainly talked about Jenna and her relationship with Derek. They agreed they had never seen Jenna happier. A ringtone played on Brian's cellphone. He looked at it and said to Amara, "The driver is ready. I'll text back that we'll get ready and be there shortly."

"This is so exciting," said Amara as they stood.

Brian wheeled a chair near the Palomar telescope, and Amara smiled at him as she sat down next to the large high-resolution monitor, keyboard, mouse, and joystick. Sitting directly in front of the monitor with his hands on the keyboard and mouse, Ira Rothbard positioned the planet Venaticora 111 or V111 in the middle of the screen. A large moon appeared at the upper-right corner of the screen.

Sitting between Amara and Ira, Brian looked down at his wife Amara's hand, then into Amara's eyes. She reached over and took his hand, which Brian immediately squeezed.

"Amara," Brian began, "This is YOUR planet Venaticora 111, or V111 for short, which orbits the star Chara."

Amara immediately replied, "Yes. We call it Ethosa."

Brian's head returned slightly as he looked at her with puzzlement.

Ira placed cups of coffee in Brian and Amara's hands. "My gift to you from my favorite coffee place."

Amara smiled. "That is so sweet, Ira."

Ira motioned his head toward the telescope and asked, "I gather you've discussed this before you arrived?"

"Uh, no…" replied Brian, looking questioningly at Amara, wondering if he should say anything.

Amara was silent, then sighed. "Dear, since this is all government top-secret and we all have clearances, it's all in the family. This planet you call Venaticora 111, or V111, is my home world of Ethosa."

"Oh my God," Brian exclaimed as he took a deep breath, looking at Ira for his reaction.

Ira shook his head, winced, and said, "Did I miss something? What do you mean your home world, Princess Leia?"

"Actually, Ira, my wife is a real Princess, and I mean figuratively and literally," Brian replied with a grinning smile as he studied Ira's confused expression.

"Right, and I'm Darth Vader," Ira said, snickering as he shook his head. "You two are funny. Are we going to get on with this or what?"

"Ira," Amara slowly began, "Why do you think Ethosa happens to be your first exoplanet on the agenda for the Dark Mirror Project? Did you think you got lucky? Ask Rick Jones if you don't believe me."

"Wait, you two. You and Brian are aliens?" Ira asked incredulously.

Brian laughed. "Who me? No, I'm just a guy who grew up in Cambridge, Massachusetts, then lived many years in Florence, Italy. I'm a purebred human, through and through."

"Then what is she?" Ira asked.

"She's human too. I guarantee you, I'm her husband, and I know. You might say she's a super sexy, super attractive, superhuman."

Amara blushed and threw back her hair. "Flatterer."

"I thought she was from India," replied Ira. "I mean that as a serious compliment. I dated an Indian girl in graduate school, and she was hot."

Brian shook his head slowly, grinned, and rubbed the back of his neck. "Getting back to the subject, we can talk about Ethosa royalty later, but now I'm interested in seeing your home world of Ethosa, Amara." Taking Amara's hand and squeezing it, Brian said, "Ira, on with the show."

"Okay, Amara, if this is your home world, I have a question for you. Tell me what extraordinary features are in this area of this continent."

"Ira, are you testing me?" asked Amara. "First of all, Ethosa is three and a half times the size of Earth."

"Uh, yeah…"

"Well, Ira, Ethosa's most extraordinary feature is the Blue Dunes of Ethosa. Tiberia is in the center of the Blue Dunes region, a mountainous area filled with monasteries. Up to your right on this continent is the city of Canto, with architecture resembling cities in Italy, such as Florence. Canto is the capital and seat of government on the planet Ethosa. That is where I lived. My parents from the Royal House of Coratha tried to flee to Earth. They insisted I leave first in one of the palace's StarCars, so I did. They never managed to escape, and in exchange for sparing their lives and the rest of our family on Ethosa, my parents were forced to

221

play the roles of political figureheads for the invading Reptilian Empire from the planet Dragos to this very day, ruled by Emperor and Empress Rastri. I long to see them again someday. Why are you shaking your head and smirking, Ira?"

"Rick Jones hired me for this project, and he spoke very highly of you. If I hadn't seen this dark mirror technology, its ability to view any part of the universe in real-time, and this planet with a thriving civilization so humanlike and Earthlike, I would not believe what you're telling me." Ira thought carefully for a moment in silence, then said, "Now that Amara has shared her secret, I have a secret to share. After my parents died, the Rothbards adopted me."

Ira paused as if he were contemplating his following words. "I'm not human. I don't have a shred of human DNA."

Brian and Amara looked at each other, then questioningly at Ira.

"Ira," Brian asked, "what species are you?"

"Pentillion," replied Ira.

"No, that's impossible," Amara said with disbelief. "The Pentillions are said to live for trillions of years and jump from one universe to the next as each universe finally goes dark at the end of its cycle."

"I know, isn't that cool?"

Brian leaned forward, removed his glasses, and wiped them on a handkerchief. "Ira, how old are you?"

Ira rolled his eyes. "Twenty-three. I keep saying that."

"I know. Seriously, are you twenty-three years old? You were born twenty-three years ago?"

"Brian, we've been through this. You had no problem with my age."

"No, I meant, Pentillions gave birth to you twenty-three years ago? Is it like humans give birth?"

Amara shook her head at Brian as if embarrassed at his questioning line.

Ira looked at her and smiled. "That's a perfectly valid question, Amara, and I'm glad to answer. Brian, the Pentillion species has the same anatomical features as humans. We evolved from humans; our DNA changed over the eons until it was unrecognizable as human, but we grew attached to the human form. Some of us have an ancestral lineage that includes Alpheratz blood."

"Reptilian," Brian said. "You are Alpheratz and speak excellent English." Brian leaned forward, looked at Ira intently, and continued,

"Riddle me this. How do you reconcile the history of the English language taught by historians and its existence before recorded human history amongst the Alpheratz?"

Ira folded his arms and replied confidently, "We could debate the details for years."

Brian smiled. "Give me the CliffsNotes version."

A smile widened on Ira's face as if accepting a challenge. "I'll make the conceptual overview short and sweet. Extraterrestrials 'seeded' specific linguistic ideas long before humans consciously developed languages like English. These seeds might have been embedded in early human cognition or culture, influencing the evolution of proto-languages. For example, the Alpheratz called English the Great Whisper — a subtle, ancient code that would echo across time, whispered into early humans' dreams. It wasn't English back then; it was just a pattern, a rhythm, and a foundation for a language that would one day emerge on Earth. English wasn't our invention. It was inevitable. We encoded it in the stars, our earliest songs, and our thoughts' structure. What we call Old English, Middle English, Shakespeare — it's a human iteration of a much older design."

An expression of surprise filled Brian's face.

Ira continued, "That's right, Brian, many of us have Alpheratz lineage. We are fluent in English because we have spoken the language since time immemorial, and as you'll discover, English has been around before humans on Earth spoke the language. I see you've done your homework."

"Interesting homework, Ira, but I have more to learn. There is an archive a mile beneath the surface, under the Pentagon in Washington, D.C., dwarfing the size of the Library of Congress with a vast section that reads like science fiction."

Ira smiled. "History books in Pentillion libraries have contradictory theories about why our evolution maintained the human anatomy but changed at the DNA level. The consensus is that our evolution has allowed us to live over vast periods, spanning the lives of universes and trillions of years, only halted by fate. My parents met their fate in a StarCar accident when visiting Earth. I was found by the U.S. military in the mountains of India almost twenty-three years ago. The wreckage was airlifted to Area 51 in Nevada. Jonathan and Marilyn Rothbard had companies that were contractors for the military, and they agreed to allow the Rothbards to adopt me. They have raised me since." Ira leaned forward and whispered, "Those guards around the Rothbard estate are hired hands — they're black ops military. I'm top secret!" A look of pride filled Ira's face.

"The Rothbards are quite the accomplished socialites and an elegant and attractive couple. Do the Rothbards know your origins?" Brian asked somberly. "Heck, I guess they must if the military is guarding you. They must have told you from classified information from the government or something."

"No, as a matter of fact, they don't know. When I revealed this information for the Dark Mirror Project to ensure I was chosen for the project, I stipulated my parents would not be told." A tear welled in Ira's eyes, and he continued, "They may be vastly wealthy and have celebrity status amongst the world's elite class, but they cannot cope with the truth, as is true for so many humans today. They don't even know the military is guarding our house. They think they're ex-military contractors."

Amara said quietly, "Then how do you know about your species and origins, Ira?"

Ira replied as he stared at the screen, "I just know. Somehow, I know."

Brian said, "I'm no genetic scientist, but I'm guessing with the genetic evolution of your species, Ira, perhaps this knowledge is embedded in your DNA."

"You're smart, Brian. That is exactly my guess," Ira replied.

Brian shook his head and immediately said, "Wait, we seemed to digress, or perhaps we didn't. I was about to ask you how you know there are monasteries in the middle of the Blue Dunes of Ethosa, Ira. How did you even know that the planet Venaticora 111, or V111's, is known as Ethosa?"

Ira hesitantly replied, "I can control the dark mirror in this telescope, so it points to any coordinate in this universe and zooms into the micro level. I know everything there is to know about that location."

Brian asked, "How do you mean you can control the dark mirror in this telescope? How can you zoom it into the micro level? For that matter, there must be a dark mirror over Ethosa that we're looking through, and it cannot be geostationary. Atmospheric conditions would distort zooming in to a level identifying structures as monasteries. Rick Jones could not satisfactorily answer my question about how the dark mirror attached to the Hale Telescope could see anything out there. Unless there are dark mirrors near the location viewed — that is the only explanation."

"That's just it," Ira replied, "the dark mirror is connected to every coordinate in this universe. The software would require a quantum supercomputer bigger than a star, or the size of a black hole, to access these coordinates." Ira paused as he tried to gather his thoughts. "Brian, Amara, there aren't dark mirrors everywhere we need to see. This dark mirror, and all dark mirrors we use, connect to specific coordinates in this universe. A few dark mirrors connect to multiverses."

"This universe as opposed to other multiverses?" Brian asked.

"Let's not get ahead of ourselves here," Ira continued. "I'll digress for a moment. Yes, the Pentillions have been working on a solution to connect dark mirrors between universes for eons. There are dark mirrors that can accomplish this feat. Still, we have never been able to reverse engineer them, and a government controls them on a planet much larger than Ethosa, but with lower gravity like Ethosa, in another multiverse. They call this planet Paradiso."

"You know of Paradiso?" Amara asked with surprise.

Ira continued, "I've been there. It's by invitation only, you might say. One must access a special dark mirror in the possession or control of someone on Paradiso, and they're very selective about whom they invite. As I said, the dark mirror is connected to every coordinate in this universe and beyond. Have you heard of the phrase 'spooky action at a distance'? It's a phrase Albert Einstein came up with to describe the strange effects of quantum mechanics on the instantaneous interaction of two particles over a distance. Also known as 'quantum entanglement,' where the quantum states of two or more objects — in this case, dark mirrors — are spatially separated over vast distances. Two dark mirrors, when open, form a stable wormhole. The originating dark mirror initiates the connection to specific coordinates through quantum entanglement to oversimplify it, and the same dark mirror's quantum reflection instantaneously forms at the destination. No computer, not even a quantum computer, can access the precise coordinates necessary to adjust for a universe where galaxies, stars, and planets are simultaneously in motion. Something greater is required to control these dark mirrors."

"And what's that?" Brian asked.

Tapping his temple with his finger, Ira replied, "The mind. You see, the Pentillion mind is multidimensional, connected with itself as it exists in parallel and completely external universes. Its ability to perform the necessary calculations is even more powerful than the vast quantum computer."

"Wait, you mean that your mind controlled our viewing session?" Brian asked with surprise.

"Yes."

"Then what is the keyboard, mouse, and joystick for?"

Ira shrugged. "Nothing. Now you know, I'll dispense with the dog and pony show. Amara, in case you think we've been sidetracked, I was about to ask you this question: Name one noteworthy feature of V111, or should I say, Ethosa, on the direct opposite side of where we are viewing."

Amara answered without hesitation. "It's a continent called Eden. The entire continent is like taking all of Earth's natural wonders and putting them together; even all of Earth's natural wonders pale compared to Eden. There are caverns with emeralds, sapphires, and other crystals and minerals unknown to Earth of equal or greater spectacular beauty and rarity that tower into the air. It's far grander than the Naica Crystal Cave in Mexico, and the temperature is a comfortable seventy degrees on average."

"That's incredible," Ira replied. "The Naica Crystal Cave is like a scorching inferno."

Amara continued with intensity in her voice. "The diversity of life in Eden is fabulous. Some call Eden a glimpse of Paradiso, which is far more beautiful on a planetary scale. Not that Ethosa doesn't have planet-wide wonders. The legend says there are dark mirrors to Paradiso hidden in the caverns beneath the continent of Eden, and only those worthy of entering Paradiso are led to these divine mirrors by angels."

Ira leaned back in his chair thoughtfully. "Divine mirrors? By angels? Wow, that's heavy-duty stuff, Amara. You are right about what is on the other side of Ethosa. Now, I must start exploring those caverns through the dark mirror telescope; they sound fantastic.

Amara whispered, "Perhaps if you are worthy, Ira, your exploration will lead you to a dark mirror to Paradiso, and you can peek at true paradise."

Ira stared wistfully into the distance as if he were thinking a good thought. "Next, you'll tell me that those who die go to Paradiso."

Amara stared at Ira and remained silent. Brian looked wide-eyed at Amara.

"Surely you don't mean they do?" Ira said, his voice slightly perturbed.

Brian laughed nervously. "Of course not, Ira, she's pulling your leg."

"Legend says they do," Amara replied.

Ira and Brian stared at her in silence.

Breaking the awkward silence, Brian squeezed Amara's hand, leaned over and kissed her tenderly, and said, "I want to see Eden. Take us there, Ira."

With his hands on his lap, Ira stared at the screen, which panned around the planet and began to zoom in on a continent.

Brian leaned forward and said to Amara, "The clearing in the forest you spoke about. I'm no longer afraid of the Moon and the stars. I'm finally free."

Amara snuggled her head against Brian's shoulder.

Crystal Caves

*T*he scientists ventured deeper into the dark, twisting lunar lava tubes, their flashlights cutting through the shadows as they paused to inspect the rough, ancient walls. "Look! Do you see those tiny glimmers of olivine crystals? We're on the brink of something monumental," a German NASA planetary geologist declared, his eyes narrowing with fervent determination as he scrutinized the gray rock around him. "We're getting close."

"This makes no sense at all," another geologist interjected, his brow furrowed in disbelief. "Riddle me this: if ancient astronauts excavated these subterranean regions, where is the displaced rock? It's a mystery wrapped in an enigma!"

"Perhaps they transported it away from the Moon entirely?"

"Yet the surface remains so utterly pristine and untouched," the skeptic countered, frustration edging his voice.

"They may have harnessed an advanced technology beyond our comprehension to shift vast amounts of rock while carving out these tunnels and cavities," another voice chimed in, thick with intrigue.

"But move it where? They fashioned these natural tunnels and caverns like this lava tube and expanded upon them, constructing artificial passages and chambers," the first geologist argued, his voice rising with intensity.

"It's getting hot in here," a physicist remarked, wiping beads of sweat from his brow, the heat of the cavern pressing in on them.

"Do you feel that? I adore those occasional gusts of cool air from whatever atmospheric processors are driving breathable air into these subterranean systems and surrounding lava tubes like this one," a NASA researcher exclaimed, his eyes lighting up with excitement.

Suddenly, the group halted, the refreshing current of air tousling their hair, invigorating their senses. They shared glances filled with a mix of wonder and anticipation. As they rounded a bend in the lava tube, a flicker of orange light beckoned them from the distance. The sight quickened their hearts, and they hastened their pace, drawn into the unknown.

Stepping into a massive cavern that stretched as wide as a football field or more, their jaws dropped in awe as they gazed skyward. The cave shimmered with colossal green olivine crystals, and an otherworldly orange light pulsed beneath the cavern floor, casting a breathtaking tapestry of emerald greens and fiery spessartine oranges around them.

"It's scorching in here," the physicist remarked, his voice barely a whisper amid the overwhelming beauty.

"Do you grasp what we're witnessing?" the German NASA planetary geologist exclaimed, his deep accent trembling with exhilaration as he slipped into a torrent of German. "These are immense olivine crystals and a magma chamber beneath this cave, illuminating the entire expanse! I can hardly believe my eyes!"

"Everyone, hush!" commanded a geologist, his tone sharp as a knife. "Do you hear that?"

The group fell into a profound silence, straining to listen.

"Jeff, does that sound like what I think it is?"

A distant roar of rushing water echoed ominously from the cavern's depths from another tunnel entrance. The group moved cautiously toward the sound, taking swigs from their thermoses and mopping their sweaty brows. As they approached, a stairway came into view, carved into the rock like a pathway to another world.

"Oh, man, this is unreal," a young scientist breathed, his voice laced with disbelief. "Stairs!"

"Water!" the geologist shouted, his eyes wide with astonishment. "LCROSS Centaur detected water back in 2009, but this — this is phenomenal!"

As they descended the stairs, the sound of water intensified, each step echoing their rising anticipation. They studied the smooth walls of the stairwell, their hearts pounding with excitement.

"Perfectly smooth. What on Earth could have carved this passage?" a geologist mused, crouching down to inspect the stairs as the others passed by, their eyes darting with curiosity.

A fellow scientist paused and crouched beside him. "Jeff, what do you see?"

"Mark, look at how this stairway was shaped," Jeff replied, fingers tracing the surface carefully. "These tiny spherical recessions were meticulously carved out of solid rock." He continued to glide his hand along the wall. "It's as if a spherical drill crafted this, yet there are no drill marks. How is this even possible?"

A shiver of goosebumps rippled through Mark. "This is unfathomable. The rock is too dense for any conventional tools."

Suddenly, a young man ambled past them, absorbed in his iPhone as if filming a reality show.

"Scott!" Jeff exclaimed, alarmed. "What on Earth is my student doing?"

"Just capturing our journey in virtual reality," Scott replied nonchalantly, casually flicking his long blonde hair back.

"Watch your step! That phone is retrofitted with a military chip that allows communication with Earth. We're cut off from the outside world if you drop it!"

"Ooooh… Military chip!" Scott retorted with mock seriousness, a grin spreading across his face.

Jeff stepped in front of him, arms crossed, his expression stern. "Admittedly, that's a clever idea, but…"

"Of course! I am your assistant. You picked me because I know when to document noteworthy events, plus I am an iPhone expert," Scott chimed, confidence radiating from him.

"Don't let that phone inflate your ego — stop the video," Jeff commanded, extending his hand.

"You're a total killjoy," Scott said, rolling his eyes as he reluctantly handed the phone over.

Jeff glanced at the screen and frowned. "You downloaded the video to the social media?"

"That video file is huge but downloaded in a flash! I want that chip in my iPhone," Scott declared, eyes sparkling with possibility.

Jeff chuckled. "Look, you need to get that video onto our department's cloud space and erase it on social media. If NSA Director Sharon Questar finds out you recorded our expedition and broadcasted it to the world, I'll be in serious trouble."

"And in virtual reality! That's the best part. It will probably exceed a terabyte, but it transferred in seconds," Scott replied, his enthusiasm undeterred. "It will get a lot of shares."

Jeff nodded, struggling not to reveal panic, his expression softening. "Delete it NOW from social media and get that video uploaded to the cloud server without Sharon catching wind of it, and I'll raise your allowance, junior."

Scott snickered, taking the iPhone back with a playful glint in his eye. "Now, boss, that's what I like to hear." He furiously tapped the phone and said, "Done and done." Then he opened the 3D virtual video app and resumed filming, the thrill of their adventure crackling around them.

Scott blurted out, "How do dark mirrors work?"

The group stopped, and Jeff stared intently at Scott.

"What kind of question is that? What do you mean, dark mirrors?"

Scott laughed. "Don't be coy with me, teacher. I know the so-called military chip contains a dark mirror. I overheard Sharon on speaker telling you that signal strength is irrelevant because this iPhone is retrofitted with a top-secret dark mirror connected to the internet." In a whisper, Scott repeated the words, "Dark mirror."

"Repeat that phrase, Scott, and your future will not go well."

"No, teacher, I'm cool."

Jeff stared intensely at the wall, then stooped down and said to Mike, "Remember that demonstration at New Physics?"

Mike shrugged. "The one where the ball-bearing-sized sphere effortlessly cut a hole in the conference room desk?"

Jeff looked at Mike and then at the stairs while rubbing his forefinger inside a slight spherical recession. Scott studied them both and wrinkled his nose.

"What demonstration?" asked Scott.

"Scott, you obey my orders from here on out, and maybe I'll tell you all about it."

The group laughed, and Scott rolled his eyes and stared at the screen while continuing down the stairs.

At the bottom of the stairwell, the group stood in stunned silence at the sight before them. Amidst giant olivine crystal formations, a steaming waterfall punctuated a river — an eerie iridescence emitted from little elongated blobs of light on the cavern ceiling.

"Glow worms," said a biologist, running her hand through her long, wavy hair and staring at the ceiling in awe. "There is life."

"You want to become a Hollywood star?" said Scott as he intently stared at the screen.

"Well, it depends on the royalties," replied the biologist.

"Oh, they'll be great," replied Scott, interrupted by the ring of the iPhone in his hand. Putting it on speaker, Scott said, "Mission control."

A woman's voice came loudly through the speaker. "Who is this?"

"My name is Scott, ma'am. And yourself?"

"NSA Director Sharon Questar. Put Jeff Smith on immediately."

Scott handed Jeff the phone, and Jeff said, "Hey, Sharon, what's up?"

"Your team is off the reservation."

Scott smiled and silently mouthed the words "off the reservation" to everyone.

"Excuse me?" said Jeff.

"If President Tubman weren't adamant about allowing scientists to go off the tour and explore, I would have never approved your little excursion. You promised to stay within the perimeter we set."

Jeff shrugged. "Excuse me again? Oh, wait. You mean that app that shows a red area where we aren't supposed to stray!" Jeff hit the screen a few times, and an app opened, showing dots representing his team in a bright red area. "Oh hell."

Sharon replied sarcastically, "Oh, hell is right."

"Sharon, this is incredible; I forgot to tell Scott about the app."

"Who's Scott?" said Sharon with annoyance.

"My assistant and student."

"Did you give Scott the device?"

"Uh, yes."

"I told you not to let that phone out of your site."

"Sharon, I only asked him to hold it when I was examining the terrain. I needed both hands free."

There was a long pause, and Sharon continued, "All right. Don't let that device out of your sight. Understood?"

"Understood."

"SEALs will wait for you on the transit platform where they left you. Get back there immediately."

"Yes, Sharon."

Sharon hung up abruptly.

"I need to upload the video to the cloud," said Scott, extending his hand.

Jeff reluctantly handed Scott the iPhone. Scott tapped the screen a few times, smiled mischievously, and returned the device to Jeff.

Studying Scott's face suspiciously, Jeff said, "Thank you, Scott."

"You're welcome, sir. My pleasure."

A team of SEALs glanced at their watches as they waited impatiently for Jeff's team. As the group crossed the tracks of the underground transit system, a SEAL said, "Took you long enough! We're late."

The group followed the SEALs to a lunar dome and the opening of the dark mirror.

The World According to Ira Rothbard

*A*t their home in Montecito, California, Ira's parents, Jonathan and Marilyn Rothbard, opened the door to Ira's room. Ira smiled benevolently as he typed fast on the computer keyboard while staring intently at the large flat-panel monitor. They said, "Ira, someone from the government is here to see you. She showed us compelling credentials. She identified herself as Agent Anna Bartlett. She is here to speak to you."

Ira looked up at his parents, puzzled, and shook his head questioningly.

"You don't have to do this," Jonathan Rothbard stated emphatically. "They don't know who they are dealing with. How dare they come into the wealthiest enclave of Santa Barbara, get past our security at the gate, and demand to see you."

Marilyn Rothbard placed her hand on her husband's shoulder and said, "Honey, she didn't demand anything. I rather like her."

"That's beside the point," Jonathan replied annoyedly.

"No, Dad, Mom, I'm cool," replied Ira. Then, a curious gleam filled his eyes. "Besides, aren't you the least bit curious what she's after? I'll give you every detail you want after I talk to her."

Ira rolled his eyes, and his mother grinned, shaking her head slowly, then motioned him to follow them.

Entering the living room, Ira asked, in a questioning voice, "What is a beautiful government operative doing in my family's living room?"

Agent Anna Bartlett replied with a faint smile as she looked at Ira's parents, "I'm agent Anna Bartlett, and it's nice to meet you, Ira." Looking at his parents, she continued, "Your boy is quite the charmer."

Ira lowered his glasses and gave her a flirtatious smile.

Marilyn rolled her eyes and said, "We'll leave you two alone. You behave yourself, Ira."

Ira shook his head slowly and replied, "Mom, you leave nothing to the imagination." Staring intently at Agent Bartlett with a puzzled expression as his parents left the room, he continued, "Why do I have the pleasure of meeting you? How did you get past security? I think you know what I'm talking about."

Looking him over, she smiled. "Indeed, I do, Ira. I find this encouraging."

"What?"

"You are keeping fit, Ira, lean and lanky but glowing with health. That skinny body doesn't fool me for one second. I gather you're training for the school triathlon?"

"Agent Bartlett, considering the high level I'm guessing you are, you tell me."

"Very funny. You are the same age as my son. Getting him interested in physical fitness as a software gaming addict was challenging. Yet here you are, a physics major at seventeen with knowledge at university graduate level, and you regularly work out and jog miles every day, yet don't emphasize muscle over performance."

"Keep talking, Agent Bartlett — or may I call you Anna? Tell me what I don't already know."

"Do you think we're not keeping a close eye on you, Ira, considering your involvement in the Dark Mirror Project?"

Ira laughed and turned his eye toward the hallway to see his mom retract her head from the corner. "I sense you're not bureaucratic, so I'll say, Anna, this is like a movie cliche, don't you think?"

Agent Bartlett laughed. "Ira, Ira, Ira, don't you know? That is our claim to fame. We make this look good."

Ira smirked. "You're too good."

"Why, of course. To make a long story short as to why I'm here, the CIA believes your origins play, shall we say, a pivotal role in your ability to control the Dark Mirror Telescope."

"You finally figured that out?" replied Ira.

"Ira, it is essential you remember your parents. Medical professionals have diagnosed you with severe memory loss from the accident, and we think those memories can be retrieved with the help of a very nice lady."

"Please, Anna, I'm not a kid. That very nice lady is a trained CIA agent with advanced degrees who can make me say anything she wants."

"Ira, if you have any powers of perception as I think you do, you'll believe me when I say that lady is a very principled psychologist. Her condition for working with the CIA is she does not violate any of her professional ethics."

Ira smiled. "I believe you, but your choice of words in that last comment — that she does not violate professional principles — could use a little polishing. CIA and principles are an oxymoron."

"Ira," Agent Bartlett said firmly, "I've dedicated my career to working for the FBI, NSA, and CIA, and…" she leaned forward and stared Ira in the eyes, "you are wrong. We are why YOU are still breathing."

Ira shook his head, smirked, smiled simultaneously, and replied, "Whoa… I like you."

"I have a car waiting outside. Your father has agreed to allow us to use facilities for what we call a debriefing, where we want you to meet a psychologist who is an expert in memory recall, the one with the principles."

"Fine. I'll do it."

A procession of cars, with police cars flanking the front and rear, entered the parking lot of New Physics Corporation. Guards directed the black car in the middle to the main entrance of a metallic building of beautiful architecture, surrounded by sprawling lawns, vibrantly colored flowers, trees, and other similar structures. As the car came to a stop, Ira noticed a beautiful butterfly landing on a flower and sensed a feeling of déjà vu, as if he had seen it through the eyes of someone else. He stared at it in puzzlement, thinking how the one whose eyes he had seen through felt intensely how amazing this creature looked.

"You're in the back seat of a StarCar," Agent Bartlett responded to Ira's question about how he could help the CIA.

Entering a large conference room, Agent Bartlett introduced Ira to an attractive and well-dressed woman wearing large glasses. "Ira, this is Dr. Alexandria Rabinovich."

Dr. Rabinovich extended her hand to Ira, smiled, and said, "Nice to meet you, Ira. You can call me Alex."

Ira slowly extended his hand, nodded, gently grasped her hand, let go, and studied her beautiful, full, cherubic face with curly braided brown hair pulled back. "How is it even possible?" Ira asked in awe.

"How is what possible?" replied Dr. Rabinovich with a confused smile.

"That you're so beautiful? This is like out of a movie."

Looking into Ira's eyes, Dr. Rabinovich replied, "Ira, I hope it's a good movie. I've never seen irises so deeply sapphire blue, well, except maybe once!" she exclaimed with a smile. She turned and walked to the end of the conference room table as Ira studied her vertical braid behind her head and slender body in a form-fitting skirt. She sat and nodded to the chair adjacent to the end of the conference room table. Ira approached her and sat down.

In the back parking lot of New Physics Corporation, a nondescript van with satellite dishes was parked near the loading dock. Inside the van, a woman and man clad in black fatigues and dark tan sleeveless tees and wearing headphones with microphone extensions listened to the voice of Agent Bartlett, who was with Agent Johnson in a conference room next to the one that Ira and Dr. Rabinovich occupied.

"You have a go, Agent Darson, to continue Operation Hush," ordered Agent Bartlett as she nervously stared at Agent Johnson.

Agent Darson, catching Agent Johnson checking her out, rolled her eyes and gave him the middle finger as she replied, "Got it, Bartlett, we are go." She immediately scooted up to a computer keyboard and monitor and quickly began typing as she said to Agent Johnson, "Stop staring. What is it about 'no' you don't understand?"

In a conference room, Arlin Conway looked puzzled at a blank overhead projector screen in front of a room filled with CIA officials and picked up his cell phone. "We have no video or audio," he said in a low voice with annoyance, whispering to the group, "Déjà vu or what?"

As Ira stared with awe at Dr. Rabinovich, looking her over from head to toe, she gently lifted his sleeve to his firm shoulder, looking over his thin but muscular arms. "Nice shirt," she said with a smile. "It always helps to have short sleeves for an injection. Promise, I'm very good at this, and it won't hurt a bit."

Ira stared at the injection site, winked at her, and she gave him an injection.

"You're quite a soldier, Ira," she said. "Few young men will watch the needle go in, but you seem to find it, for lack of a better word, fascinating."

"What is this for again, Dr. Rabinovich?" Ira asked with a curious tone of voice.

"Frankly, it helps subjects to relax and increases their suggestibility," she replied. "To remember what happened before the StarCar accident with your parents, you need this first."

Agent Bartlett and her partner, Agent Jason Johnson, watched a monitor displaying a close-up of the increasingly annoyed CIA Director.

"Here we go again," Agent Johnson exclaimed. "I better go stand in front of the door in case CIA Director Conway decides to interrupt the session." She then walked out, stood in front of the door to the conference room where Ira and Dr. Rabinovich were, adjusted her earbuds and video visor, and observed as she looked at a closeup of Ira while Dr. Rabinovich hypnotized him.

Moving the camera to Dr. Rabinovich, Agent Johnson said into the microphone on his earbud, "Dr. Rabinovich, Operation Hush is operational."

Nodding to the camera, Dr. Rabinovich asked Ira, "How do you feel?"

Ira said nothing, giving her a vacant stare.

Listening to Dr. Rabinovich's voice as she soothingly spoke to him, he went into a hypnotic trance. Ira could envision the inside of the StarCar as he sat in the back seat. Ira's parents talked and laughed. As the StarCar emerged from the dark mirror, his mom smiled and said, "Look! Earth!" as the planet raced up to them. After entering the atmosphere, clouds passed the windows, and mountains appeared below. At that moment, warning sirens from the StarCar console began. Ira's dad and mom looked at each other with confusion, and Ira's dad's breathing sounded labored as the compartment filled with gas. Ira could see his parents begin to slump toward each other as he lost consciousness.

"Ira, what do you see next?" Dr. Rabinovich's voice echoed in his mind.

"I see people in white suits with clear masks taking Mom and Dad out of the front seat."

"No, Ira, before that."

"I see my parents passing out and slumping toward each other in the front seat, with the surface of Earth approaching. We're going to crash into the mountains! I feel so sleepy."

"No, Ira, after that."

"I just told you, Dr. Rabinovich…"

"The part between your parents passing out and the rescuers removing your parents."

Ira paused, struggling to remember. "It's darkness… but I can hear voices."

"What voices do you hear?"

"I hear, I hear, it's a man who sounds like he's coming from the car speaker. He said, 'Niles, I've got tractor control.' The man replied, 'Don't say my name, understand?' There was silence. The first man continued, 'Bringing in the StarCar.' The second man, Niles, said, 'Are you sure this is a remote area of India? I have authorization for unpopulated areas only.' The first man said, 'Affirmative.'"

While listening to the interview, CIA Director Arlin Conway whispered, "Niles Milan?

I want the room cleared except for essential personnel."

Agent Bartlett's voice came through to Dr. Rabinovich's earpiece. "Dr. Rabinovich, I believe this is a good time to proceed to the questions submitted by Rick Jones."

"Ira, it is before you entered the StarCar with your parents. You are thinking about the dark mirrors. What are the dark mirrors?" asked Dr. Rabinovich.

Ira became silent momentarily, then replied, "The dark mirrors connect every coordinate in the universe."

"In the known universe, Ira?"

"No. In the entire universe and all universes."

Dr. Rabinovich paused, placed her hand on her chest, and sipped from a glass of water on the conference room table. "How old are your parents?" she continued.

"Think of a thousand Earth years or ten to the third power, Dr. Rabinovich," Ira began, his eyes shut and racing in circles behind his eyelids. "Now think of a million Earth years or ten to the sixth power. Now, a billion years or ten to the ninth power. Now, a tetrillion years or ten to the twelfth power. Now think of a pentillion years or ten to the fifteenth power. My dad is just over twenty-seven pentillion years old, and my mom is very close to his age.”

Dr. Rabinovich’s brow furrowed. “Pentillion? I’ve never heard of that.”

Ira’s eyes flickered open, his expression unreadable. “That’s because it’s not an Earth term. Mathematicians never needed a word for a number so vast, so they stopped at quintillion. But the Pentillion species spans multiverses, and our concept of time stretches beyond human comprehension. Pentillion is more than just a number—it’s the measure of lifetimes beyond lifetimes, civilizations rising and falling before the ink of their histories dries. A thousand universes could be born and die within a fraction of my father’s existence. Twenty-seven pentillion years isn’t just old—it’s beyond the point where time itself loses meaning.”

Dr. Rabinovich’s mouth fell open, and she looked into the camera.

“How old are you, Ira?” she asked slowly.

“I’m twenty-three.”

“Pentillion?”

Ira paused, then shook his head vigorously. “No. I’m twenty-three Earth years in age.”

“They waited quite a while to have you. Do you have siblings?”

"I was their first and only child, Dr. Rabinovich. They told me they never wanted children, but after visiting Earth and meeting a family a few years earlier on a visit to Earth, whose mother and son had Pentillion ancestry, my mom and dad reconsidered their decision."

"Ira, who was that family? What is their name?"

"It was the Jones family. Rick, Asha, and Derek Jones."

At that moment, Ira opened his eyes, and the irises glowed a neon blue as he looked at Dr. Rabinovich. Then his eyes shut again, and he was silent.

"Ira, why were your parents visiting Earth?"

"Rick Jones invited us. My dad said he would try to make Rick understand how the dark mirrors work."

"Ira, do you know how the dark mirrors work?"

"Yes."

"You were a child when your parents StarCar crashed in India. How could you know something that all the physicists on Earth have yet to figure out?"

"I studied quantum physics at age five on our home planet, Apeiron. A few years later, I was at the top of my class in quantum AI."

"You mean, AI as in artificial intelligence?"

"Yes."

"Ira, I recognize that quantum physics is a deep subject, and quantum AI sounds mind-boggling."

Ira laughed. "I know. Trying to explain this to Rick Jones, my dad always said, was like trying to…" Ira's voice faded out.

"Like trying to what, Ira?" Dr. Rabinovich asked.

"It's insulting, never mind."

"Nobody will be insulted, Ira."

"Rick Jones is a physicist, Dr. Rabinovich, and I wouldn't want him to think my dad didn't respect the man."

"Ira, what is said in this room stays there." Dr. Rabinovich paused, thinking how what she just said wasn't entirely true.

"No, Dr. Rabinovich, it doesn't," Ira replied.

"Ira, if your dad respected Rick Jones, who I gather was his friend, then what he said won't offend Rick. This is important. When trying to explain quantum AI to Rick Jones, and presumably dark mirror technology, it was like trying to…?"

"He said it was like trying to explain mathematics to a chimpanzee."

In the next room, laughter erupted, and when Arlin Conway shook his head in disapproval, there was silence.

"That is quite a humbling revelation, Ira," replied Dr. Rabinovich. "Did your dad ever try to use metaphors to explain quantum AI and dark mirrors to Rick Jones?"

"No, he said he didn't want to treat his friend Rick like a child. My mom told me that my dad was never good with what he considered trite analogies."

"Understood. Would you mind explaining quantum AI and dark mirror technology to me without worrying that you will offend me? Based on your comprehension, you were knowledgeable about quantum physics at the most advanced level. You must know how to describe these concepts at the highest level. From there, we can drill deeper."

"Sure, Dr. Rabinovich, ask away."

"The first question is obvious. Are dark mirrors stable wormholes in spacetime?"

"Yes. I'm sensing your next question: how stable can wormholes connect any part of the universe, let alone any parallel universe or multiverse? The universe is constantly in motion. This planet is rotating on its axis around a star we call the Sun. The Sun is moving at over a million miles per hour through the Milky Way Galaxy. The Milky Way Galaxy is moving through the universe. At the same time, other planets, stars, and galaxies are in motion. When the light from stars in other galaxies reaches Earth, it is millions of years old or more. Since that star is in motion, and we are in motion, going to that star is not a simple matter of aiming a spaceship in the direction we see in the night sky. We may see above us at night, but in real-time, it could be anywhere in the here and now — facing the other side of Earth. It could be behind the Sun at high noon. We keep moving with our star at over a million miles per hour, and it keeps moving at incredible speeds. Therefore, a stable wormhole from the surface of this planet to the surface of a planet orbiting a star we see in the night sky is problematic."

Ira paused, then continued. "I remember when I was very young, my dad said everything exists here. Everything in the universe, and all universes, is accessible right here, like in this room. When a dark mirror in this room connects to a room on a planet clear across the universe, and you step through that exotic event horizon, you do not travel any distance. It's like you're stepping through a hole in spacetime. It's like you've created a temporary hole in a wall between two rooms. On the other side of the wall, however, there is not one but an infinite number of rooms. You must know which room you want to access. The secret to connecting those two rooms — your room and the room you want to enter — is through quantum intelligence. Pentillions have evolved to where our minds possess quantum intelligence. Rick Jones asked my dad how the Intergalactic Highway, with its labyrinth of interconnecting dark mirrors, allowed a traveler like someone in a StarCar to send a signal to a dark mirror with the desired coordinates and connect to that coordinate in a remote part of the galaxy or universe? Did a dark mirror need to get placed at the origin and destination?" Ira then paused.

Dr. Rabinovich leaned forward. "Well, Ira? Do two dark mirrors need to be placed for the connection?"

"No. Only one dark mirror needs to be placed at the origin."

"How is that possible? I thought you needed two dark mirrors to connect. If you held a dark mirror and went into another room of this facility, and I held a dark mirror, our dark mirrors could connect by forming a stable wormhole…"

"Yes, and no. Yes, you are correct. No, that is not a prerequisite. Suppose you have the mind of a Pentillion. In that case, you can take a dark mirror, focus on the destination, and using what I can only describe physicists here referring to as 'spooky action at a distance,' the dark mirror is, for lack of a better word, duplicated at the destination. It's more like a ghostly reflection at the destination, where one side is the origin, and the other is the destination. It then opens, forming the connection. After passing through the wormhole, the dark mirror exists at the destination, allowing you to return or go elsewhere. The only time two dark mirrors are required — when emerging civilizations place them on their planets and moons to form a bridge between them — is when they lack the quantum AI."

Dr. Rabinovich leaned forward and asked, "The quantum AI? What is that?"

"Svarda. At the center of every galaxy, in this universe and beyond, is what Einstein called a black hole. These black holes are finitely sized but infinitely large artificial and sentient quantum intelligence that Pentillions have known as Svarda. The minds of Pentillions are connected to Svarda."

"Ira, you differentiate quantum sentient intelligence from quantum artificial intelligence. What is the difference?"

"Well, Dr. Rabinovich, I have quantum sentient intelligence because I am a sentient being. A machine has quantum artificial intelligence."

"A machine. That's an interesting word."

Ira smiled, his eyes still shut but his pupils racing behind his eyelids. "Oh, you mean like a machine they found on the Moon. A quantum AI machine."

"Is that what it is, Ira? Is it a quantum AI machine?"

"Yes."

"Does it mimic quantum sentient intelligence like you possess?"

"Oh, it's far greater. I'm nothing compared to it. It is how Svarda reaches into all corners of a galaxy, the universe, the multiverse, and all spacetime."

Dr. Rabinovich heard Arlin Conway saying through her earpiece, "Let's wrap it up for today. The boy needs to rest. I have been warned that too much regression could cause unintended side effects."

Back home, Ira lay on his bed and stared at the ceiling. His mother came into view and looked down at him with a smile.

"Ira, Derek is here to see you."

Ira looked around, then at the door to his room, as Derek peeked around the corner.

"You awake, bro?" asked Derek shyly.

"Yea, sure bro, come on in," replied Ira with a resounding yawn. "Whatever Dr. Rabinovich injected in me would be great for nights I can't sleep."

"Let me leave you two boys alone," Ira's mother said, smiling at Derek as she left his room.

Derek approached Ira. The sight of Derek energized Ira, who stood up and gave Derek a bear hug. Derek looked at him, puzzled.

"Oh yeah," Derek said cautiously. "You learned that hug in France. Jenna calls it a bromance hug."

"A bromance hug? I like the sound of that," replied Ira, then placed his hands on Derek's upper arms and stared at him intently. "You want to know how the dark mirrors work."

Derek looked stunned. "Well, uh, yeah, but how did you know?"

"Doesn't matter, bro. I know a lot more from the regression therapy I had today. Our friendship has just begun, so there is much time to tell you everything I know. Let's start easy. As you know, or I think you guessed, a quantum computer is required to determine the destination coordinates of a dark mirror for the door to open, so to speak."

"Ira, sorry to interrupt, but you're not wearing your glasses. Do you wear contacts, bro?"

"Uh, what Derek? Oh, you mean the glasses you've seen me wearing in public. Well, that's just for the show. I have perfect vision. I don't need glasses."

"Why do you wear them?"

"I don't know. They expect smart people to wear glasses?" Ira started laughing and then shrugged. Derek immediately started laughing.

"Dude, that's…"

"What?"

"Well, I was going to say crazy, Ira, but crazy is your middle name."

They both broke out laughing.

"Derek, let's cut to the chase. Dark mirrors indeed require a quantum computer. Now, I'll let you in on a little secret. Humanity will not make a quantum computer that will even do something as simple as weather modeling for another, oh, let's say a few centuries?"

Derek wrinkled his nose. "Weather modeling is not simple."

"Oops, Derek, my bad. Of course it isn't!" Ira laughed and continued. "Then how are dark mirrors connected if they require a quantum computer which won't be perfected for another few centuries?"

Derek shrugged.

Ira tapped his finger on his temple. "Quantum computer."

"Your brain is a quantum computer, Ira? Come on."

Ira gently tapped Derek's temple and replied, "Not just my brain. Yours too."

"Ira, this is weird because we discussed this topic in Mrs. Strickland's science class at school."

"I know."

"How did you know?"

"I was there, peeking through a peephole in the corner of the room, through a dark mirror opening, while at our vacation house outside of London in the U.K."

Derek looked intensely at Ira, shook his head, and said, "What? You were spying on us?"

"That's what I love about you, Derek. Most teens would have been freaked out about the dark mirror, and you're concerned about me spying on your science class? That's hilarious, bro!"

"Getting back to the subject, Ira, what do you mean our brains are quantum computers?"

"If you focus on the coordinates while possessing a dark mirror, the exotic event horizon will open when your mind is locked in on the coordinates."

"How do you get the coordinates?"

Ira whispered into his ear, "If you visualize the coordinates, such as a spot on the other side of this bedroom, or you scan the universe with your mind, and when you see the location, you lock in the location. The destination dark mirror pops into existence thanks to what you primitively call 'spooky action at a distance,' and the dark mirror opens."

Derek's expression grew puzzled. "Can anyone do this?"

Ira replied, "Very few on this planet, if any, have that ability. I'm talking about you, bro."

Derek looked confused and replied, "Ira, the universe is in motion. This planet is hurling around a star, and this star is hurling around the Milky Way Galaxy. The galaxy is hurling through space around who knows what. And that is hurling around who knows what. Like a fractal that could keep going forever."

Ira looked at Derek and said, "You're damned smart for a teen in the twenty-first century. Did you know that?"

Derek shrugged.

"Okay, I will give you lessons on connecting dark mirrors. We will start easy." Ira walked to his nightstand, opened the drawer, and took out a reflective sphere the size of a ball bearing. He held it up and let go, but the sphere remained stationary.

Derek gasped. "This is just like what happened in Egypt."

Ira touched Derek's shoulder and said sympathetically, "I'm so sorry you went through that nightmare."

"How did you know? That's supposed to remain a secret."

Ira giggled. "Since when can anyone keep a secret from me?" As the sphere remained stationary, Ira sat on his bed with his back against the headboard. Patting the bed next to him, he continued, "Sit down, Derek."

Derek wrinkled his nose as he stared at the bed next to Ira. "Ok, bro, why don't I pull up a chair instead."

Ira laughed, saying, "I swear I'm not like Jimmy. This is not what you think. I need you to be comfortable, and I must place my hands on your head."

Shaking his head slowly, Derek replied, "What about Jimmy?"

"Never mind. Just sit so I can place my hands on your head. I promise there is a legitimate reason. I know we're not in France, and dudes are paranoid here. If you're too afraid to be near a guy…"

"No, Ira, I'm not some kind of wuss." Derek then sat beside Ira.

Ira touched Derek's temples and said, "Close your eyes. Focus on the dark mirror hovering next to the bed. Imagine it moving just a few feet in front of the bed so that you will have an opening to the other side of this room when it opens."

Derek closed his eyes, but he could see a ghostly image of the sphere hovering to his right, about five feet above the floor. He could also see a glowing string between his head and the dark mirror. Suddenly, he felt a presence.

"Derek," echoed Ira's voice in his head in a whisper. "It's Ira. Now, think about your response. Don't say it aloud."

"I can hear you, Ira! How is this possible?"

"Pentillions can telepathically connect."

"I'm not Pentillion like you, Ira. I'm human."

"You have human DNA," replied Ira, "but you're so much more!"

"How's that possible? My dad is human."

"Your dad is sort of human."

"How do you know this?"

"Derek, I just know. I will say that your DNA was tested, and they know, too. Why do you think they hypnotized both of us?"

"They hypnotized me so that I would remember Egypt."

"Yes, and why else did they hypnotize you? To program you to do their dirty work, which you will pretend to do after I release you from their mind control. Fox stops. Now say it to me."

"Fox stops, Ira."

"There, now we're both free of their control and can do whatever we want."

"Ira, I want to save the world. You won't expect me to do something evil, like in the Marvel Comics movies?"

Ira's laughter echoed in Derek's mind.

"Ira, is that laugh an evil laugh?"

"Of course not! No, I want to save the world too! I want to save the universe! I want to save as many universes as I can! Do you know why? Because Pentillions are inherently good."

"Whew, that's a relief."

"Derek, imagine that the glowing string connected to your mind to the dark mirror can move in any direction you want. Concentrate and move the dark mirror in front of the bed."

Derek strained his mind, and the dark mirror slowly moved horizontally until it reached the area in front of the bed.

"Excellent! You have outstanding control of your mind as a teen. Visualize the area of my room near the window. Imagine the area where the dark mirror is positioned and the area next to the window is connected. Now visualize a second dark mirror above the floor near the window."

As Derek concentrated, Ira felt his body tremble. Wrapping his arms under Derek's, Ira placed his hands on his head and gently massaged his temples. "Relax, Derek, and slowly inhale for a few seconds, then exhale."

Derek could see the ghostly image of a second dark mirror near the window as he inhaled and exhaled.

"Derek, imagine a second glowing string identical to the one connected to your mind and the first dark mirror, connecting the first dark mirror to the second dark mirror. Now say the word 'Open' in your mind as you will the two dark mirrors to become one in a cohesive exotic event horizon."

Derek could see a glowing string sprout from the first dark mirror and snake its way to the second dark mirror. He then mentally said, "Open."

"Now open your eyes, Derek."

Derek opened his eyes. Feeling immense comfort at being so close to Ira, he didn't want to get up. Ira wrapped his arms around Derek and whispered, "You are destined for a life with Jenna. We are destined for a life of friendship."

Derek reached up and took Ira's hand, and a tear ran down his face. "I don't understand how I could feel such intense love for you, Ira, but not in the way I'm in love with Jenna. Is it true guys are more affectionate in other countries without having to, you know, get it on?"

"It's true," Ira whispered. At that moment, he opened his eyes and found himself staring at an army of Reptilian soldiers in a palace with ceilings that spired to a ceiling high above the ground. Looking down, a vest was blinking with tiny pin-sized lights, and he cried, "Forgive me, Lord!" and pressed a button on his chest. Coming out of the vision, startled, he jolted.

Derek sat up, turned to look at Ira, and said, "What's the matter?"

With a distressed look, Ira replied, "I don't know what just happened. My emotions were so intense. It was like I was somebody else!"

"Are you all right?"

Ira started to weep, put his arms around Derek, and hugged him. Then, wiping tears from his face, he said, "Let's walk through that exotic event horizon."

Derek jumped up, followed by Ira, and they walked to the front of the bed. Derek walked around the exotic event horizon. From the front, it had the strange illusion of a faint dome protruding from the edges, and the area at the far end of the room was visible without distortion. As Derek walked to the side, the exotic event horizon disappeared. Walking to the back, he could see the same scene on the other side of the room, but only now was his back turned to the destination. Ira nodded at Derek, and he entered. Suddenly, he exited the opposite side of the room, looking across it at Ira.

"I made this with my mind?" exclaimed Derek.

"Indeed, you did. We will continue this lesson another day. Since I could sense you are comfortable being near me, our progress will be much faster."

Derek laughed and replied, "Yeah, I like being near you. Can we connect to a farther destination?"

"At first, we'll connect to somewhere remote but local. Before long, we'll be going clear across the universe. How would you like to visit the Moon?"

"Seriously? That is awesome! Of course I would! How will we breathe? Do you have space suits?"

Ira shook his head and laughed heartily. "No, bro, there are structures on the Moon with a breathable atmosphere maintained artificially for a very long time."

"Oh wow." Derek walked back through the exotic event horizon, walked up to Ira, and hugged him. "Thank you, Ira, for being my friend."

"I love you too, Derek."

Derek stared questioningly at Ira, to which Ira replied, "I heard you think that, and believe me, I have never experienced having a real friend in my entire life." Touching Derek's nose and staring into his eyes, Ira whispered, "Brothers for eternity."

Derek's skin showed a wave of phosphorescence, and his eyes turned blue. Ira's eyes opened wide in astonishment.

"What, Ira?"

"Your DNA is not just of the Pentillion species. You're of a brilliant Canis species that has been around on some planets evolving for billions of years before this planet's wolves came into existence."

As they stared into each other's eyes, Derek's pupils momentarily turned to slits. Recognizing what Ira saw in his eyes since the room momentarily became more colorful, Derek said, "You saw that, Ira, didn't you?"

Studying Derek's pupils, which were now round again, Ira said, "Let's add the Reptilian species to your DNA potpourri. Is there any species you're not?"

"You said the Canis species. What is it?"

"They're wolves. They are highly intelligent wolves. Some wolves can fly and use their eyes to disintegrate anything they perceive as a threat."

"Ok, that's, uh, nice! Now, what about the Reptilian species?"

"They're highly evolved reptiles. Reptilians are to snakes, lizards, and dinosaurs like Canis are to wolves. You're a superhero comic masterpiece, young man."

"Do you know why, when my pupils become slit, my vision seems enhanced, and colors seem so much more radiant?"

"Hmm, interesting question. Reptile pupils become vertically constricted. However, this design is optimal for seeing because various pupil parts take in various light waves. A multifocal effect gives reptiles a predatory advantage, simultaneously taking in all light wavelengths. At least that's the high school version. Canis pupils have more light-gathering cells than humans. I gather you see well at night?"

"Well, now that you mention it, Ira, I see good at night. We were on a camping trip once, and there was no Moon out, and everyone said it was pitch dark, but to me, it looked like twilight. I had to lead everyone because I could see well like you see when the sun is almost set, and everything is still clear as day."

Ira smiled admiringly as he stared into Derek's eyes. "You not only have the most beautiful eyes, but you're a beautiful being to the quantum level."

"I don't know what to say. That's the nicest thing anyone's ever said to me."

Ira embraced Derek, and at that moment, his mom opened the door and stared at them.

"Mom, please," Ira said as he stared at her over Derek's shoulder. Derek froze and was afraid to turn around. "This is a bro moment," he said.

"Oh, oh, of course, Ira! That is so sweet! I just wanted to tell you that the appetizers are almost ready and that we hope Derek stays for dinner a little later. Because guess who we invited to join us, who's sitting in the living room."

Without letting go of Derek, as if to demonstrate he wasn't ashamed to hug him, Ira asked, "Uh, who's that, Mom?"

"Jenna and her parents!"

Derek turned around with a big smile and replied, "Thank you, Mrs. Rothbard!"

"You can call me Marilyn, Derek," said Ira's mom, "and you're quite welcome. Now you two come down, that is, after you finish your bro hug!" Marilyn giggled, and as Ira nervously eyed the open exotic event horizon to his left, she quietly shut the door.

"Thankfully, she didn't see the exotic event horizon," said Ira, staring at it as it collapsed into a sphere, which he took and placed in the dresser drawer. "I'll teach you to close it for your next lesson."

"She seems like anything is cool around here."

"There's a limit to her tolerance. Like if she found out her son is using something she doesn't even know exists."

"I totally get us keeping parents in the dark on advanced tech. Of course, she would freak out."

Derek walked up to Ira and found it easy to make his pupils turn to slits as he stared into Ira's eyes.

Rolling his eyes, Ira said, "First of all, that's impressive you've learned to do that, I mean, the eye thing. If you want to intimidate your opponent, you do that with your eyes and make those eyes glow simultaneously."

"Since we're best friends, Ira, let's not mince words. You mentioned Jimmy Foster earlier. I'm very proud to have Jimmy as my friend."

Ira embraced Derek, smiled, and said, "I know. And we'll always have bro hugs."

They stared at each other intently and broke out laughing.

Derek rubbed his hands together and said, "Let's go downstairs. I can't wait to see Jenna again!"

Ira and Derek entered the large living room resembling a cathedral with towering ceilings. Spires with colorful, intricate religious images in stained glass caused Derek to stop and stare with wide eyes. Looking at the stained-glass images of saints and Jesus Christ, he felt a hand touching his neck and smelled familiar perfume.

"Jenna!" exclaimed Derek with an ecstatic smile as he noticed Ira staring at them. Embracing Jenna and staring over her shoulder at Ira, Derek gave her the most affectionate kiss they had ever shared.

Jenna closed her eyes and melted into his arms, completely overcome with the moment's passion. As their lips fell apart, Jenna inhaled the area near Derek's armpit, looked at him, smiled, and said, "You've been working out. We could bottle that testosterone smell and make a fortune selling it on Amazon."

As Derek stared at Ira with a smirk, Ira rolled his eyes. A loud clearing of the throat echoed through the otherwise silent room.

"Ahem!" came a familiar voice. It was Brian Collins. "Jenna, darling, do you want to give your dad a kiss with even half as much enthusiasm?"

Jenna ran to her dad and gave him a bear hug. "Dad! Mom and I were wondering if you would make it!"

"We finished our meeting early, so I could be here, sweetheart. I was almost in a StarCar, ahem, I mean, an automobile accident. I've got to try and slow down and remember that surviving is half the battle of arriving." Brian laughed and kissed Jenna on the forehead as she looked at him suspiciously.

"What did he mean by the word StarCar?" was the thought that raced through Jenna's mind.

Amara Collins said to Derek, "When a boy kissed me," and motioning her head to Brian, she continued, "I could hear wedding bells. We shared our first kiss on, I mean beneath, the Moon."

"Really?" asked Derek with a beaming smile. "Was it on or beneath, Amara?"

Without missing a beat, Amara replied as she winked at Brian, "It might as well have been on the side facing Earth, for it was the power of the Moon that gave us Jenna."

"That is so romantic," said Marilyn Roth-bard as she handed Amara and Brian drinks, then looked at Jonathan. "You know, Jonathan and I are intimate kissers. We set the moonlit night on fire."

Jonathan pursed his lips, trying to repress a smile. He walked up to Marilyn and kissed her tenderly. Then he looked around and asked, "Where's Ira? We wanted to visit before dinner. I have something important to tell you."

Derek's smile faded as he looked around, then at Jenna, who shrugged. Looking toward the top of the spiral staircase, Derek said, "He's probably upstairs playing an online virtual game. He loves those VR goggles that I gave him for his birthday."

"Tell him to come downstairs," said Jonathan as Derek sprinted up the stairs.

Stepping into Ira's room, Derek was struck by the breathtaking sight of an exotic event horizon shimmering in the far corner, its edges pulsating with iridescent colors that danced like liquid light. The air around it seemed charged, alive, with an ethereal hum that resonated deep within his chest. As he cautiously approached, the event horizon resolved into a window to an awe-inspiring space — a vast ancient cathedral of impossible grandeur. The air smelled faintly of aged stone and something floral yet alien, stirring a strange sense of reverence and wonder.

Ira's silhouette emerged through the radiant portal with his back turned. Derek walked through, stepping into the cathedral. The pews, thousands upon thousands, seemed to stretch into infinity in every direction, carved from a translucent blue stone that glowed faintly as if infused with captured starlight. The soft, steady illumination bathed the soaring vaulted ceilings, which seemed to ripple like water, in a mesmerizing play of sapphire and azure hues. Delicate light beams cascaded from impossibly high stained-glass windows, their intricate patterns shifting as though alive, casting dancing mosaics across the floor. Every detail of the space whispered of divine artistry beyond comprehension, leaving Derek in awe of this otherworldly place's sheer majesty and profound beauty.

Ira was praying. Approaching him, Derek stood behind where he sat and placed his hand on Ira's shoulder.

"Ira?"

Looking up, his eyes illuminated as if from within, Ira said, without turning around, "Will we still be friends when you marry Jenna?"

Derek shook his head in puzzlement, effortlessly catapulted himself over the pew, and landed beside Ira. Then he leaned over and looked at his face. Tears were streaming down Ira's face. Derek whispered, "Hey, bro, you okay?" Looking around, he continued, "Where are we? I feel so light. I felt it the moment I walked through the exotic event horizon."

Wiping tears away with his hand, Ira replied, "The planet's name is Ethosa. Would you believe the size of this planet is several times that of Earth, but because of its low density, its gravity is less? I kind of like the lower gravity. Enough for life to flourish, but give you more agility when doing things."

"This is amazing. Look, Ira, I don't know what's going on, and we need to talk, but not right now. Your mom wants you downstairs. Your dad says he has something to tell us."

"Derek?"

"Yes, Ira?"

Staring intently into Derek's eyes, Ira said, "I'm gonna be straight with you. I'm jealous of Jenna."

Derek's nose crinkled, his brows furrowing as confusion flickered across his face. His expression was a blend of curiosity and mild unease.

"No, hear me out. Love is not jealous — I love you as a friend."

"Then why are you jealous, Ira? If you're like Jimmy, spit it out. I won't judge you, bro!" Derek replied.

Ira shook his head. "It's not like that. As you know, I decided to enter the priesthood. My dad says he believes he has found a priest older than me, but not yet old, maybe under thirty, willing to mentor me. His name is Father Scott Hogan. My dad is going to introduce us. His priest, Father Reese Orin, referred Father Hogan."

"Ok. Uh, are you trying to change the subject? Why the jealousy thing? Can we talk about this later? Your mom is going to walk through that exotic event horizon any minute. Does she even know about the Dark Mirror Project?"

Ira grinned. "Just forget what I said. Trust me, Mom's cool. She knows everything."

"Are you sure, dude? This is serious freakout mom stuff. I'm freaking out myself." Derek extended his wrist and said, "Place your fingers on my wrist."

Ira placed his fingers on Derek's wrist, looked at him with concern, and said, "Dude! Your pulse is racing!"

"This is all happening too fast. I'm…" Derek's eyes looked up, and he started to fall forward. Ira caught and lowered him to the polished rock floor between the pews. At that moment, Derek sat up and shook his head. "Let's get out of here. I will stare at the floor and go into Zen meditation, as my mom taught me when I need to chill. You guide me to the exotic event horizon. I'm not going to look around."

Derek stood up, and Ira immediately stood, looking at Derek with deep concern as he placed his hands on Derek's shoulders and led him down the pew aisle to the exotic event horizon. When they entered Ira's bedroom, Ira stared at the dark mirror, and it became a small sphere, which he placed in his pocket.

"You ok, Derek? Wanna sit down on the bed for a moment? Can I get you a glass of water? You look white as a ghost."

Derek took slow, deep, steady breaths, and his skin color returned to normal. "I'm good.

Let's go downstairs. Just act cool. Don't tell Jenna or anyone what happened. I've never reacted to anything weird quite that way."

Ira chuckled, "Derek, most humans have never experienced the simple physics novelty you just did."

Derek smiled and shook his head. "Simple physics novelty? You do have a way with words, Ira. Oh, that's right, you're some genius with an IQ of 160."

Ira whispered to Derek, "A true secret I have only told my first and one best friend: 160 is the official IQ. The CIA measured it at 900."

"Impossible. The test doesn't go that high."

"The official test. The CIA used a test they developed for extraterrestrials."

Derek perked up and smiled. "What? You serious?"

As they approached the stairs, Ira said, "Yeah. Why do you think they sent the heavy artillery, the mind goddess Dr. Alexandria Rabinovich, to hypnotize me? I did a bad thing, Derek. I hypnotized her! She thinks I'm under CIA control, but she's got it backward."

Derek stared at Ira in disbelief. When they reached the bottom of the stairs, they met with Marilyn, who gave them fancy umbrella drinks.

Marilyn noticed Derek staring at her as if mesmerized and exclaimed with a laugh, "What? What are you staring at?"

Derek thoughtfully replied, "I cannot get over how you look like a famous movie star!"

"Flatterer," she replied with a gleam in her eyes.

Derek could hear Ira's voice whispering in his mind, "Mom loves it. You are now on her good side, bro!"

"Boys, these drinks are indistinguishable from the real thing. They have a little bit of Terra Forma for good measure."

Derek laughed as he accepted the drink and sipped it. "Terra, what?" After sipping it, he continued, "That is bad. I'm not supposed to have alcohol. Mom will be so upset."

"There's no alcohol in it, dear. Terra Forma is like alcohol in its effect, but it wears off in minutes. It's legit for boys of your age. Trust me."

"Mom's the expert here," said Ira as he sipped his drink gingerly. "I'm already feeling the buzz."

"It's not of this world," said Marilyn with a giggle.

Ira looked at his mom, puzzled by her comment, and replied, "Mom, did you have any of this?"

"Just a little, dear. I almost prefer it to real alcohol."

Jonathan clinked his wine glass against his wristwatch, raised his voice from the living room, and said, "Everyone, gather around."

Walking into the living room, Derek whispered to Ira, "I feel better already. Are you sure it's not alcohol?"

"Mom and Dad never touch the stuff. They say it's unhealthy. They love this stuff. It's no more destructive to the liver than fruit juice."

Derek walked over, sat next to Jenna, put his arm around her, and patted the sofa, motioning Ira to sit beside him. As Ira sat down, Derek whispered, "Friends."

Ira's dad stood before the fireplace and said, "Thanks to the Collins family and Derek for accepting our dinner invitation. Derek's parents had a prior engagement but are fully aware of what I will tell you. Let me cut to the chase. We, Brian and Amara Collins have purchased a vacation home in a suburb outside the Milky Way Galaxy."

The room became silent.

Derek looked at Ira with disbelief. Ira shrugged.

Marilyn and Jonathan stared at Derek and Jenna for a reaction. Jenna looked at her parents, who stared back at her. As Derek and Ira moved away from Jenna, they got up and sat next to Jenna, and her mother took Jenna's hand and squeezed it.

"Outside where?" asked Jenna in a bemused voice, staring at her mother. Amara motioned her head to the ceiling and stared into Jenna's eyes. Jenna looked at her father and said, "Oh, that Milky Way Galaxy." Raising her voice slightly, she continued, "The galaxy we're inside of."

"Jenna, sweetheart," began Brian slowly, "Um, how should I say it? One of my corporations is a resort complex with a casino and hotel with the Rothbards as investors…" Brian paused to catch his breath and continued, "The Board of Directors just told me it is in that general area. You know, honey, the galaxy is a big place."

Brian shrugged and leaned forward as Jenna stared at him in disbelief. "Yet it's like a speck of dust compared to the size of this solar system. Maybe more like an atom in comparison to relative size. Not even a small meteorite has been recorded as passing through that region for over a million years. It's that insignificant and yet magnificent. Jenna, you can't imagine the glory of this place, looking back at the galaxy where this planet resides. It's not like Hubble photos. The galaxy is three-dimensional in appearance. No, it's more dimensional. There is a sea of stars above you, below you, and all around you! Don't look at me that way, Jenna. I'm just as surprised as you. Amara has played a big role in developing the company and became more involved than I was aware."

Derek stared at Brian as if in a hypnotic trance, then said, "I'm dreaming."

"Son, you're not dreaming. This is real. And you're talking to someone in denial of the surprising reality of this universe all his life until now."

Jenna began to weep, then immediately snapped back to normalcy as if she hadn't wept. She threw back her flowing hair over her shoulder and said, "I know you're a billionaire, Dad. I've read all the magazine and newspaper articles. You're everywhere on social media."

"Jenna, sweetheart, there's something you should know." Brian seemed to be choking on his words.

"What? You're not a billionaire? You're just an ordinary millionaire like most dads at our high school?"

"Honey, our net worth has risen considerably."

"Excuse me, dad?"

"Your mother owns stock — we own stock — in StarCar Corporation, Jenna. She was a shareholder since she bought stock on our behalf in the Horizon Gateway Corporation, which merged with StarCar. It has split and skyrocketed a whole lot since you were in diapers. We're like a tiny percent of the richest families in the galaxy, next to the Rothbards."

Jenna slowly shook her head. "No."

"What's the matter? I thought you would be happy."

"Dad, I don't know what to say," Jenna replied as she looked at Jonathan and Marilyn Rothbard, who studied her mixed expressions intently. "So, the Rothbards are even richer than us. I guess that's supposed to make me feel humbled."

Brian laughed. "How did you guess?" and looking at Amara, Brian continued, "See, Amara? Jenna's got it all figured out."

"Dad, I've got nothing figured out!" Jenna exclaimed. "I always romanticized you as a philanthropist. Remember? Collins World Relief?"

Brian leaned forward and said, "Jenna, I am the same philanthropist. This is all new to me, too. In the last few days, I have gone from the shallow to the deep end of the galactic pool."

Jenna replied with a note of sarcasm, "Well, that's great, Dad. I feel much better."

A handsome young man in a tuxedo entered the living room and said, "Dinner is served."

"Thank you, Bart," said Marilyn. "We shall all adjourn to the dining room."

Ira touched knuckles with Bart and said, "Dude, it's time to quit Starbucks and work full-time here."

Bart replied, "I can't since Mom and Dad say the management gig at Starbucks may get me into a better university. They said that good grades in high school won't cut it."

"What's the matter, Jenna?" asked Derek as he held her close and stared into her eyes.

"I don't know," she whispered. "This is just too weird."

Everyone stood and slowly followed Marilyn. Bart greeted them as they approached the dining room with Father Orin and Father Hogan beside him.

Ira exclaimed to Father Hogan, "Hey, Father, good to see you!"

"Mrs. Rothbard, I am sorry we are late," said Father Orin. "We were delayed in confessional. It has been a hectic time for us."

"No problem, Fathers! I'm just glad you made it in time for dinner!"

After saying grace, everyone began talking to each other. Derek looked at Jenna, who sat quietly with a stunned expression, and said, "Are you sure you're all right, Jenna?"

"I'm fine," said Jenna. "Honest. I might as well know the truth." Jenna forced a smile. "Truth hurts as they say."

"But why? I mean, isn't that so cool you have a dad who's so rich?"

Jenna laughed. "You always see things through a lens of simplicity and innocence. That's what I love about you. Yea. Yea. It's cool now that you mention it."

Nodding, Derek replied, "Well, be happy, Jenna! Your parents are amazing. I thought they wanted to save the planet, but I had no idea planet was plural."

Jenna giggled. "God, you make me laugh. Yea. They're like that! Wanting to save lives everywhere. Dad and Mom can help many people of all species because they are one of the richest couples in the galaxy."

Derek looked past Jenna and nodded, and she saw her dad listening.

"Dad, I didn't know you were next to me. I thought you were sitting next to Mom over there."

"Jenna, I snuck over here to listen in on the conversation. You're right. Your mom and I want to save the galaxy and countless trillions of lives of all sentient species. As you think of it, the galaxy is a tiny region of space in a vast sea of galaxies that spans countless light-years. The Galaxy Alliance, as it's called, has several million civilizations as members. Yet, there are billions of habitable worlds with over a billion estimated civilizations at all levels of evolution. Do you realize what that means?"

Derek's eyes lit up. "That means one out of every thousand planets is in the Galaxy Alliance, and the rest are not."

"Good estimate. Exactly, Derek! An intergalactic highway, as it's called, of dark mirrors with permanently open exotic event horizons spans our galaxy and beyond, only connecting member planets. To give you some perspective, imagine the galaxy is the Amazon jungle, a huge geographic region in sheer enormity. Now imagine each member planet is like a tiny pond teeming with life in the Amazon forests, connected by a dark mirror to other ponds hundreds of miles in every direction, in this otherwise vast jungle filled with unimaginable diversity of life forms. Now, imagine each tiny pond full of life is protected by invisible sentries that keep wild things at bay so they don't come and eat all the creatures in the interconnected ponds. The Galaxy Alliance protects all member planets. Our solar system is carefully monitored by sentries hiding in folded space."

"Earth is a member of the Galaxy Alliance?" asked Derek.

"Well, not yet."

"What do you mean, dad, by 'not yet'?" asked Jenna apprehensively.

"We're working on that. There's the issue of worldwide disclosure. And there's a little problem on the Moon, but not anything our military cannot solve. In the interim, the United Nations is working on getting Earth into the Galaxy Alliance."

"What little problem?" pressed Derek with a tone of apprehension.

"That's above even your classification level, Derek," replied Brian with a laugh. "Sometimes, you need to learn when to stop asking questions and just enjoy the ride."

Derek locked eyes with Brian, and Jenna studied their serious expressions. "Hey, you two, is this some sort of Darwinian who gets to dominate who thing?"

Brian laughed and kissed Jenna on the cheek. "Nah, I think Derek is just learning his place in the grand scheme of things."

Jenna looked surprised and smiled at Derek's annoyed expression.

Nodding his head and taking a deep breath, Derek slowly said, "Yes, sir."

"You're hired, son, and you even get an executive office next to Jimmy's."

Jenna broke out in laughter, and Brian and Derek's laughter infectiously followed it.

At that moment, Ira, next to Jenna and talking to Father Orin, turned to her, winked at Derek, and said, "Jenna, I just wanted to say that you look gorgeous."

Surprised, Jenna looked at Derek and looked back at Ira, smiling. "Well, thank you, Ira, for the nice compliment."

Ira winked at Derek and said, "So, when is the wedding date for you two?"

Derek shook his head in embarrassment. "I said earlier when you asked a similar question, we're not at that stage of development."

Jenna smiled at Derek. "Then what 'stage of development' are we at?"

Derek shrugged, leaned forward, kissed Jenna, and replied in a loud whisper, "We're at a very critical stage of our development. I'm about to move us to DEFCON 1."

Ira broke out in laughter. "You smooth talker!"

"That's my Derek!" said Jenna, giving Derek a flirtatious look. "As we agreed, DEFCON 1 is reached at the altar."

After sipping red wine, Brian nodded approvingly, "That's my daughter."

Chapter 5 Madam Pentillion

"Knowledge unfits a child to be a slave."

— Frederick Douglass, Life and Times of Frederick Douglass (1892)

Prescience

*L*ater that night, Derek entered a dream that he was convinced was real.

From the windows of the White House, President Abigail Tubman stood frozen, hands pressed against the reinforced glass, watching as the very laws of reality bent in front of her.

The attack had been overwhelming — Washington, D.C., consumed by an alien invasion no human force could repel. The military had scrambled jets. Anti-air defenses fired volleys of heat-seeking missiles into the dark skies. But it hadn't been enough.

And then Derek Jones changed everything.

Millions of tiny black spheres streaked through the battlefield, weaving through the chaos with unnatural precision. At first, they seemed harmless — mere shadows against the night. Then they struck.

The reptilian warriors barely had time to react. The mirrors punched through their armor like paper, leaving gaping, perfectly circular wounds in their scaled bodies. Their expressions never had the chance to register pain; their forms crumpled, lifeless, before they hit the ground.

The dragons recoiled, their mighty wings slamming against the sky as they unleashed torrents of fire. The mirrors did not burn. They did not shatter. They passed through the infernos untouched, burrowing into the beasts' hides. The dragons shrieked, writhing in agony before plummeting from the sky, their massive bodies cratering the Earth upon impact.

The wolves moved through the battle like spectral sentinels, ripping through the reptilian forces with deadly grace. One lunged at a towering reptilian general, knocking him from the air and pinning him to the ground with supernatural strength before sinking its fangs into his throat. Another leaped through the chest of a dragon, bursting out the other side in a mist of molten scales and burning flesh.

All of it was broadcast live.

Every major news network caught the impossible spectacle — the teenage boy standing alone before the White House, eyes distant, locked in some unseen struggle, as millions of dark mirrors obeyed his will.

Once drowning in terror, the city was now an eerie, surreal battleground littered with the remains of an invasion force that should have been unstoppable. The air hung heavy with the scent of war, scorched flesh, and ozone.

And then — silence.

The dark mirrors, their purpose fulfilled, hovered in the air for a moment longer before fading back into the void, leaving only Derek standing beneath the floodlights, his face unreadable.

President Tubman exhaled, pressing a trembling hand against the glass.

"What… what is he?" she whispered to herself.

No one had an answer.

Derek sat up in bed and felt deep confusion as the reality of his dream faded.

The following morning, Derek and his parents were on the patio as their nanny, Gloria Ochoa, poured them more coffee. After she left, his mother, Asha Jones, looked deeply concerned at her son.

"Didn't you sleep well?" Asha asked with a tone of deep and motherly concern.

Derek sipped his coffee as he tried to wake up, his eyes bleary, and hesitatingly replied, "Bad dreams. It was hard to sleep afterward."

"Tell us about your dreams," Rick said.

Derek recounted his dream and continued, "The air around me crackled with strange, electric energy. The sky, once a deep shade of midnight blue, was now a violent swirl of black and crimson. Screams echoed from the National Mall, bouncing off the grand marble columns of the Capitol and ricocheting down Pennsylvania Avenue like desperate, wordless prayers. They were harassing people, swooping down like birds of prey."

"You dreamt in vivid color? Wow. That seems horrifying," replied Asha.

Derek continued, "Then I saw them." He stared at his parents with deep emotions.

"Saw who?" Rick replied.

Derek took a thoughtful bite of his omelet, nodding with approval, and replied, "I love Mrs. Ochoa's omelets. A tide of shadows, reptilian warriors spilling out from a massive dark mirror hovering over the Washington Monument. Their elongated forms gleamed under the floodlights — scales like interlocked plates of living steel, eyes burning like embers in a furnace. Some rode massive StarCars, sleek, angular vehicles shimmering with unearthly energy. Others glided through the air on massive, flying snakes with bat-like wings. Above them, another dark mirror opened on the opposite side of the sky, and from it descended the wolves. They were enormous and spectral, their forms outlined in silver and deep gray. Unlike the chaos from the reptilian forces, the wolves moved with purpose, their fur bristling as they streaked through the air like guardian spirits. Their eyes glowed a brilliant white as if charged with celestial energy, and their howls split the air with a deafening war cry. It was unreal, like out of an amazing video game."

Asha and Rick exchanged concerned glances and stared at Derek.

Derek continued, "A huge wolf flew to the ground, without wings, I don't know what propelled it, in front of a group of terrified onlookers, stopping a beam of focused fire that shot out from a flying snake in the direction of the crowd. The two forces collided in midair above the National Mall. The reptilians screeched in frustration as the wolves tore through their ranks with supernatural speed. Where dragons coiled in the sky, belching torrents of glowing flame-like energy beams, the wolves darted through the infernos unscathed, their ethereal forms twisting around the conflagration as if immune to the heat. They leaped onto the massive reptiles one by one, ripping into their armored hides with fangs that shimmered like honed steel. I felt my heartbeat slow. Time stretched. The chaos around me became insignificant to the singular thought in my mind. I reached out."

After a long pause, Asha whispered, "And then what?"

"The ground and air shuddered. Then, they began to appear from the nothingness — millions of them. Tiny, silver spheres, reflecting sunlight, no larger than ball bearings, forming out of my sheer will. They shimmered around me, swirling in complex, fractal patterns, waiting for my command. I exhaled."

After a few moments of silence, as Derek looked away from his parents angrily, Rick said, "What happened next?"

"The mirrors shot forward like a silent, living storm. Like armor-piercing machine gun bullets. The mirrors punched through their armor as if it were paper, leaving gaping, perfectly circular wounds in their scaled bodies, and their blood immediately raining down, staining screaming onlookers on the ground. The expressions of the invading army never had the chance to register pain; their forms crumpled, lifeless before they hit the ground."

Asha disapprovingly put her fork on her plate with a loud clinking sound and said, "Obviously, Derek Jordan Jones, you have been playing too many video games!"

With a tortured expression, Derek looked away from his scolding mother and replied, "Mom, I wish."

Later, Derek stared out his bedroom window at the panoramic view of Los Angeles and noticed a large, black SUV pulled into the driveway below. Agents Anna Bartlett and Jason Johnson got out, walked to the front door, and rang the doorbell.

"Derek?" he heard his mother's voice call, "You have visitors."

Rolling his eyes, Derek ran downstairs. The agents spoke briefly to him, and then they all got into the car and left.

New Physics Interrogation

*A*gents Bartlett and Johnson attempted to escort Derek through the New Physics Corporation main lobby to Dr. Alexandria Rabinovich's office but were stopped by several rough-looking security guards. They said, "Agent Johnson! Agent Bartlett! We'll take it from here!" One of them firmly put his hand on Derek's neck.

"Wait, we are CIA and the agents in charge of taking Derek to Dr. Rabinovich's office."

Another muscle-bound security guard said, "Dr. Alexandria Rabinovich is away, and Dr. Samantha Spindler will take over. Due to enhanced security concerns, your presence is not required. We'll take it from here!"

The agents looked at each other, nodded, and Derek was led through metal detectors that had not been there earlier. After closing the door behind him, the two agents looked at each other with puzzled expressions and sat in the lobby.

"Jason, who is Dr. Samantha Spindler?" asked Agent Bartlett.

"I'll find out," Jason replied, tapping his iPhone.

Derek was marched down a carpeted corridor that felt familiar, its deceptive warmth contrasting with the cold purpose of his escort. The security guards led him through a heavy, reinforced metal door, the echo of its closing reverberating ominously behind him. They descended several flights of stark concrete stairs, the air growing colder and heavier with each step. At the bottom, the concrete stairwell gave way to the harsh austerity of a dimly lit concrete hallway, its walls oppressive, as if the weight of the building above was pressing down.

Derek was ushered into a sterile, cavernous room at the end of the corridor. The walls, made of dark, reflective concrete, seemed to drink in the faint light filtering through narrow, horizontal slits high on either side. The harsh, white illumination from fluorescents flooding light through these horizontal openings cast unforgiving shadows that stretched and shifted like specters across the polished, mirror-like floor. The air was heavy with the antiseptic tang of chemicals, sharp and unyielding, as though it sought to strip away any trace of humanity.

Derek wondered if his dad, Rick Jones, knew about this place in the lower bowels of New Physics Corporation that defied the otherwise warmly designed interior and richly landscaped exterior of the building.

The room's only furnishings were minimalist in simplicity: a cold, bare metal chair facing a sleek table accompanying a single ergonomic upholstered swivel chair on the other side. A lone glass of water stood on the table, its presence more disconcerting than comforting. Behind the table sat Dr. Samantha Spindler, a German woman whose sharp brown eyes betrayed no warmth, her bleach-blonde hair pulled harshly into a severe bun. Her clinical detachment while looking Derek over felt more like dissection than observation. Leaning forward, her form-fitting white suit, artificially youthful appearance, exposed cleavage, and oversized glasses appeared pretentious. Dr. Spindler gestured to the metal chair with a gloved hand, her gaze never leaving him. Reluctantly, Derek sat with his back to the door, pressing against the cold metal and feeling unnerved as he faced her.

The guards nodded silently, their boots echoing on the floor as they left the room. She turned her attention to the open notebook before her, the scratching of her pen the only sound in the oppressive silence.

She tapped her fingers against the table, her nails clicking softly against the surface.

Looking over her glasses, she said in a thick German accent, "Derek, we're going to try something different today. We need clarity."

Before he could protest, a small, sharp prick in his arm from someone behind him sent a cold sensation rushing through his veins. His vision blurred, his body slumping as the room seemed to tilt around him.

His breathing slowed. The world dissolved into light and shadow.

"Tell me about your dream," Dr. Spindler's voice echoed in his mind.

Derek found himself floating between consciousness and memory. Images flooded his thoughts as he articulated them—the reptilian warriors spilling from the dark mirror, the massive wolves leaping into battle, and the sheer destruction he had wrought with his will alone.

"How did you know?" Dr. Spindler's voice prodded. "Where did you learn this?"

Derek's lips moved, but he wasn't sure if the words were his own. "I… I don't know. I just saw it. I felt it. Like it had already happened."

The pressure in his mind intensified. A presence lurked at the edge of his thoughts, something foreign, trying to extract what it sought. He looked at the dark, almost reflectionless mirror on the wall, and for a moment, he saw a flash of light in the middle of the mirror, as if someone was lighting a cigarette.

"Who told you?" she pressed. "Is this classified intelligence? How do you know about the Reptilian Empire?"

He gasped, fighting against the weight pushing down on him. The visions flickered, twisting into something deeper beyond what he had seen in the dream.

Then, just as suddenly, the pressure lifted. Derek jolted upright, gasping for air, his body drenched in sweat.

Dr. Spindler leaned back, studying him with unnerving calm. "Fascinating," she murmured. "Your subconscious is more advanced than we anticipated."

She stood and smoothed the front of her knee-length suit. "A United States ally on planet Velmora Prime wishes to speak with you. You are to answer all of her questions."

Still struggling to steady his breath, Derek stared at her. "Who?"

"You will address her as Madam Pentillion," Dr. Spindler replied. Then she reached under the desk, which triggered a faint ringing sound.

Moments later, Derek was escorted by men in United States military uniforms down the stark hallways of the underground facility. Derek recognized biometric readers next to metal doors without knobs along the corridor's length. The air grew colder as they approached the hangar. His pulse quickened when he saw the massive 20-foot dark mirror shimmering with an abyssal glow that he had seen before when visiting his dad's lab. The polished surface distorted reality around it, an endless void within a perfect frame.

Military soldiers flanked him as he stepped forward. The government had connected the mirror to a secure building on Velmora Prime, less than three hundred light-years away from Earth.

Derek swallowed hard.

With a nudge from behind, Derek stepped through the dark mirror.

Velmora Prime Meeting

*T*he golden spires of Velmora Prime, the capital world of the Galaxy Alliance and less than three hundred light-years from Earth, shimmered in the fading twilight of the planet's twin suns. Beneath the opulent skyline, sprawling metropolis streets bustled with dignitaries, merchants, and emissaries from countless worlds — each bound, knowingly or not, by the invisible grip of Madam Pentillion.

In a secluded chamber within the Grand Assembly Hall, she sat alone. Next to her sat a golden retriever. The silence in Madam Pentillion's high-rise suite was not just physical — it was the silence of a woman who had lost something beyond the grasp of time, beyond the boundaries of even this universe. She traced her fingers along a polished obsidian pendant around her neck, the last relic of her husband, who had been lost to the void while passing through the dark mirror from a dying multiverse.

A soft chime signaled her guest's arrival. She straightened her shimmering indigo robe and turned as the doors hissed open.

Derek Jones stepped inside, his youthful curiosity barely masked by a composed expression. The gravity of the moment did not seem lost on him.

"You look at me as if I am a tyrant," Madam Pentillion mused, offering a faint smile. "Yet I am the reason a million worlds do not collapse into anarchy."

Looking Derek over, she continued, "If that pesky doctor mistreated you, tell me, and I will deal with her."

"Dr. Spindler's bedside manner could use a makeover, Madam Pentillion. I sense that I know you."

"As a Pentillion, Derek, your mind has deeply perceived me."

"I perceive you as if you think control is the same as stability," Derek countered. "If freedom must be an illusion, then isn't peace just another form of enslavement?"

She admired his defiance. It reminded her of the earliest Pentillions, those who first dared to breach the confines of dying multiverses and forge dominion across countless realities. And yet, there was something different about Derek. He was untouched by the weight of power, uncorrupted by the hunger that had driven her people across the infinite divide.

The dog was wagging its tail, and Derek smiled warmly as their eyes locked. Madam

Pentillion petted the dog, looked at Derek, and said, "He likes you. He trusts you. You would have been ripped to shreds if you had been a foe. Yet here you stand, and he sits trustingly, wagging his tail."

"What's his name?" asked Derek with a smile.

"Solara," she replied. "Derived from 'solar,' Solara symbolizes light, warmth, and guidance. He was a gift from your President, Abigail Tubman, and Solara has filled a cavernous void. My late husband would have loved him. Dogs have been a constant in our household throughout the ages, even though I have always undervalued them — until now."

Her words "throughout the ages" echoed through Derek's mind as he pondered the phrase's meaning. Madam Pentillion nodded, and Solara immediately ran to Derek. Instinctively falling to his knees, he basked in Solara's affectionate licks.

Although the tragedy occurred billions of years ago, it was like it happened yesterday. The surprised face of her husband protectively cradling their golden retriever in the last moments of his and his dog's lives before they vanished haunted Madam Pentillion in dreams. In discussions at the United Nations of Earth becoming a member planet of the Galaxy

Alliance, after Pentillion scientists deemed it at a level of advancement qualifying it for membership, President Tubman had invited Madam Pentillion into her office in Geneva, Switzerland, and presented Solara as a gift.

Staring at Solara, Madam Pentillion whispered as a tear briefly appeared, then disappeared, "The choice of gift seemed like an impossible coincidence, almost like a divine sign, and coming from someone who knows God doesn't exist, it affected me deeply. It was almost as if my husband had returned Solara to watch over me, like he was sending me a message from a place that couldn't exist."

Her emerald-green eyes, once burning with the arrogance of a conqueror, now flickered with something else — a chasm of memory, of longing buried under eons of calculated governance. But grief was a weakness she refused to acknowledge. The illusion of control had to be preserved. Solara was her only connection to a side of her that barely survived the loss of her husband and his beloved dog.

"The civilizations under our protection flourish," she said, pouring a deep crimson liquid into two crystal glasses. "Their cultures are preserved. Their wars are managed. Do you believe they would be better off if left to their devices?"

Derek met her gaze. "Now that you ask, I believe they would be better off if allowed to become what they were meant to be."

A silence stretched between them, tense yet unspoken. Madam Pentillion set down her glass, the ghost of a smirk playing at the corner of her lips. She pondered Derek's innate Pentillion abilities. "Idealism is charming. It is also a child's game. But I will entertain the notion. You intrigue me, Derek Jordan Jones."

He studied her as if trying to discern the sincerity behind her words. "My mom always uses my full name when she calls me into a room to discuss something. Why did you call me here?"

She leaned forward. "Because I have been watching and listening to you like a hawk. You remind me of something that was lost." Her voice was softer now, almost reverent. "A time when the Pentillions were explorers, not rulers. Before power became our only currency."

Derek tilted his head. "And you want to change that?"

"I want to control it." Her lips curled slightly. "But perhaps you can teach me a better way."

His expression hardened, and she could sense his wariness. "You think I can be molded."

"No." Madam Pentillion smiled, the first genuine smile she had allowed in ages. "I think you can teach me to remember."

She had not expected her own words to unsettle her. But something about this boy — this descendant of her kind — was unraveling the careful mask she had worn for so long. He asked her whether governance had to be a game of control or if true freedom could exist without the destruction she had long feared.

Before she could speak again, a tremor passed through her mind. A presence — one she had not felt in centuries. The shadows at the edges of her suite seemed darker than they should have been. Her peripheral vision always revealed an otherworldly presence.

Something else was here. Watching.

The sensation tightened her chest, and she felt cold for the first time in a millennium.

Derek sensed it, too. "What is it?" he asked, his voice quiet but alert.

Madam Pentillion exhaled slowly, masking her unease. "A ghost of the past."

She turned toward the vast and illustrious cityscape, but her mind was elsewhere.

Something was stirring in the depths of the Galaxy Alliance, in the corridors of power she had thought unshakable.

And she had a worldview-shattering epiphany: Whoever it was…

They had followed her here.

Chapter 6 Lunar Underground

"The moon like a flower in heaven's high bower, with silent delight, sits and smiles on the night."

— William Blake

Inside the Dome

*T*he lab at New Physics buzzed with preparation for a highly classified military product demonstration to Pentagon officials, referenced as "Project Dark Mirror," built upon the continuation of scientific research into dark matter by scientist Dr. Ethan Conrad. Rick Jones prepared his introductory presentation to explain the concept of dark matter to non-technical military and government officials in a large conference room.

These words from a Pentagon official overseeing the project resonated in Rick's mind as he flipped through notes: "Dumb it down! Your audience members are not rocket scientists, but they control the purse strings!"

Rick's cell phone resonated with his newly downloaded ringtone. Asha Jones appeared on the caller ID. "Hello, Asha?"

"Mrs. Ochoa is back," Asha said with a hint of unease. Just then, a man wearing a military uniform stood at the conference room door.

"Mr. Jones, I was instructed to remind you that time is of the essence. The alignment is in place. The mirror is ready. The lab team has entered."

Rick nodded to the man in the military uniform, "Thank God, Asha. I have many questions, but we're on a time-sensitive project. I've got to go. Love you, sweetheart!" Rick turned off the cell phone display, locked it, clipped it to his belt, and walked around the long conference table toward the gentleman. His name on his name tag read Major John Stevens. Rick shook Major Stevens' hand and said, "General McNab asked me to prepare a brief presentation to introduce observers to the basic concepts behind the project."

The large conference room began filling quickly. It could seat at least fifty people and had room for twenty-five more. Name badges on the lapels of guests to New Physics showed a who's who of agencies and professional titles, from the military and other government agencies to private industry. Two visitor badges displayed "CIA" under their names.

The project related to cutting-edge physics, specifically using dark matter to coat giant mirrors in large astronomical telescopes, from the Atacama Desert to mountaintop observatories and orbiting telescopes.

The nano-thin coating of dark matter particles was grown in the lab as crystals on large sheets of super-thin titanium film. Nano-sized robotics made the assembly process possible, yielding a near-perfect mirrored surface. Developed for recent military applications, the dark matter particles were obtained from a recent defense contract project using the Stanford Linear Accelerator to capture the illusive substance never before measured, let alone studied firsthand.

"Dark matter has eluded the scientific community for years," said a woman from the back of the conference room. Everyone turned to see an attractive young woman in her mid-twenties, formally dressed in a black business suit, a white blouse buttoned to the neck, a knee-length skirt, and high heels. She had stylish medium-length reddish brown hair. The bold capital letters CIA were on the visitor badge under Anna Bartlett.

"Welcome to your non-disclosure agreement, Agent Bartlett," boomed General McNab's deep voice as he stood rigidly postured. He was sporting an array of military medals and other brass glistening off a perfectly pressed uniform, and a New Physics badge with his frowning face and name, Harlan McNab, was pinned to the uniform lapel.

"That is correct. Is it agent Bartlett?" said Rick, slightly adjusting his necktie tightly knotted by Asha before he rushed out of the house earlier on that balmy Saturday.

"Agent Bartlett, agency CIA."

"My apologies, Agent Bartlett," General McNab replied.

"And pardon me for asking," Agent Bartlett continued, "but how many years ago was dark matter measured and captured? I thought it was all theory and conjecture."

"Let's just leave the answer at many years," interjected General McNab.

Agent Bartlett continued, "Then you have solved what NASA and others consider one of astronomy's, particle physics', and astrophysics' grandest mysteries," as agent Anna Bartlett exchanged glances with a top NASA official across the room.

"That is quite correct," General McNab replied.

"I gather Dr. Ethan Conrad's research led to this discovery, and shall we say unintended application?" Agent Bartlett queried.

"Agent Bartlett, can we take this offline?" General McNab replied with a stern undertone. "We are on a tight schedule."

Smiling, Agent Bartlett stated, "Most certainly, General McNab."

Rick continued his presentation and answered questions, using photos as a background on the large flat-screen monitor on the wall next to him. Guests sipped coffee and listened with rapt attention.

"That is correct," Rick replied to a question from somewhere in the room. "The dark mirror, abbreviated DM on related classified documents, increases magnification exponentially. During field testing, telescopes such as Paranal, located in the Atacama Desert, can 'see' distant galaxies outside Hubble's range. If we were to replace Hubble's mirrors, imagine the possibilities."

Outside on the New Physics grounds, military guards turned away traffic except for authorized vehicles, and military helicopters hovered in the air. Observers at the nearby Starbucks commented, "Something is going on over there."

"The capabilities of DM," Rick continued, "extend beyond capturing distant images no ordinary mirror can reflect. New Physics has gathered you together to announce a discovery that may shock many of you into disbelief, but General McNab will vouch for me. As the good General reminded our visitor from the CIA, we must remind everyone of our non-disclosure agreement vows. They say that with the government, at the top-secret clearance level, it is 'till death do us part in analogy to marriage vows." Rick then made a silly grin as if to imply, 'Just kidding! It's not that serious!' in an attempt to take the edge off just how severe it was.

This remark succeeded in eliciting a chuckle from General McNab. Glancing at General McNab and grinning, Rick continued. "If you're single, you just got hitched to Uncle Sam." A few laughs punctuated an otherwise hushed silence. Visitors exchanged nervous glances. "Project scientists theorize dark mirrors act differently when the Moon is near a DM, say, on Earth or in orbit."

"Differently?" asked a voice from the room. Agent Bartlett's partner, Jason Johnson, was a handsome and athletic African American CIA agent wearing a black business suit, matching tie, and white Oxford shirt. He winked at an attractive young woman in military uniform, wearing glasses with her hair pulled back severely into a bun across the conference table, whom he observed checking him out. "Our non-disclosure prevents us from delving too deeply into DM, meaning 'dark mirror' and 'dark matter,' the latter also used to coat the telescopes. Didn't Dr. Conrad believe the Moon emitted an unknown form of energy that activated these mirrors when the Moon was at perigee or closest point to Earth during orbit, forming an Einstein-Rosen bridge or a traversable wormhole?" Jason hoped the last sentence would impress the young lady, and glancing at her, she looked more interested in him.

Amid total silence, a few hushed whispers punctuated the looks of puzzlement and disbelief. Visitors looked at General McNab, who remained silent and expressionless.

Rick lowered his head and paused as if to consider his following words. Lifting his head with a movement as if he were about to shake his head and stopping short of shaking his head, Rick looked at the audience across the conference table with a glassy stare.

"That is correct," Rick replied in a matter-of-fact tone. "Seems our CIA visitor has done his homework."

Jason Johnson immediately replied with pride, "CIA Director Arlin Conway has given Agent Bartlett and me the highest level of security clearance next to President Abigail Tubman. I always come prepared." He noticed the young lady across the conference room table grinning and glancing at Agent Bartlett; she quickly rolled her eyes and checked her wristwatch.

A hushed silence filled the room, and then there was barely audible conversation.

Outside the facility, CNN reporter Nancy Cunningham, standing in front of cameras on a hill overlooking the New Physics corporate campus, spoke to the camera. "Live from a hilltop above the corporate campus of venture capital-funded startup New Physics Corporation, this sunset and unusually bright full Moon couldn't provide a better backdrop. These gleaming buildings are covered with sparkling solar panels, with enough output to take New Physics off the grid and pump excess power back into PG&E's system. The sprawling lush green lawns, sprinkling systems going full blast during this water shortage, and large magnificent fountains gushing into the air down there won architectural, landscaping, and energy savings awards. All water circulating continuously through the landscaping, fountains, and inside toilets is filtered and reused with processes like those used on the space station."

The camera zoomed in and panned the grounds as she continued, "The entire facility is powered 100% by solar energy from those gleaming solar panels on the roofs of buildings. Although the inside is equally magnificent and showcases green technologies and stunning architecture, punctuated by art on consignment by the world's great artists, including a massive warehouse-sized area of one building that looks like a hangar fit for super-sized aircraft,

I cannot show you. Why? As you can see, the facility is surrounded by military vehicles. See the helicopters overhead? CNN received word from an insider at New Physics that the greatest discovery in modern history surrounding dark matter is being demonstrated for top military officials from the Pentagon and brass from other government agencies from Washington, D.C., as I speak."

The conversation continued in the conference room.

Agent Anna Bartlett repeated her question with a tone of incredulity. "You have a functional wormhole?"

"That is correct," Rick answered again in a matter-of-fact tone, looking at General McNab.

Agent Bartlett exchanged a nervous glance with partner agent Jason Johnson.

A man in a navy blue business suit and tie raised his hand. After Rick acknowledged him by nodding, the man asked, "At least according to modern theory, wormholes require two locations in space and time. These two places, or times, are connected through the curvature of spacetime, a theoretical entity permitted by Einstein's theory of general relativity. My question to you, Dr. Jones, is about the second 'spacetime mirror' location…"

"Excellent question," Rick replied. "Indeed, it is a spacetime mirror and a rather sophisticated one where matter from the connecting mirror is projected to coordinates for the destination, using the principle of spooky action at a distance. That's the short, layman's answer. Our live demonstration in New Physics' main laboratory will answer your excellent question. I don't want to spoil the surprise. And so, without further ado, our military escorts will lead you in groups down to our facility's main laboratory, where the mirror is set up."

Again, Bartlett walked beside her partner, following their military escort down the wide, carpeted corridor of closed office doors and magnificent artwork on the walls.

Carter Smith caught up with them and said with a chuckle, "Very elementary presentation, wouldn't you say?"

Agent Bartlett laughed and replied, "To say the least. Typical conference room posturing for those who don't know a dark mirror from dark matter from their bathroom mirror. It's the lab part I would camp out to see like an Apple iPhone groupie waiting at dawn for the next phone."

They all laughed. Agent Bartlett opened her briefing packet and began flipping through the pages as they walked. She stopped at a curious insert that looked typewritten and faded, like several generations of copies.

NATIONAL AERONAUTICS AND SPACE ADMINISTRATION

APOLLO 17

TECHNICAL AIR-TO-GROUND VOICE TRANSCRIPTION

Prepared by

Test Division

Apollo Spacecraft Program Office

Excerpt from Transcript:

The Apollo 17 mission was flown from December 7 to 19, 1972; lift-off occurred at 05:33:00.60 GMT (12:33:00.60 a.m. EST) on December 7.

Excerpt from Tape 59/18:

03 15 30 32 Lunar Module Pilot: "We can see the area where MariusHills should be, although it's not an obvious topographic feature in this light. Still see Aristarchus off up there shining like a star, if the Moon could have stars."

Excerpt from Tape 91B/8:

05 17 42 51 Command Module Pilot: "You know something - the observation that I think is pretty significant is that most of the 30-

kilometer craters on the back side of the Moon seem fairly fresh. And any of them that are fresh - by fresh, I mean you don't have any real definite ray pattern to them, but you've got a real smooth - not smooth but streaked straight - slope, 45-degree angle going down into the crater and the crater wall. Then you get down to the bottom of the crater and have a flat floor, or sometimes a domical type of floor. And the domical material there resembles nothing like the stuff slumped down the side."

Excerpt from Tape 93B/1:

05 19 33 13 Command Module Pilot: "There's the ole Earth. It's about a half Earth now.

Command Module Pilot: "Houston, America."

Mission Control Center, CAP COMM: "Go ahead, Ron."

Command Module Pilot: "Okay, Robert. I guess the big thing I want to report from the back side on this one here is that I took another look at the - the Cloverleaf in Aitken, with the binocs, and that southern, domical crater of the Cloverleaf - it has a breach on the east - east side of it. I can't tell. There's a flow. In other words, the domical structures are part of a flow material that partially fills the breach. In other words, the breach had either flowed into that little domical structure before the domes were built, or else all of that stuff on the mare floor had flown out of that domical structure before the domes came in. In other words, the domical structures are different in relationship to the floor. They are - are younger than the floor it-self."

Mission Control Center, CAP COMM: "Roger, Ron. We copy that."

05 19 35 20 Mission Control Center, CAP COMM: "Ron, is there a difference in the color between the dome and the mare in Aitken?"

Command Module Pilot: "Yes, there - yes, there is. The dome-type material is - the colors again are tough, you know? I'm just going to say that it's slightly darker than the mare floor - that is how it looks to me right now. Also, the texture is coarser than the floor itself; in other words, the floor is a standard mare flat-floor-type stuff to me. And I have to compare the tex-ture of the domical hills to - Oh - I guess what I would imagine is some of the dacite flows I've seen in California. You know, the heavy viscous-type flows."

Excerpt from Tape 109B/1:

06 19 28 50 Command Module Pilot: "Oh, I hope we got a pan-camera picture of that. The one I was describing had a little diamond down in it."

Mission Control Center, CAP COMM: "Roger."

Command Module Pilot: "Because that little diamond was with the binocs. It's a dome of material in there, and it looks like a diamond because you have slide material or talus-type stuff slumped around it. And in that dome-type material, there are three or four black spots. I call it black. I consider it a greenish — a greenish-black, you know?"

Mission Control Center, CAP COMM: "Roger."

Command Module Pilot: "Why don't you see if our pan camera coverage covers that crater? I think it probably did. That's an interesting one to look at anyhow."

End of Voice Transcription quotations.

Flipping to the next page, Agent Bartlett's mouth immediately dropped open.

MILITARY Top-secret

NATIONAL AIR FORCE AND SPACE ADMINISTRATION

APOLLO 18

TECHNICAL AIR-TO-GROUND VOICE TRANSCRIPTION

Prepared by

Test Division

Apollo Spacecraft Program Office

"Look at this," whispered Agent Bartlett, "on page 287, there is something curious. Directly after Apollo 17 excerpts of voice transcripts between the astronauts and Mission Control about mysterious dome-like structures on the Moon that sparkle like diamonds is a page labeled 'Military Top-Secret' referring to a 'National Air Force and Space Administration' and 'Apollo 18' voice transcription!"

Agent Johnson glanced curiously at the open briefing in Agent Bartlett's hands as they stopped at an elevator and whispered, "Was that Apollo 18 mission by NASA?"

"No!" she exclaimed in a terse whisper. "Apollo 17 was the last of the Apollo missions by NASA, and I've never heard of this National Air Force and Space Administration or NAFSA."

Carter Smith looked over her shoulder at the report as she slowly closed it and stared at him.

"I know all about it," Carter said.

"Really!" Agent Bartlett exclaimed in a whisper.

"All cell phones off," ordered the military escort as the elevator doors opened. "Not airplane mode. Power down."

Voices resonated throughout the cavernous, high-ceiling laboratory in an adjacent New Physics corporate campus building. Visitors conversed with one another while sipping coffee or drinks and frequently glancing at the sizeable 20-foot circular mirror, which appeared embedded in the floor. Hence, the bottom of the opening was flat. The mirror reflected their images.

The high-pitched sound of a microphone pierced the air, causing voices to fade as visitors turned toward the source of the sound. Rick Jones stood at a podium and microphone in front of the large mirror, tapping the microphone to test the sound. "Testing, testing," he said into the microphone and looked toward the back of his anxious audience. Rick's secretary, Barb, tapped her ear and nodded with her usual signal that the microphone was working fine.

"May I have your attention? Ladies and gentlemen," Rick began, leaning toward the microphone. "The mirror behind me measures 20 feet in diameter and extrudes into the floor, allowing access by military personnel and vehicles of large sizes."

The audience broke out in hushed whispers.

"There will be time for questions," Rick continued, motioning for silence. The lab became silent except for the humming of computers and other equipment. Audience members stared at themselves in the mirror.

"Ordinarily," Rick continued, "you would be staring into another parallel universe or dimension of spacetime. The only theory in physics that comes close to explaining such a dimension, as touched upon earlier, is Dr. Hugh Everett the Third, Ph. D. In 1957, he first proposed the many-worlds interpretation of quantum physics. It did not take over 100 years to verify his theory as accurate, as it took scientists to figure out that the famous $E=Mc^2$ theorem is correct and has led physicists down a path to this." Rick turned his head, glanced at the mirror and his reflection, and looked back at the wide-eyed audience.

Rick paused and sipped a glass of water, his throat feeling rough from the dry air of the lab. "There is a reason you're now staring into what appears like an ordinary mirror, with such a perfect yet resilient finish, coated with a form of matter scientists have always theoretically referred to as 'dark matter.' You are staring at an exotic event horizon that passes, not into a parallel universe, but a distant place that exists in this universe here and now, at this very moment in time. That place for this particular dark mirror is a subterranean structure beneath Earth's Moon's lunar surface."

All whispering ceased, and complete silence filled the cavernous airport hangar-sized lab.

Rick continued. "We can now activate the dark mirror's exotic event horizon independently of the perigee Moon's natural ability to activate the mirror. We are also capable of using an artificial source of energy, found on the Moon itself, to cause the mirror to transform from a passage between parallel universes or 'many-worlds' into a traversable wormhole between places in our spacetime, here and now, within a certain radius of the energy device."

General McNab approached the podium, and Rick continued, "I will hand over the podium to General McNab."

A voice in the crowd asked, "Structures on the Moon? Is there an atmosphere?"

General McNab, stepping to the podium as Rick stepped aside, replied to the voice, "We will field your questions later, but the short answer is yes, you won't suffocate. There is too much for you to digest quickly, so we shall begin with a demonstration. Rest assured, we have been testing this technology for over a year, and you will be in no danger."

Visitors looked at one another with surprise at General McNab's suggestion that there was 'no danger,' as if he were implying *they* would participate in the demonstration.

"Dr. Brown," said General McNab toward a man in a white lab coat seated at a control panel across the lab, "Activate Project Dark Mirror."

The man, identified as Dr. Brown, lifted what looked like a radio or cell phone and said in a low voice, his words indiscernible to visitors, "Is the Paranal telescope aimed at the correct coordinates?"

The voice of astronomer and astrophysicist Dr. Jacques Bullialdus, holding a telephone while staring at a computer screen at the Paranal Observatory, replied in his deep French accent, "That is correct, and the dish is dark as ever and aimed at near lunar surface's southeastern rim of the Mare Serenitatis. I'm sending you the exact coordinates for verification right now."

General McNab continued, "Some interesting trivia may help clarify this demonstration as we do the walk-through. In the southwestern Montes Taurus, the southeastern rim of the

Mare Serenitatis was the Apollo 17 landing site in December of 1972. Of interest to the United States government and our military were highly unusual craters that scientists at the time theorized could be volcanic in origin. The crew members were Harrison Schmitt, a geologist who became the first scientist-astronaut, and Eugene Gene Cernan, Commander. These two astronauts drove a lunar rover that reminds me of a dune buggy for 34 kilometers or 21 miles through the Taurus-Littrow Valley. Noteworthy in the news media, reports about the last Apollo missions were about their discovery of unusual orange-colored soil and leaving a set of instruments behind on the lunar surface. Apollo 17 was the last lunar landing mission sent by NASA. Apollo 18 was the last lunar landing mission sent by NAFSA, or the National Air Force and Space Administration, a highly classified 'black box' agency of the government administered by NASA, the United States Air Force, and the NSA or National Security Agency. Of course, to elaborate on the issue, discussing anything you learn on this tour outside this facility will violate your NDA and subject you to prosecution."

"I've never heard of the NAFSA's existence," said agent Bartlett, "and I have a fairly high access level, you might say, the highest."

"Not the highest, Agent Bartlett, that I assure you. That is why everyone's clearance in this room was temporarily increased to a level that allows access to this information and what you are about to witness. Now you have heard about it, as will the public at a point to be determined by the President soon."

An email message from Dr. Bullialdus immediately arrived in Dr. Brown's inbox. Opening it, he nodded approvingly toward the screen.

"Thanks. We're good. How's the weather in your area of the Atacama region?" asked Dr. Brown.

"Skies are clear," Dr. Bullialdus replied, "as one would expect high on a virtually rainless plateau here in Chile, South America."

"You have a bird's eye view of the domes," said Dr. Brown with a hint of curiosity.

"They are spectacular. The dark spacetime mirror effect, for lack of a better way of putting it, is like looking at the lunar soil with a microscope, then panning back a bird's eye view and everything in-between."

"You lucky sap," Dr. Brown replied, shaking his head slowly and smacking his lips. "What I wouldn't give to trade places with you."

Dr. Brown quickly entered commands on his keyboard while staring at the screen.

Suddenly, the mirror lost its reflection in complete silence and momentarily seemed dark. Amazed visitors moved forward and squinted into the darkness. As the lab lights dimmed, objects and topography in the view behind the mirror began to take shape. Across a floor that appeared like slick black granite or concrete, transparent and semi-transparent geometric shapes jutted up from the floor.

A musty smell rushed into the lab like in an Egyptian tomb, and a cool breeze blew as air pressure seemed to equalize between it and the other side of the mirror.

An officer in military uniform moved the podium aside as General McNab grabbed the microphone. "Ladies and gentlemen, if you recall the old 'Star Trek Experience' some years ago in Las Vegas, this may sound like a similar amusement ride as I ask you to form groups of seven starting at the neon orange lines on the concrete floor ahead of you."

In formation, eleven officers in military uniform stood at attention to the side of the lab, walked between the crowd and mirror, and stood in front of each of these neon orange lines. About 20 feet separated the officers from the mirror. Visitors and others in the lab, including Rick Jones, looked around and gathered with those they knew or had met into eleven groups, with six in the last group.

"These officers will be your guides," continued General McNab. At that moment, a jeep with military-armed personnel and plastic capsules containing supplies appeared from around the right side of the mirror and drove behind the officers. A few gasps echoed through the cavernous lab as the jeep continued driving into the mirror and across the black floor, tires squeaking on the glassy floor's surface, the smell of rubber and exhaust punctuating the lab.

"Oh my God," whispered Agent Bartlett to Agent Johnson, "I wonder if it's safe to go in there."

"I don't get what this has to do with the Moon and Apollo 17, Bartlett, or the supposed top-secret Apollo 18 mission," whispered Agent Johnson.

Agent Bartlett's hand brushed against Agent Johnson's hand as he stood closely next to her. Instinctively, with a hint of veiled fear on her face, Agent Bartlett began to put her fingers around Agent Johnson's palm and the back of his hand to take hold of his hand. Pulling away quickly, she glanced at him with a hint of embarrassment. Looking down at their hands, inches apart, Agent Johnson grinned and tried to act like nothing happened. Then, without looking at her, he reached over and took her hand, squeezed it, and whispered, "You have nothing to feel ashamed about, Bartlett."

Behind Agents Bartlett and Johnson were five other people. A heavyset man puffed a cigar he just lit. Two young women whispered back and forth. One interrupted their conversation to answer the melodic ring in her purse of a cell phone call. An officer in military uniform approached her, took the phone, deactivated the ring, and placed the phone in his vest pocket.

A young man in more casual khaki trousers and a blue blazer with an open-neck Oxford shirt intensely studied the scene behind the spacetime mirror. A young woman in a semi-formal pantsuit, whom Agents Bartlett and Johnson recognized as Barb, Rick's secretary, nodded and walked toward them.

"The boss lets you join us on the tour?" asked Agent Bartlett with a smile.

"Sure, I'm on the classified up and up," the young woman replied with a squeaky voice. "So how does the CIA get interested in the world's greatest discovery since sliced bread?"

Grinning nervously, Agent Johnson looked up and down the young woman in a pantsuit and replied, "I thought you knew. Doesn't your boss tell you everything?"

"Not," Barb mumbled while stuffing a stick of chewing gum in her mouth. "Want some? It's Wrigley's Spearmint."

"No thanks," Agent Johnson replied with a hint of amusement.

"We're following up on the case of Dr. Ethan Conrad's disappearance, with some co-incidence, after discovering the science that made all this possible," Agent Bartlett replied.

"What, Agent Bartlett, or may I call you Anna," Barb whispered, motioning her head toward the spacetime mirror. "You think he's in there?"

"Good question," Anna Bartlett replied. "Yes, you can call me Anna. We're so used to titles at the CIA; it's refreshing to be on a first-name basis."

"And can I call you Jason?" asked Barb.

"Sure, we're not formal at the CIA," Jason Johnson replied, looking at Anna in his usual attempt to get a rise out of her. This time, it didn't seem to work. Something finally caught her attention so overwhelmingly, her eyes just wandered everywhere from the officer before them, to the lines of people to her right, to the neon orange line in front of her feet, to the spectacle before her.

General McNab's voice boomed through the microphone, punctuated by a feedback squeal. "All right, everyone. Starting at my right, which is your left, your military escort will lead you into the next room, shall we say?"

Anna was the first in line and followed the military officer.

"Stay in line. Don't stray from the group. Always keep close to your military escort," cautioned General McNab.

Approaching the opening that once appeared like a propped-up twenty by a twenty-foot mirror, Anna could feel her heart beating faster. A dizzying sensation momentarily jolted her, leaving her feeling emotionally overwhelmed. "What am I doing?" she thought to herself, continuing her thoughts. I cannot believe what is happening! Where are we going?"

Anna blurted out, "Where are we going, General?"

Calmly looking into her eyes stoically, General McNab replied quietly, "You have first to see. I guarantee you will immediately understand where you are when you're there.

You will immediately feel a lot lighter from the Moon's gravity."

With frustration and an almost overwhelming curiosity, Anna thought, "That's great. Thanks for the elucidation!"

Walking through the point where it seemed one should run into a solid mirror surface, Anna instinctively closed her eyes, wrinkled her nose, and hunched her shoulders as if expecting to run into something. The air immediately felt chilly as she opened her eyes, and she felt much lighter in the Moon's gravity. The musty, tomb-like smell, initially pungent, seemed to grow stronger. The large room they were in, without lighting, was lit by the glow of a white light coming from glass that was visible several hundred yards away. Almost sixty feet in the air, the glass was much higher than the lab's ceiling. The glass looked very thick, and it curved at a descending angle. Between the glass and floor was a lattice of geometric shapes that formed an open ceiling for the room they stood in. This ceiling looked like concrete or perhaps dull metal, like the black floor, but not shiny, with more of a matte finish.

As the eleven groups, each with seven people, streamed in following their military escort officer, Anna wandered toward what looked like a large transparent tube. She placed her hand on it, and the tube felt more like plastic or acrylic, cold to the touch. Inside were metallic objects that formed more geometric shapes. The wall was recessed four feet above the floor and of the same black granite or concrete. Large squares of the same type of transparent material were embedded into the wall behind the recessed areas like computer monitors, but only these were not illuminated.

"Alight, people," said General McNab with a raised voice to compensate for the lack of a microphone. "Stay with your escorts always, and do not wander!"

Jason tapped Anna's shoulder as she stared mesmerized at the recessed walls and squares, startling her. She turned around quickly, her face glowing in the shadows from the white light emanating from the glass above them.

"Don't do that!" Anna exclaimed.

"Sorry," Jason replied, "but we're going."

Their escort shouted, "You two get over here and follow me!"

Anna and Jason walked quickly toward the young man who was their escort. Anna's high heels briefly slid against the slick floor, and she caught herself as Jason reached to keep her from falling. "If I only knew, I would have worn tennis shoes! They should have warned us!"

Jason shook his head, chuckled, and replied, "They did, Bartlett. Didn't you get the memo?" A female officer approached Anna and handed her slippers, which she quickly changed, and handed the officer her high heels. They quickly followed their escort and the rest of their group. As they walked toward the glass overhead, it curved at a downward angle, leaving the area of the room, and the floor changed texture. The black ceiling over the room they left no longer separated their view of the glass overhead, which increased in height as it curved upward at an angle.

"This is incredible," exclaimed Anna, gazing at the glass above and ahead of her, turning around in a circle and looking down as she surveyed the scene. "It's a giant underground geodesic sphere! It looks like the top of this geodesic sphere is surrounded by soil, and the sunlight is so bright."

"You're right; this is a geodesic sphere, partially buried under the ground with a small curvature above the surface," said their escort as he and their group stared straight up.

A woman in a military uniform approached Agent Bartlett, carrying some hiking boots.

"Based on your profile, these boots should fit you nicely."

"Thank you," Agent Bartlett said, removing her slippers and putting on the hiking boots. "They're just the right size."

"I don't understand," Anna said aloud, her hair falling behind her back as she craned her neck backward to look straight up and around her. "Where is this place?"

"Just take it in," her escort replied, "and get used to it. There is plenty of time for questions."

"What's your name?" asked Anna, squinting at his name badge in the now bright white light and making out the name William.

"Bill Camden," he replied. Looking at her New Physics Visitor Badge, with large lettering, he continued, "Nice to meet you, Anna Bartlett, CIA. Now that's funny."

"What's funny, Bill?" Anna replied, mesmerized at the complexity of the outer transparent geodesic sphere and all the levels inside the sphere without apparent connection to the inner shell.

"Seems strange to see a CIA poking around in a top-secret military installation."

"So that's what this is, a military installation?"

"Well, not in the sense that we built it. Perhaps I should have referred to it more accurately as an archeological site of military interest. You know, like in one of the pyramids of Egypt."

"What kind of archaeological site, and what do you mean 'one of'?" said Jason, exchanging glances with Anna.

"Don't you know?" Bill replied, looking around to see if the General was on site. Bill continued, eager to spoil the General's surprise, "These go on and on. They're interconnected by tunnels so large we can drive large vehicles through them. You could get lost for days, weeks, or months if you started wandering around. In that respect, it's like a cave system, only a manufactured one interconnected with a natural network of caves."

"Not of terrestrial origin, I gather," came the young man's voice in the blue blazer.

"Excuse me," said Barb, approaching Anna and Jason. "I heard you say this is the inside of a geodesic sphere. What is that?"

"You want the long or short version?" asked Anna.

"The shorter, the sweeter," Barb replied, checking her lipstick in a compact mirror and depositing it in her purse.

"Alright, I'll keep it simple. A geodesic sphere comprises interconnected polygons that create a nearly perfect sphere. The edges follow arcs of great circles, making the structure strong and efficient."

"This is no run-of-the-mill geodesic sphere," said Bill. "There are some amazing properties about this sphere…"

As they all exchanged glances filled with wonder and curiosity, General McNab's voice echoed from above, "Camden! Get your team up here!"

Motioning for the group to follow him, Bill quickly walked toward a wide, open ramp with no railing that ascended at a 45-degree angle to the next level. The sheer drop on either side of the ramp made ascending it a foreboding prospect.

"No, no, no," said Anna in a trembling voice, surveying the 45-degree angle of the wide ramp with a very coarse concrete-like finish. Turning to Jason, she whispered, "I'll get halfway up and slide back down, breaking my neck! Even in this low gravity!"

"You would have never made it in high heels, but those boots are perfect for climbing," Bill replied with laughter. "Be patient. Our ride will arrive any moment."

"Our ride?" said Jason with a doubtful look.

From around the corner, a large military Hummer sped toward the group. They stared at it with open mouths and expressions of disbelief as it pulled up to the ramp.

Bill opened the door and motioned with his head for the two young women in their group to enter the vehicle, followed by Agents Johnson and Bartlett.

After they all squeezed into the back seat, Bill slammed the door and said to the remaining three members, "Wait here with me for the next Hummer to arrive." Bill motioned his head for the driver to proceed up the ramp.

The Hummer sped up the ramp on the steep incline. Anna looked for something to grab onto. Finding nothing, she sat tensely, looking at the sheer drop to her left. The interior of this geodesic sphere, as seen from this vantage point, made Anna realize the sheer enormity of its size. She estimated its diameter to be the size of many football fields.

"I wonder how many football stadiums you could fit inside the void created by this sphere?" she exclaimed.

"Like a ton of them?" one of the young women exclaimed, looking around excitedly. "This is so cool."

"What agency are you with?" Anna asked with a hint of skepticism, grabbing the open window frame and squeezing it.

"We're not with any agency! My dad is the head of Marketing at New Physics. Dad pulled some strings and got us on the tour. The real question is, where are we? I'm Cynthia, and this is Veronica."

The other young woman, Veronica, frustratedly said as she pushed buttons on her cell phone, "No signal. That figures."

"No cell phones are allowed on the Project Dark Mirror tour!" yelled the driver. "Turn that thing off and put it away."

The young women rolled their eyes and exchanged annoyed glances. Anna rolled her eyes and shook her head as she looked at Jason, who seemed very nervous at their steep ascent up the ramp.

The Hummer sped up the ramp so fast it seemed to catapult from the ramp into the air and then onto a flat surface, the lower gravity giving its bounce an air of strangeness. The tires squealed as they jolted to a stop. "I love driving her in low gravity! Get out here and wait for your escort," said the driver, motioning to an open area where all the groups congregated.

Anna opened the door, and her legs felt wobbly as she stepped onto a course surface. She was thankful she was wearing hiking boots. Jason, Cynthia, and Veronica got out, and Veronica slammed the door hard while staring down the driver with a look of scorn. Shaking his head and pursing his lips as if to throw a kiss at Veronica, then laughing when she stared angrily at him, the driver drove in a circle in a large open area near the ramp until facing another ramp. Anna was in awe at the economies of scale in this structure and was awestruck at the next ramp to the top level. The ramp started at an incline of 45 degrees, gradually entered a longer 50-degree incline that almost appeared straight up, and ended at the same 45 degrees, including the last ramp.

"Oh, boy," she murmured, "what is that all about? No way am I driving further up there unless we find another way!" Anna's curiosity about what was up there continued to grow. Looking at her wristwatch, she noted it was almost 3:00 in the morning, over eight hours since they arrived at New Physics, had an excellent dinner in its executive dining room prepared by a famous New York chef, attended the meeting, and entered this insane lunar amusement park.

Yet strangely, the sun was shining brightly, almost too brightly, through the top of this massive geodesic sphere. Bill's referring to this place as an archaeological site seemed all the stranger, considering this entire structure seemed so otherworldly.

"I wonder if Dr. Conrad knew about this place. It's so massive it seems anyone could get lost or injured somewhere without any means of calling for help," Anna said to Jason. Looking at her cell phone instinctively, not even the lowest signal bar appeared.

"Bartlett, you better put that away before they confiscate it," Jason whispered.

Anna looked at him and slipped the cell phone into her pocket. She said, "I wonder where Dr. Conrad hid his binder of notes. His assistant insists she kept the binder organized, and it contained every detail on dark mirror technology, including equations and maps to a mining complex in an underground area she thought was in Area 51, Nevada, but which we believe is located on the Moon."

"Maybe the two are connected by another of those mirror things?" Jason replied. "All I know, Bartlett, is that Rick Jones stated in a meeting that the Moon is filled with underground complexes, underground transit systems and roadways, and natural cave systems. There's a labyrinth that could span tens of thousands of miles. Maybe there are connections to the surface."

"To the Moon's or Earth's surface?" replied Anna with a brief, faraway gaze.

Jason slowly nodded. "That, and more."

Anna continued, "Finding a binder hidden in such a superstructure would take forever. Where do we even begin?"

Jason shrugged as he stared into the giant dome's chasm and then upwards at the geodesic, transparent, and complex network of interconnected triangular panels connected by dark grey metallic struts. Shaking his head, he replied, "It beats me."

Dr. Ethan Conrad's Binder

*D*erek and Jenna opened the door to the attic. Walking across the dusty floor, they looked out over the foothills dotted with large stately homes and then gazed at the skyscrapers of Los Angeles in the distance.

"This would make a cool bedroom," Derek said.

"I know, Derek! It's so it. These huge octagonal windows let in so much light! This house is so well built. Look at these floors."

"The house is only a few years old. You know those roof shingles, according to Dad, are the latest solar panels designed to look like conventional tiles. That roof is stronger and lighter than most."

"Interesting. I love your house. Did you ever come up here before?"

Shaking his head as he stared at all the boxes and antiquities in isles filling the ample space, he replied, "No. I know my parents collected stuff, but this is a lot."

"Didn't you say this house was owned by one of the founders of New Physics, and your dad is the CEO?"

"Oh, you mean Dr. Ethan Conrad? Yes. After the company jet disappeared between Los Angeles and Dubai, after having strayed off course in Canadian airspace and lost contact with the ground, an investigation concluded it likely crashed. A science vessel ran across the wreckage of the company jet on the ice near the North Pole. It had exploded on impact."

"That's terrible, Derek."

"I know. Dr. Conrad's estate put the house up for sale, according to my dad, and dad immediately made an offer; it was accepted, and here we are."

Jenna noticed Derek's eyes fixated across the room and followed him through an aisle of boxes and antiquities. Derek stopped at a pile of boxes, furniture, and a roll-top desk.

"What's the matter?" Jenna asked.

"I just get a strange feeling and was drawn here. I've never seen that roll-top desk," Derek replied. "Look, it's solid oak." Slowly opening the desktop, he noticed a small metallic sphere with a mirrored surface, no larger than a golf ball, on a pile of envelopes. Lifting the sphere, he took the first envelope and read it. "It's a letter addressed to Dr. Ethan Conrad at this address. It's from an address in Washington, D.C."

Derek immediately looked at the sphere in his hand.

"What's the matter?" Jenna asked again.

"There's no weight," Derek replied, looking at Jenna with wide eyes. "This can't be."

"No weight? What do you mean?"

"Watch."

Derek opened his hand and lowered it, and the small sphere remained stationary above Derek's hand. Jenna's mouth dropped open as she stared at it, as it remained stationary and motionless in the air space where Derek unclasped it.

"This is like Egypt," Derek said. The sphere then unfurled into a flat circle before them. Derek and Jenna could see their reflections on its surface.

"Derek, I'm scared," Jenna said, her voice trembling, and he placed his arm around her. "What do you mean it's like Egypt?"

"Dr. Zeyad Hassan of Egyptian Antiquities walked into this mirror, Jenna. It opened."

"What do you mean it opened? Like a doorway?"

"Yes, Jenna, like a doorway."

Derek flashed back to Egypt momentarily:

"What is it?" asked Derek as he stared at the orb intently.

Dr. Zeyad Hassan spoke in Egyptian Arabic to a young Egyptian woman in the chamber. She replied and began taking photos of the object. Zeyad put on a glove. Carefully placing his thumb and forefinger on each side of the tiny orb, he lifted it carefully.

"This can't be," Zeyad whispered in astonishment.

"What?" Rick replied.

"There's no weight. None whatsoever. This… this is impossible. It is lighter than a balloon. It is lighter than air itself." Zeyad widened his thumb and forefinger. The object remained stationary in space, floating several feet above the ground before him.

"No, this can't be real," said Derek loudly. At that moment, the mirror became flat, and the expedition team could see their reflections as they stared at the mirror with puzzled and vacant expressions, like a herd of deer standing in the headlights of an oncoming truck.

"This is the same object we found at Area 51," said Zeyad as he walked around the flat disc and inspected the area behind it. "It was 1947. How did it get here?"

As Rick and Zeyad exchanged puzzled, wide-eyed glances, the vertical, flat, mirrored object expanded in diameter until its circular edges extended into the chamber's floor and ceiling.

"There's something inside. It's another chamber," said Zeyad. "This could explain everything."

"No!" exclaimed Derek. "Where are you going? Something moved in there. Don't go!"

Derek started crying. "Dad, stop him!"

Derek then felt Jenna hugging him, and he realized that he was weeping. Jenna put her head against his chest and looked at their reflections. The mirror was now extruding into the floor. Then, the reflection vanished, and they could see a dark room with hieroglyphics covering the walls. Taking a deep breath, Derek said, "This may sound crazy, Jenna, but we must go in there and investigate. Maybe that's where Dr. Conrad is."

Jenna shook her head with a panicked look on her face. "Derek, you said Dr. Conrad died aboard the company jet after it crashed at the North Pole. How could he be in there?"

"I don't know," Derek said in a confused voice. "I sense it. He's in there."

"No, Derek, no," Jenna replied in a fearful voice and fought back tears. "Where is Dr. Hassan?"

"He's still in there."

"And if we go, Derek, we'll be in there! What if nobody ever finds us?"

Derek turned to Jenna, gently took her shoulders, stared into her eyes, and she looked at his deep blue irises as they began to illuminate. At that moment, she felt spellbound and compelled to follow him. "Don't be afraid, Jenna."

A gentle, chilly breeze was coming out of the mirror, along with a musty smell that reminded Jenna of a basement or parts of a museum where fossils were displayed.

"I'm suddenly not afraid," Jenna replied. Placing her hand in his, she said in almost a whisper, "Promise you won't let go of my hand."

Derek squeezed her hand and said, "Are you ready, Jenna?"

"To go in there?" Jenna replied. Squeezing his hand tighter, he lifted her hand and kissed it. Looking at his hand, then into his eyes again, she said, "I'm ready. Take me to your leader."

Derek gave her a puzzled look, and then they both giggled. "You're funny, Jenna."

Jenna grinned.

Derek's eyes suddenly became fixated on a notebook with the words in handwriting, "Dark Mirror Project," inside an open drawer.

"What is it?" Jenna whispered, looking at the notebook.

Shaking his head, Derek reached into the drawer, took the notebook, and started leafing through the pages covered with furiously scrawled handwriting. He glanced at the handwriting, stopped at a page, and began reading aloud from the heading at the top.

"Jenna, this page is dated yesterday. This must be Dr. Conrad's diary or something. It says: Dark Mirror Project. (See my binder for details.) Our discovery points out how the dark mirrors work! It is very akin to the holographic universe theory. The dark mirrors can connect to any coordinate in the universe by accessing any coordinate in two dimensions. The Pentillions must have figured out how to control the dark mirrors to access any coordinate. Through something akin to spooky action at a distance, a duplicate mirrored sphere appears at the coordinates, and the mirror (or, should I say, the mirror and its counterpart) connects. This explains the Dark Mirror Telescope retrofit on the Hale at the Mount Palomar Observatory. Who is the conduit making it function? OMG. It's

Ira Rothbard." Derek suddenly stopped and stared into the distance.

"Ira Rothbard?" asked Jenna, looking at Derek's distant stare with puzzlement.

"Dad mentioned the dark mirror telescope at Palomar could not function without Ira. Dad wouldn't elaborate."

Jenna looked at Derek, then the notebook. "I don't understand. Dr. Conrad wrote that Ira is the 'conduit.' He said earlier that the Pentillions must have figured out how to control the dark mirrors. Surely you're not thinking…"

"That Ira is a Pentillion? That his parents who died in that StarCar were Pentillions?" Derek said, finishing her question and then adding his own.

"Is he? Are they?"

Derek continued rereading the notebook from where he left off, and replied, "This makes sense! The Rothbards adopted Ira, who survived the StarCar accident that dad told me about after the StarCar was taken to Nevada for study. Dad said the autopsy revealed his parents' physiology contained extraordinarily advanced human DNA." Derek stopped and wrinkled his nose. "Jenna, do you think Dr. Conrad is referring to Area 51?"

"I know that name; it was in a movie about an alien invasion. Does he say anything about Area 51?"

"Well, no, I'm glancing through his notebook and don't see that reference." Looking toward the open dark mirror, Derek looked at Jenna and motioned his head toward it. Looking anxious, Jenna grabbed Derek's hand and squeezed it.

Glancing at Jenna's hand in his, Derek held the notebook in his other hand tightly to his chest and slowly led her through the opening. She warily watched the familiar polished and dusty wooden floor underneath her feet transform into a shiny black, seemingly polished floor with fine patches of what looked like gray talcum powder. Jenna's running shoes provided adequate friction on the slick surface, which left her tracks with each step, and she noticed Derek wearing a new pair of basketball shoes that appeared to provide as much friction.

The door to the attic slowly opened, and a Special Forces team carrying weapons and wearing weapons on black combat uniforms with helmets and visors equipped with 3D overlays of the terrain cautiously entered the attic. Motioning to the dark mirror across the large attic, the team leader immediately radioed, "The exotic event horizon is open, I repeat, the exotic event horizon is open," to the acknowledgment of a woman's voice. Cautiously approaching the dark mirror, weapons at the ready, the team surrounded the edge of the opening.

In a control room, Secretary of State Roland Nichols and NSA Director and Commander of U.S. Cyber Command Sharon Questar watched the Special Forces team through monitors on the attic ceilings.

Aiming his helmet camera into the dark mirror's opening, Special Forces team leader Carter Smith said, "Sharon, do you see this?"

"Affirmative, I see Derek Jones and Jenna Collins," replied Sharon Questar, wearing a black blazer and white shirt. She nervously brushed her dark blonde hair to the side of her face and adjusted her earphones while studying Secretary of State Roland Nichols's intense expression near her.

The young Secretary of State's handsome, unshaven face gave Sharon a sense of his thinking, and he looked uneasy. Her eyes wandered to his closely cut sides and densely thick buzz cut that remained just like in his military days, a time that ended just a decade before he became the youngest Secretary of State in United States history. His thick eyebrows and large, intense eyes betrayed his deep concern. Running his hand through the dense, sweaty hair on his head, he pressed his lips together.

"What's the plan, Carter?"

"We need to go in and ascertain the coordinates of this location so we can relay it to Agents Bartlett and Johnson. They're on the tour," Carter Smith replied.

"Carter, if anyone on that tour gets wind of their plan to leave the tour, this could jeopardize the mission," Sharon Questar said in a deliberately calm voice.

"Understood," Carter replied. The seventy-two-year-old and still youngish-looking former Navy SEAL and NASA astronaut felt a renewed strength as if he were back in 1975. He flashed back to the youthful face of his friend, recently the United States President Arthur Wilson, who died when Air Force One was sabotaged and exploded in the air. He briefly pictured what the last moments of his friend's life must have been like when the Presidential aircraft exploded, and he briefly closed his eyes.

Secretary of State Roland Nichols' voice said to Carter, "How are you doing, Carter?"

"Just fine, sir," Carter replied.

"Listen up," Roland continued in a deliberately deep and authoritative voice, one that Sharon recognized when he was concerned an operation could go sideways, "This must go by the numbers, or we are fricking screwed. Do you read me, soldier?"

"Yes, sir," Carter replied.

Sharon looked at Roland and said, "Do you want me to take over from here? If this operation goes sideways, I feel it would be best if you are out of the loop."

Roland stepped back and scratched the back of his head. "Sharon, I know the Secretary of State doesn't get involved in these matters as a matter of policy, but my background qualifies me to command this operation."

Sharon replied, "Well, if necessary, Roland, there's always plausible deniability. You weren't officially uninformed."

"Right, Sharon, you're always understanding."

Sharon nodded, placed her hand on her headset mouthpiece, and said in almost a whisper, "Carter, follow Derek and Jenna, but do not let them see you. We believe Dr. Ethan Conrad will try to contact Derek inside the complex."

Carter shook his head slightly, squinted, rubbed perspiration from his eyes, and said, "Need to know, I know! Now you tell me Dr. Conrad is alive. Can you give me a quick elevator summary of how someone gets from a crashed corporate jet to the Moon? He wasn't on the jet, is that it?"

Sharon and Roland exchanged nervous glances, and Roland nodded to Sharon.

"Carter, he entered an exotic event horizon before impact. That's all you need to know," Sharon said, paused, and continued, "but there's a Starbucks at CIA headquarters where I'll buy you a coffee or bar drink, your choice, and I'll tell you all about it off the record."

Carter grinned and replied, "Got it. My team will shadow Derek Jones and Jenna Collins. You said the package is the binder." Stopping, Carter then said, "Wait, what about Arthur? You said Dr. Conrad entered the exotic event horizon. What about Arthur?"

"Need to know, soldier. Focus. The package and its owner," Sharon replied.

"Right," Carter said, his jaw dropping slightly as the thought of his best friend surviving sent a wave of goosebumps across his body and the hairs of his body standing on end. "We're going in now."

"Excellent," Roland said. If anyone can retrieve the package and its owner," he continued as he grinned at Sharon, "it's you and your team."

"They're the best SEALs in the United States government. This is a cakewalk," Roland added with admiration.

Sharon laughed. "It's a walk on hot coals, and you know it."

Carter said, "We're going in. Out."

"This floor is so weird," exclaimed Jenna in a quiet voice to Derek. "Is this concrete or some stone…? What's all the whitish-gray dust in patches?"

The Special Forces team peered around the corner of the exotic event horizon opening.

Derek gave her hand a gentle squeeze. Their eyes caught each other as they stood in the shadows of a room. Jenna squeezed Derek's hand tightly. Derek instinctively looked toward the opening, but Carter and his team had moved quickly out of sight. "I could have sworn I saw something move from the attic opening at the corner of my eye, Jenna," Derek said. "It must have been a floater. Dad says floaters make you think you see something in your periphery when nothing's there."

Gazing toward the illumination source by bright white light from an open area outside the room and beyond its ceiling, Jenna commented, "Where's the light source?"

Derek looked at his watch. Leading Jenna by the hand toward the light, they passed recessions in the wall that reminded Jenna of kitchen countertops. Transparent glass squares that looked like recessed computer monitors lined the walls behind these countertop-like surfaces, but there were no controls.

Walking into the open space, Derek and Jenna were awestruck by the spectacle.

Above them and to all sides was the glass-like interior of a hollow sphere, the size of a football stadium or more, with honeycomb recessions in the transparent material.

"This is unbelievable," exclaimed Jenna, eyes and mouth wide open.

"A geodesic sphere," Derek replied with a matter-of-fact, calm voice.

"You mean like Spaceship Earth in Epcot at Walt Disney World?" Jenna replied. "I ran across that on the Internet. This seems a lot bigger!"

"Space was not an issue for whoever built this structure, probably long ago," Derek replied as their eyes moved up toward the source of light at the top.

"Look at the edges of the circle; it is irregular like soil, the same light gray color as the dust on the floor," Jenna observed. "Is this sphere buried in the ground? Only with the very top exposed above the surface?"

"You know, Jenna, you have a good point. I think we are under the surface of the ground."

Jenna pulled Derek's hand toward a wide ramp that ascended at a 45-degree angle. "Let's go up there. Look, Derek, there appears to be four humongous tunnels halfway up." The tunnels were spaced apart by 90 degrees.

"Before we go up there, Jenna, I want to show you something exciting I can see."

Derek led Jenna by the hand away from the ramps and open space into an area that appeared like a subway station. At the edge of the black concrete-like surface was a dark cavernous tunnel exiting the lowest curvature of the geodesic sphere.

At least 30 feet in diameter, the circular tunnel appeared to have been excavated through solid dark gray rock. Bright LED-like lights in panels illuminated the rock, which sparkled with specks of green. On the tunnel's floor, a monorail track trailed off into the far distance, where a tiny hole of light punctuated the darkness. From the opposite direction to the distant light came a rushing sound of movement that sounded like the rush of air.

Suddenly, a sleek, tubular train-like vehicle sped past them and stopped, doors automatically sliding open.

"Come on, let's take a ride," said Derek excitedly.

"I don't know," Jenna replied. "We don't know where it goes. This is crazy."

"All the more reason to check it out," Derek replied, laughing and pulling at Jenna's hand. Intense curiosity overwhelmed her sense of caution, and as if Derek's enthusiasm and childlike glee were infectious, she giggled and followed Derek into the door.

Sitting next to one other, Jenna's smile turned into a somber look, and she remarked, "Comfortable seat. It looks so unusual. The design of this train is like nothing I've ever seen."

Outside the large windows of thick transparent material, Jenna was in awe at the beauty of the rock striations on the cut surface of the tunnel walls that sparkled green. The rock appeared like gray marble or granite, with orange veins running in marble-like patterns.

Derek observed, "Can you see the patterns? It's like some giant tunnel machine excavated this tunnel through solid rock!"

"What is the glittery green, Derek?"

"Tiny olivine crystals, I'm guessing!" Derek replied. "The Moon has a lot of olivine, and the deeper you go, the more you'll find. My science teacher said the surface is mostly light to dark gray, but you might spot hints of green if you look closely. Deeper down, there's even more—if I'm not mistaken."

Derek and Jenna stared out the window in silence as the train-like vehicle began moving, accelerating quickly until the tunnel walls blurred. Suddenly, white light bathed into the seating area. At first, the light seemed blindingly harsh as they transitioned from gloomy low lighting to bright sunlit lighting. As their eyes adjusted to the light, they appeared to be standing on a recessed track out in the open, brightly sunlit by a grayish-white landscape of rolling hills covered with craters. The ground rushed by at the level of their heads. They stared at the ground's surface at an angle that made it difficult to focus on the surface but made hills in the distance visible. Looking up, expecting a blue sky, their eyes were met by what seemed like a black void.

The train-like vehicle seemed to ascend a steep incline and still recessed partially below the ground surface, and suddenly, they were looking down from a hill across a crater and boulder-filled valley. In the black sky, a star twinkled momentarily, even though the sun brightly illuminated the landscape. As the train-like vehicle curved slightly, they instinctively turned around in their seats and could see what appeared to be a glass dome inside a large crater. Gazing upward, an object caught their attention. It was a distant but familiar orb, distinguishable as blue with white cloud formations blanketing it, a few parts of its surface red, green, and brown.

Looking at one another in disbelief as the train-like vehicle ascended, a large crater appeared out the windows to the right. Jenna pointed at the crater, and Derek nodded in acknowledgment. Inside the massive crater was the glint of what seemed to be another transparent dome.

Derek and Jenna thought the same thing: that the first dome in the large crater was the giant geodesic sphere they were just in, buried in the crater, and the second dome was another buried geodesic sphere. This transit system interconnected all of these domes.

The train-like vehicle snaked around a bend and started to descend. Darkness surrounded them as the tunnel was no longer transparent.

Lights appeared to the left of the train-like vehicle as it stopped at another platform area that seemed identical to the first.

"Come on, let's get off," said Derek, grabbing Jenna's hand and hurrying out of the opening sliding door. They stepped onto the platform and looked around. It appeared they were in the same area, except Derek noticed something on a bench carved out of the wall to one side of the platform. As he walked over to the bench, the doors slid shut and appeared to coalesce with the metallic walls of the train-like vehicle as if there were no doors. The train-like vehicle quickly sped away from the platform in the same direction it was heading.

"I wonder if there's another sphere in that direction?" asked Jenna, folding her arms and rubbing them as if she were cold while gazing in all directions. Strange and eerie shadows filled the area, and white light illuminated the area in the sphere's direction.

Derek approached the bench and picked up a few sheets of paper stapled together.

"Listen to this, Jenna," Derek exclaimed, his voice brimming with urgency as he began to read. "'NASA briefing. Top-secret. Project

Dark Mirror. Congress has terminated funding for Project Dark Mirror due to escalating pressure to mitigate the budget deficit and rising military expenditures in the Middle East.'" He continued, "'All personnel are instructed to prepare for potential long-term storage, powering down all computers, network servers, and other equipment prior to returning to Earth via the exotic event horizon mirror. Paranal will focus on this location. Upon activation of Dark Mirror, all personnel must undergo a biometric scan upon exiting at the Earthside to ensure complete accountability. Signed, General McNab, NASA-AF.' Jenna, can you even fathom this?"

"Derek, I was thinking how I recognized your house for some reason. When my mother busted me after she saw you drop me off, and of course, Marilyn gleefully confirmed over the phone that I was not at Dad's house last night, Mother insisted I tell her all about you. Where you live, all that stuff. When I told her where you lived, guess what? She said that house once belonged to Mr. and Mrs. Ethan Conrad, the same Dr. Conrad who first disappeared before he was declared dead in a plane crash."

"You're kidding."

"That NASA Air Force memo ordering all personnel to leave through the dark mirror, I suspect, refers to another mirror at the Paranal Observatory in the Atacama Desert of northern Chile," continued Jenna, "where she and my dad have toured that observatory. They said it's like an underground city in the middle of nowhere. I'll bet anything Dr. Conrad returned here through one of those mirrors, like the one we came through, to continue his research."

"Well, if Dr. Ethan Conrad's here, Jenna, where is he?"

"Good question. This complex is so huge, and who knows how many of these domes are spread across the lunar surface?"

Entering the lowermost level of the geodesic sphere, Derek pointed to a wall. Against the wall was a desk with a computer, and a large NASA emblem was mounted above it. Next to the desk, a large area of the wall had a mirror finish. Derek and Jenna approached the mirror, their reflections appearing as if facing an ordinary mirror.

As they approached closer, the mirror immediately seemed to disappear, revealing an opening. The scene behind the opening appeared like the interior of another sphere, only looking at the very top with curvature immediately overhead.

Derek took Jenna's hand, and they walked into the opening.

Derek took Jenna's hand inside another massive dome, and they ran to the open space. Derek looked at another mirror in the distance in the sphere's interior.

"You know what I think?" he asked Jenna. "I think there's another mirror connected to somewhere else."

Jenna gazed up, then at the mirror, and shrugged. Taking her hand, Derek ran with Jenna toward the mirror. Holding Jenna's hand tightly, Derrick and Jenna walked into the mirror.

The area Derek and Jenna entered through the dark mirror was brightly illuminated. White light reflected off the dark polished floor from a curved transparent ceiling only 30 feet above their heads. The view of the sphere from the top was like looking into a surrounding canyon, which they realized was a massive crater surrounding transparent walls forming a gigantic geodesic dome.

"This is spectacular!" Jenna exclaimed, walking toward the edge of the black platform and looking down. Looking up, they could see the surrounding walls of the massive canyon-sized crater, and the boundary around the exposed tip of the sphere was surrounded by soil and rocks.

Taking in the view, Derek replied, "Let's go back down and see if NASA left anything behind that might shed light on all of this."

"I just want to stay here for a while and take this all in," said Jenna with a sigh. "This is too cool."

"Jenna, we need to find out what this is all about. This looks like something NASA is studying. You know, like ancient astronauts and alien civilizations?"

"You're right, Derek. Besides, my mother will find me missing and wonder about my whereabouts. We've only been gone for a few hours, so we have time to look around."

Turning toward the mirror, they were stunned to face a middle-aged man in a jumpsuit embroidered with the same NASA emblem on a wall above a desk. Under the emblem was embroidered the name Dr. Ethan Conrad. He was holding a large binder.

The silver-haired older man who stood before Derek and Jenna looked healthy and statuesque for a man of his advanced years. Dr. Conrad seemed to recognize them and smiled.

"You must be Derek and Jenna." Looking at the notepad in Derek's hand, Ethan continued as he extended his hand, "I see you found my diary. May I…?"

Derek took a double-take at the name tag and handed the man the notebook. "Your Dr. Ethan Conrad? That's impossible. You died in a company jet crash over the North Pole."

Dr. Ethan Conrad smiled. "Come again, Derek?"

"You're dead."

"Do I look dead?"

"Well, no, not exactly. Everyone thinks you're dead. We went to your funeral. Dad collaborated with you at New Physics and said your loss was humanity's."

The smile faded from Ethan's face, and he looked sad. "I never wanted to put her through this, but the stakes are too high. I couldn't risk my wife telling anyone." Then Ethan's expression lit up. "Humanity's loss? Wow…"

"How did you survive the crash?"

At that moment, Derek heard a man's voice and the clicking of guns. A group of men in military uniforms, helmets, and carrying weapons approached Derek, Jenna, and Ethan from out of the shadows beyond the mirror and walked through the mirror toward them.

Looking at the binder and notebook, Carter said, "My name is Carter Smith of the United States Special Forces. Dr. Conrad, Derek Jones, and Jenna Collins, you must come with us."

Ethan, Derek, and Jenna looked at each other, and Carter motioned his head to follow his team as he eyed the binder in Ethan's hand. Walking from the black platform into the mirror, the dome close above abruptly changed to the same dome hundreds of feet higher.

Jenna studied Derek's face as he looked around with a puzzled expression. "What is it, Derek?"

"Jenna, this is not the same dome. It looks similar, but not the same. It's like the opening we traversed entered another similar dome."

"That is correct, Derek," said Carter. "The connections of these dark mirrors are like a labyrinth. We are miles from the dome where you entered from your attic."

"Do you know the way?" asked Derek with a sense of growing panic as he gazed around in confusion.

"Yes, I do. You must follow this team; we must not get separated, and you must follow my exact orders. Do you two understand?"

Derek and Jenna nodded.

Suddenly, the soldiers stopped dead in their tracks.

"What is it?" asked Carter.

"I thought I saw movement down in the transit system," said one of the soldiers. "Roy and I will investigate. You wait here."

The two soldiers entered the transit system opening, and the other soldiers surrounded Ethan, Derek, and Jenna. Suddenly, gunfire erupted, echoing through the transit system.

"Get down!" yelled Carter as the soldiers raised their weapons.

"Come here, Carter!" yelled one of the soldiers.

"You wait here!" said Carter, sprinting onto the transit platform and crouching down with his weapon. Slowly standing up, he walked out of the soldiers, Ethan, Derek, and Jenna's sight. Derek put his arms around Jenna protectively.

On the transit platform, Carter approached the soldiers, who were stooped over a body in a metallic uniform with strange insignia with bazaar hieroglyphics-like lettering. Standing over the body, Carter shook his head and looked at the soldiers. "They never usually venture this far from their home base on the far side."

The body looked human except for iridescence and fine gray scales, like a snake. There was green fluid oozing from the gunshot wound. As Carter stared into the eyes with pupils that had vertical slits, he saw the humanoid creature starting to raise its weapon. Without any hesitation or emotion, Carter shot it in the head, and green organic matter that reminded Carter of human brains ran down the side of its head, its eyes staring vacantly.

"Sharon, are you there?" Carter said into his cellphone. After a pause, he said, "We've got trouble."

One of the soldiers standing watch at the entrance to the transit system platform said, "Holy crap! We have company."

Carter hovered his hand over what looked like a console, whispering, "Come on!" Suddenly, a rushing sound and a sleek, long train-like transport vehicle raced onto the platform. "Get in!" Carter yelled, pushing Derek and Jenna toward the doors as they opened. "Ethan, get in! Everyone, get in!" As the last soldier entered, the doors closed. As the transport moved away from the platform, Carter and the group leaned toward the windows and watched a group of the same humanoid creatures that Carter killed run onto the platform, holding weapons and staring at them as the transport disappeared into the distance.

Chapel on the Moon

"*I* feel light!" exclaimed Jenna, looking down at the transport floor. "Now I feel heavier again."

Derek put his arm around Jenna and gently pulled her close. They stared into each other's eyes, their expressions reflecting the same unease.

"Those are artificial gravity fluctuations," Carter explained. "The transport's field is compensating for motion. At high speeds, the stabilizers adjust, but sometimes they lag, making you feel lighter or heavier."

The transport raced out of the long, dark tunnel, and everyone squinted as intense sunlight flooded the cabin. The artificial lights shut off, and the transparent roof bathed them in unfiltered brilliance. As their eyes adjusted, their mouths fell open at the breathtaking view—an endless expanse of craters and jagged mountains stretching into the distance.

"Where are we on the Moon?" Derek asked.

"We're approaching the far side," Carter replied. "Right at the terminator—the dividing line between lunar day and night." He inhaled deeply through his nose, then frowned. "Smell that?"

Jenna wrinkled her nose. "Yeah… what is that? It's like something burning.

Carter leaned closer to the window and inhaled again. He frowned. "The Apollo astronauts said lunar dust smells like 'spent gunpowder.' And as a SEAL, I'd say that's dead-on. That sharp, metallic bite in the air? That's it. Like the acrid tang after a rifle's been fired—smoky, burnt, with a hint of something almost electric. The dust is fine, clingy, like talc, but it shouldn't have a smell here. The air scrubbers should remove every trace. This is fresh—someone tracked it in."

"Yeah, it does smell like that!" Derek exclaimed.

Carter laughed. "How would you know?"

Derek grinned. "Just the way I'd imagine spent gunpowder, freshly tracked in, would smell, I suppose?"

The soldiers chuckled, and one smirked. "You've never shot a gun in your life, boy. You wouldn't know the difference between gunpowder and your girlfriend's talcum powder." More laughter erupted.

"Now come on, SEALs," Carter scolded. "He should be glad to have never fired a weapon."

"Yeah!" Derek said, causing Jenna to giggle."

As the transit tube raced by the surrealistic lunar landscape and the group stared out of each side of the cabin, Derek and Jenna stared mesmerized into the distance, with emotional flashes of iridescent blue filling Derek's pupils. Carter approached them, crouched down, looked toward the horizon, and then studied Derek's eyes.

"Magnificent desolation," whispered Carter. "That's how Buzz Aldrin described the Moon when he saw it up close—the stark beauty of a place so few have ever set foot on."

"What an amazing way to describe all of this," said Jenna quietly as Derek nodded.

"No place on Earth, even Antarctica, can compare," said Carter. "All of this hasn't changed for an unfathomably long time, for eons."

The transit tube glided to a halt with a soft hiss, the doors sliding open to reveal a starkly different environment than the one Carter Smith and his team had grown accustomed to. Stepping out, they found themselves in an expansive corridor carved directly into the moon's crust, illuminated by a series of glowing panels embedded seamlessly into the smooth walls. The ambient lighting cast a warm, golden hue contrasting sharply with the cold, lifeless surface they'd traversed above.

Dr. Conrad was the first to speak, his voice tinged with awe. "A self-contained habitat this deep within the lunar surface… it's remarkable. The air pressure, the temperature, even the humidity levels — perfectly regulated."

"Feels like we just walked into a high-end resort," Derek quipped, though his tone carried more curiosity than humor.

"A resort with a view," Jenna Collins added, her eyes drawn to the series of large windows along the far side of the corridor. Beyond them, the jagged edges of the lunar crater stretched out like a natural amphitheater, an ethereal glow bathing the barren landscape.

Carter glanced around, his instincts sharp as ever. "Stay focused. This might look like a tourist spot, but we're on business. Keep your guard up."

The team nodded in agreement, their collective unease tempered by the undeniable beauty of their surroundings. They moved forward as a unit, their boots echoing faintly in the cavernous space.

As they continued down the corridor, they noticed subtle architectural details — intricate patterns etched into the walls, symbols, and designs that seemed almost organic.

Dr. Conrad ran a hand along one of the carvings, his expression thoughtful. "These symbols… they're not just decorative. They're functional. Likely tied to the structural integrity of the habitat."

Jenna frowned. "Functional? How does a carving help hold up a wall?"

"It's not just the carvings," Dr. Conrad explained. "It's the material, the placement, the energy dynamics. The Pentillion's technology integrates seamlessly with their artistry."

Derek smirked. "Great. So, the walls are pretty *and* smart."

Carter silenced them with a glance as they approached a set of double doors at the end of the corridor. They were massive and made of a shimmering material that seemed to shift colors subtly under the light. As they drew closer, the doors parted soundlessly, revealing an enormous chamber that took their breath away.

The room was vast, its ceiling arcing high above in a series of interconnected domes. Along one side, a row of massive windows offered an unobstructed view of the lunar crater.

At the same time, the other walls were adorned with murals depicting celestial scenes — nebulae, star clusters, and galaxies rendered in astonishing detail.

At the center of the room stood a raised platform, surrounded by rows of benches arranged in a semicircle. The setup was unmistakable.

"It's a chapel," Jenna said, her voice barely above a whisper.

Dr. Conrad nodded. "And not just any chapel. Look at the ceiling."

They all tilted their heads, gazing upward at a breathtaking fresco. Instead of religious iconography, it depicted scenes of cosmic creation—the birth of stars, the formation of planets, and the swirling dance of galaxies. It was as if the Pentillions had sought to tell the universe's story.

"It's like the Sistine Chapel," Dr. Conrad continued, "but for the cosmos."

"Impressive," Carter admitted, his tone neutral but his expression betraying a hint of respect.

A figure emerged from one of the side doors as they stood, marveling at the room. He was tall and regal, dressed in flowing robes that seemed to shimmer like liquid metal. His silver hair fell to his shoulders, and his piercing blue eyes carried a calm intensity.

"Welcome," the man said, his voice resonant and warm. "I am Father Pentillion. This is our place of reflection, where the wonders of the cosmos are honored."

"Father?" Derek asked, a hint of skepticism in his tone. "As in a priest?"

Father Pentillion smiled, his expression serene. "Of sorts. Here, we do not separate science from spirituality. We believe that understanding the universe deepens our connection to it."

Carter stepped forward, his posture firm but respectful. "We're here to learn. We've heard much about the Pentillions, but meeting one firsthand is entirely different."

"And there is much for you to learn," Father Pentillion replied. "Come. There is someone I'd like you to meet."

The team followed Father Pentillion through another set of doors, leaving the chapel behind. The corridor they entered was narrower, lined with shelves holding books, devices, and artifacts that seemed both ancient and futuristic. Finally, they arrived at a laboratory filled with sleek equipment and glowing monitors.

"Dr. Conrad," Father Pentillion called, addressing a figure hunched over a workstation.

The woman turned, her face lighting up with a smile. She wore a fitted lab coat and had a sharp, intelligent gaze. "Ah, visitors. Welcome to my lab. Good to see you, Ethan!"

Derek exclaimed, "The wife of Dr. Ethan Conrad?"

Dr. Ethan Conrad approached and said, "Yes, this is my wife, Mary."

Father Pentillion looked at Dr. Mary Conrad and said, "This is Carter Smith and his team, accompanied by your husband. They're here to learn more about our work."

Dr. Conrad extended her hand, which Carter shook firmly. "Then you've come at an interesting time. We've been making breakthroughs in understanding the threshold between life and death."

"Life and death?" Jenna echoed, her brow furrowing. "What does that mean?"

Father Pentillion looked benevolently at Jenna and said with passion in his voice, "Dr. Mary Conrad is a scientist working with the Pentillions, studying the threshold between life and death with humans on Earth, with the objective of learning if what we consider a primitive belief in God creates a mental connection to outside the universe and multiverses into a hidden area of reality where the 'Grand Architect' or 'God' exists."

Dr. Mary Conrad said, "Follow me."

Chapter 7 Man in the Moon

"What can we gain by sailing to the moon if we are not able to cross the abyss that separates us from ourselves? This is the most important of all voyages of discovery, and without it, all the rest are not only useless but disastrous."

— Thomas Merton

Outer Veil of Eternity

*D*r. Mary Conrad led Father Pentillion, Derek, Jenna, Dr. Ethan Conrad, Carter Smith, and his team to another transit system like the one that brought them.

Emerging from the sleek, metallic transit tube, the group stepped into an expansive corridor illuminated by soft, ambient lighting that seemed to radiate from the walls. The air inside was crisp and faintly scented with something earthy, contrasting with the cold sterility one might expect beneath the lunar surface.

Jenna Collins adjusted her jacket, her eyes wide as she took in the sheer scale of the place. "This is... incredible. Who built all of this?" she murmured, her voice tinged with awe.

"The Pentillions," Dr. Mary Conrad replied, her tone reverent. "Their architecture is as much art as it is functional design. Look at the curvature of the walls — perfectly aligned to distribute weight and pressure from the crater above."

Ahead, Derek walked with his usual casual confidence, though his eyes betrayed curiosity. "Big rooms, bright lights... does not feel like we're in a crater."

"That's because we're not just in it," Carter said, his voice steady. "We're integrated with it. Everything here was designed to harmonize with the environment." He gestured toward the far end of the corridor, where large double doors beckoned them forward. "Let's see what's waiting."

The team moved together, their footsteps echoing softly against the polished floor. When they reached the doors, they slid open soundlessly to reveal a vast space that seemed to defy reason.

They had entered a massive room carved into the side of the lunar crater, with one wall entirely made of reinforced glass. Through it, they could see the crater's rugged interior, bathed in a ghostly, pale light from the Earth's distant reflection. The other walls were lined with intricate carvings and towering arches that led to smaller chambers. At the center of the room, rows of benches faced a raised platform adorned with a simple yet elegant podium.

Jenna gasped. "This… it looks like…"

"Another chapel," Derek finished, his voice quieter than usual.

Dr. Ethan Conrad nodded, stepping forward. "Modeled after the Sistine Chapel, by the looks of it. But with its distinct elements." He pointed to the ceiling covered in murals — not of biblical scenes, but of stars, galaxies, and cosmic phenomena.

"This place isn't just for worship," Carter said, scanning the room. "It's a testament to the Pentillion's philosophy — a blend of science, art, and spirituality."

From a side door, a figure emerged, his robes flowing gracefully as he walked. He was tall and slender, his features sharp yet serene. His silver hair shimmered faintly in the ambient light, and his piercing blue eyes seemed to see into their souls.

"Welcome," the man said, his voice rich and melodic.

Derek raised an eyebrow. "Are you a priest?"

The man smiled gently. "Not in the traditional sense, perhaps. I am a guide, a historian, and a keeper of knowledge. This chapel is where we honor the unity of the cosmos."

Dr. Ethan Conrad stepped forward, extending his hand. "I'm Dr. Ethan Conrad, and these are my colleagues. It's an honor to meet you."

The man shook his hand, then nodded to Dr. Mary Conrad. "You've come at an opportune moment. There is much to see."

They followed the man through a side corridor that led to a smaller chamber.

Dr. Mary Conrad gestured toward a sleek, pod-like machine in the center of the room. "This device allows us to explore what lies beyond what we consider reality. The transition, as we call it. But it's not something to be taken lightly."

Derek raised an eyebrow. "You're talking about near-death experiences?"

"Precisely," Dr. Mary Conrad said. "Under controlled conditions, we can bring someone to the brink and back, allowing them to explore that threshold safely."

Jenna glanced at Carter, her concern evident. "This sounds risky."

"It is," Carter said, his tone cautious. "But if it helps us understand what we're dealing with here, it might be worth the risk."

Dr. Mary Conrad's gaze shifted to Derek. "It's entirely voluntary. But the insights gained could be invaluable."

Derek studied the machine, then looked back at his team. "All right. I'll do it."

Dr. Mary Conrad nodded. "Then let's begin. This device induces a controlled near-death state. Volunteers report experiencing a tunnel of light, feelings of transcendence, and profound revelations. Under controlled conditions, we can study the phenomenon in detail."

Derek stepped closer, studying the machine, and looked at the others. "What do you think?"

Carter's jaw tightened. "It's risky. But if you're sure, we'll support you."

Jenna touched Derek's arm. "Just… be careful, okay?"

Derek gave a lopsided grin. "Always am."

He turned to Dr. Mary Conrad. "All right, let's do it."

Moments later, Derek lay inside the pod, the lid sliding shut over him. The monitors came to life, displaying his vitals. The team watched anxiously as Dr. Mary Conrad operated the controls.

"Initiating the process," Dr. Mary Conrad said.

Inside the pod, Derek felt a sudden weightlessness. His vision darkened, then filled with a soft glow. A tunnel appeared before him, drawing him forward. At the end, there was a brilliant light, warm and inviting. As he moved closer, he felt a wave of peace and understanding.

Father Pentillion stood in the brilliant light, motioning Derek to come forward.

"This place is called the Outer Veil of Eternity," Father Pentillion said, describing the mysterious place where they stood. "It is beyond the known universe."

The two stood on a platform overlooking a sea of what appeared to be universe orreries. Like bubbles containing universes filled with tiny galaxies, Derek found the sight breathtaking. When he turned to Father Pentillion, he was gone.

Someone moved in the corner of his eye. With a start, he looked over to see the woman who had tended to him during his captivity in Egypt. She wore a beautiful robe, and her deep, lustrous brown hair was intricately braided.

"It's you again. Where am I?" Derek exclaimed to her in a forced whisper.

"You are between life and death," she replied. "This is the Outer Veil of Eternity."

"Will I die?" he said, his voice hoarse and cracking with emotion, his eyes welling with tears.

"No. Your purpose here is to return to tell the tale."

"What tale?"

Looking out over the expanse of orreries, she asked, "Derek Jones, give me your first impression of what you see."

Derek gazed over the horizon over orreries and replied, "They look like bubbles with universes inside."

"That is correct."

Derek felt dizzy and felt as if he was losing his balance. His body felt extremely light in the low gravity. Suddenly, Derek was sitting in a meadow near a forest, his legs crossed, each foot placed on the opposite thigh, and the woman was facing him in the same sitting position. Derek looked at the sleeves covering his arm. He wore an ornate robe that seemed to glisten with very faint but distinct pinpoints of light.

Derek asked, "What is your name?"

The woman replied, "My name is Seraphina."

"That is a beautiful name," Derek replied.

"Well, thank you, Derek."

"Where am I."

"Where you just were."

"You mean the sea of universes? I don't understand, Seraphina."

Looking around, Seraphina replied, "Derek, all the universes you could see, an infinite 'sea' as you call it, is here. Human physicists call these multiverses. The fabric of this beautiful ecosystem is like your apparel, made of these glistening universes, one from where you came. Each pinpoint of light on your apparel is a vast civilization of sentient beings."

Gazing around with wide eyes filled with wonder, Derek asked, "Seraphina, where is my universe?"

At that moment, a greenish-blue lovebird fluttered down, landing on the grass beside him—a mirror of the ones his mother once raised with care. It regarded him curiously before taking flight, perching on a nearby branch.

Seraphina followed its gaze. "Your universe is but one of the countless stars within that little bird, a spark nestled deep in its heart. No matter where she flies, your connection remains—unbroken, unseen, eternal."

As if summoned by her words, another lovebird, identical in form, alighted beside the first. Their padparadscha-hued beaks met in a fleeting caress before they vanished into the sky, two souls bound beyond distance or time.

Derek's eyes followed them as they soared through the azure blue skies above, vanishing over the forest's trees.

"Pentillions have jumped through the multiverses you beheld," Seraphina continued, "from one universe to the next. They have lived countless quadrillions of your Earth years in this manner. They have been unable to leave the membrane or bubble encompassing each universe. They have exploited an effect like two soap bubbles that stick together. When two universes get too close, their outer membranes intersect. This juncture provides an escape from one universe about to 'pop' out of existence to another that is stable. No other intelligent beings have accomplished this."

"Seraphina, a Pentillion told me that Earth was the center of their research into the existence of a supreme being we call God. They called God the Supreme Architect. They said that a 'wormhole bridge' is formed at the moment of death. They said that the bridge exits known spacetime and goes to a mysterious place that theoretically is non-existent or nothingness. They said this is impossible, that, on the other hand, it is non-existent, yet their scientists have observed this phenomenon. Here I am to prove there is a place, somewhere."

"Like the song Jenna used to sing," Seraphina murmured. "When I visited Earth before you were born, I heard a voice unlike any other—Barbra Streisand, singing Somewhere. I fell in love with that song, for it holds the same longing, the same boundless promise, that this place embodies."

She gazed into Derek's deep blue eyes, now shimmering with the iridescent glow of his other race. For a long moment, she was silent, as if listening to something beyond words. Then, in a near whisper, she said, "Pentillions know the truth."

Derek tensed. "What truth? What is 'truth'?" His voice, edged with frustration, cracked the stillness.

Seraphina's smile was gentle, knowing. "An age-old question," she mused. "But you, of all people, should not need to ask it." She tilted her head slightly, studying him. "Pentillions have always known — humans are unlike any other. A race more ancient than even they, woven with something the universe itself cannot contain.

"When a human dies, their mind does not fade. It generates what you might call a 'micro-wormhole'—not a passage to another world, but an escape beyond all worlds. A tunnel to the very edge of the bubble... and then, beyond it.

"You are standing at the threshold of that beyond. What you see here is only the faintest glimmer of what lies past the veil. This is not a place within spacetime—it is the place spacetime cannot touch."

"Then how will I return?"

"You are still connected. Everything you are that makes you a conscious being is connected to your lifeless body back on your Earth's Moon, just as I am connected to my body on a world far from yours."

"Seraphina, you are mortal, for lack of a better word?"

"It's a long story, Derek. I volunteered to preside with another angel…"

Interrupting Seraphina, Derek exclaimed, "You're an angel?"

"Yes."

Derek stared in astonishment at Seraphina.

"As I was saying, Derek, I volunteered to preside with another angel as a human from Earth. Perhaps I will tell you about it sometime. As I was saying, you are still connected. Normally, that tunnel immediately closes, but it remains open and stable for a purpose. That purpose is for you to return and tell the Pentillions the tunnel exits where they have come to know as their eternal unconscious tomb. They must view that place not as a tomb but as a cocoon. One is not destined to remain in a cocoon forever, but take comfort in it, grow strong in it, and exit it like a butterfly into the eternal light you can only glimpse from where we sit."

"Why me?"

"You are destined for greatness."

"You said that in Egypt."

"You will learn more, Derek, when the time is right."

"Why is there evil in the universe, Seraphina? Why isn't everyone good?"

"Derek, the truth as you now know it, when propagated throughout the infinite multiverses, will set countless civilizations free. Before that truth can fully propagate, you must return and tell the Pentillions that the beauty of life is worth fighting for and even dying for. Evil exists because of fear. Love conquers fear."

Looking intently into Seraphina's eyes, Derek asked, "That is a very profound yet cryptic statement, Seraphina. Let me ask you, how old is God? I mean, I always thought, if there were this higher intelligence that religions call 'God,' he must be the most advanced extra-terrestrial being that ever existed."

Seraphina smiled. "You think deep thoughts. Let me ask you a question, Derek. If I told you there was an extra-terrestrial being from a civilization that was one trillion Earth years in age, greater than the age of many universes combined, would you be impressed?"

"Well, yeah, of course I would. Who wouldn't?"

"Derek, a simple math question. What is 10 to the 10th power?"

Derek grinned as he let out a breath and shook his head. "I hope I get this right, Seraphina. That's ten multiplied by itself ten times. The result is 10,000,000,000."

"Simple math." Seraphina paused, looking intensely into Derek's eyes as he stared at her in wonder. "What is one trillion to the trillionth power?"

Pursing his lips together with wide eyes, Derek replied, "Uh, it's one huge number."

"Derek, whatever the answer is, take that answer and take it to the second power. Keep doing that a trillion times. That might as well be one 'year' in the life of your 'extra-terrestrial' being your religion called God. This being God is not just advanced beyond your limited comprehension. God invented the concepts of physics, time, and the realm beyond."

"Seraphina, if you're an angel, is this Heaven?"

"Such allegorical words."

Seraphina stood, started walking toward the forest, looked over her shoulder covered with flowing brown hair, and said, "Follow me."

Derek stood and followed her into the forest. The euphony of bird songs gave him a deep inner feeling of peace.

"The sound of this forest is so beautiful!" Derek shouted out over the increasing complexity of multiple bird sings.

She smiled and replied, "I know."

"My mom, in her studies of Earth's ecosystem, insisted that birds are a critical component to life on habitable worlds. I always wondered why she said that instead of referring to Earth itself."

"Your mother is a sage woman," replied Seraphina with a knowing smile. "The birds are the voices of many worlds."

Approaching a stream, Seraphina knelt next to a still pond, next to the flowing water, and grasped a handful of sand that sparkled like flawless diamonds. As Derek stared mesmerized at her hand, the forest birds fell silent as the sand fell into the water. Only the sound of a gentle breeze punctuated the hushed silence.

After a pause, smiling while gazing upward at the trees, she looked into Derek's eyes and said with force, "'To see a world in a grain of sand and a heaven in a wildflower; hold infinity in the palm of your hand, and eternity in an hour.' The Pentillions have studied this stanza of William Blake's poem Auguries of Inno-cence for centuries. I encourage you to read it."

Gazing into the flowing water, Seraphina continued. "'A horse misused upon the road calls to Heaven for human blood. A fiber from the brain tears with each outcry of the hunted hare. A skylark wounded in the wing, a Cherubim does cease to sing.' Derek, do you know why he might have penned these words? Do you know how relevant these words are to the Pentillions and, ultimately, humans and every living species?"

Seraphina's voice echoed in Derek's mind with her final question. Suddenly, he was pulled back, the sensation jarring. Opening his eyes, Jenna looked down into the pod at him, her eyes filled with tears.

As the pod's lid opened, Derek gasped for air, his eyes wide with shock.

"What did you see?" Jenna asked, her voice trembling. "I was so worried. You must have been in there for twenty minutes!"

Derek sat up slowly, his expression unread-able. "I was dead."

"For twenty minutes," Jenna whispered.

"It's... it's hard to explain, Jenna, but I saw something. I felt something. Like I was part of something bigger."

Dr. Mary Conrad said, "We may finally have the proof we need for the Pentillion Council. You didn't just have a near-death experience." Choking her words, she continued, "You *were* dead."

Derek gazed into Dr. Mary Conrad's eyes confidently and said, "No, I wasn't. Because death does not exist, I have it on good authority that we never cease to exist."

Father Pentillion stepped forward, his gaze steady. "What you experienced is but a glimpse of the interconnectedness of all things. There is much to learn from it, Derek. And much you can teach others."

Derek nodded, still catching his breath. "Yeah. I'd say that's an understatement."

"Thank God," Jenna exclaimed.

"How long was I out again, Jenna?"

"Twenty minutes."

Derek thought to himself, "It seemed like hours."

A Pentillion in a lab coat stood beside Jenna and said to Derek, "We measured a micro wormhole exiting the known universe in your cerebral cortex. Again, it went nowhere."

Derek sat up and replied, "But nowhere is somewhere. It's *not* a wormhole to nowhere,"

Derek replied emphatically to the Pentillion, his blue eyes flashing with luminescence and his voice so deep with conviction that the Pentillion looked startled.

"Yes!" exclaimed Dr. Mary Conrad.

"Easy, Derek!" exclaimed Jenna with a soothing voice, gently trying to make him lay down. "Be still, relax."

Reptilian Mining Operation

Carter Smith led his team through the winding corridors of the lunar structure, their footsteps echoing faintly. The expansive chapel behind them faded into silence as they ventured deeper into the uncharted surroundings.

"Are you sure about this?" Jenna's voice crackled over the commlink, her unease evident from the chapel.

"We won't go far," Carter replied firmly. "Stay with the Conrads and Derek. We'll be back soon."

Turning a corner, Carter and his team entered a section of the habitat that time had forgotten. The lighting dimmed, and the walls, once smooth and adorned with carvings, were now marred by scratches and scorch marks. At the end of the corridor, they found a peculiar object — a tall, reflective surface that seemed to shimmer with an unnatural blackness.

"What the hell is that?" one of the team members, Lt. Harris, asked, stepping cautiously closer.

Carter's eyes narrowed. "A dark mirror," he muttered. "The same kind of technology the

Pentillion warned us about. We need to see where it leads."

Harris hesitated. "Sir, are we certain about this? It doesn't exactly look… safe."

"If it's tied to what's happening here, we need answers," Carter said, his tone leaving no room for debate. "Stay alert and keep your weapons ready."

The team stepped through the dark mirror, the surface rippling like liquid as they passed through. On the other side, they stood on the Moon's far side, beneath a black sky devoid of Earth's comforting glow. The air was thick with dust and a faint metallic tang.

Outstretching before them was a sprawling mining colony, its architecture alien and harsh. Towering machinery belched smoke into the thin lunar atmosphere while reptilian figures — tall, sinewy, and draped in crude armor — moved purposefully among the structures. Carter's stomach clenched as he saw the rows of human and otherwise prisoners toiling under the reptilians' watchful gaze.

"That's not just any mining colony," Harris whispered. "Those are slaves."

Carter nodded grimly. "And they're mining something important. Look at that."

He pointed to a central pit where glowing, crystalline ores were extracted and transported. The ore shimmered with the same unsettling energy as the dark mirror they had passed through.

"That's the source," Carter said. "They're mining whatever creates the mirrors."

"We can't just leave them here," Harris said, his voice tight with anger.

"We won't," Carter assured him. "But we need to report this first. Let's move."

Retracing their steps, the team passed back through the dark mirror, emerging again into the lunar habitat. Carter activated his commlink.

"Sharon, this is Carter," he said. "We've found something big. There's a covert reptilian mining operation on the Moon's far side. They've got prisoners from Earth and other planets working as enslaved people."

Sharon Questar's voice came through, steady and measured. "Understood, Carter. This aligns with some intel we've gathered, but this confirms it. Can you gather more information without exposing yourselves?"

Before Carter could respond, a frantic shout erupted from down the corridor. One of the team members, Private Allen, sprinted toward them, his face pale and sweaty.

"They're coming!" Allen gasped, pointing back toward the dark mirror. "Rather large spiderlike creatures — half machine, half organic! They're coming through the mirror!"

"What?" Carter barked, already moving toward the chapel. "Seal that mirror off now!"

"I tried," Allen stammered, "but they're too fast. We need to bolt the doors!"

The team burst into the chapel. Carter's voice cut through the chaos.

"Everyone, help us secure the doors!"

Derek was already moving, dragging a heavy bench toward the main entrance. "What's going on?" he demanded.

"Something came through the mirror," Carter replied, his voice grim. "Spiderlike creatures — part machine, part organic. They're hostile."

Jenna's eyes widened in fear, but she grabbed the other end of the bench, helping Derek shove it into place as it screeched across the smooth floor. Everyone joined them, working to reinforce the barricade with whatever they could find.

A faint scratching sound grew louder outside, followed by a metallic clattering. The creatures had reached the doors.

"Keep it together!" Carter ordered. "We hold this position until we figure out what we're dealing with."

The team worked furiously, their movements synchronized. Soldiers positioned themselves by the windows, their weapons drawn, while Jenna and Ethan reinforced the remaining entrances.

The scratching turned into pounding, each impact reverberating through the room. Carter tightened his grip on his rifle, his jaw clenched.

"Sharon," he said into the commlink, "we're under attack. Hostile entities are coming through the dark mirror. We're requesting immediate backup."

Sharon's voice was calm but urgent. "Understood. Hold your position. Reinforcements are enroute. Stay alive, Carter."

The pounding grew louder, and a high-pitched screech filled the air. Carter glanced at his team, their faces mixed with fear and determination.

"Whatever happens," he said, his voice steady, "we don't let them through. Understood?"

The team nodded in unison, bracing themselves as the pounding reached a crescendo. The battle for the chapel had begun.

Escaping Into the Galaxy

*T*he crashing sounds in the chapel intensified, reverberating through the walls of the lunar habitat. Father Pentillion's expression remained calm but resolute as he pushed the heavy bolts into place, sealing the massive double doors.

"This will hold them for a time," he said, facing Carter and his team. "But not indefinitely. We must move quickly."

Carter nodded, gripping his rifle tightly. "Lead the way."

The priest gestured to a side passage, its entrance marked by intricate carvings like those adorning the chapel. Beyond it lay a vast, spiraling staircase that seemed to descend into infinity. The walls glowed faintly, providing just enough light to navigate.

"This reminds me of the Vatican spiral staircase," Carter murmured as they stepped onto the topmost landing.

Father Pentillion glanced back with a faint smile. "An astute observation. The inspiration was mutual. But be cautious. The gravity flooring here is weaker and closer to true lunar conditions. You'll descend faster, but you must control your movements."

"Noted," Derek said, his voice tight. "Let's not trip over each other."

The group began their descent, their footsteps light and rapid. Sounds of splintering wood from the chapel grew louder, as did the pounding on the bolted doors at the top of the stairs.

"They're breaking through," Jenna said, glancing upward nervously.

"They'll find the doors resilient," Father Pentillion assured her, though his pace quickened. "But we mustn't test their limits."

Weapons at the ready, the soldiers took point, their sharp eyes sweeping the spiraling staircase below for any sign of danger. With each step downward, the air grew colder. After what felt like an eternity, they reached the base, emerging into a vast, domed chamber.

"This way," Father Pentillion instructed, leading them through a narrow passage into a long, dimly lit tunnel. The floor here was smoother, and faint tracks ran along the tunnel's length.

"A transit system?" Dr. Ethan Conrad asked, his voice tinged with relief.

"Precisely," Father Pentillion replied. "It will take us to the StarCar hangar. From there, your path will become clearer."

They followed the tracks to a small platform where a sleek, enclosed transport awaited. Its design was minimalist but unmistakably advanced, with smooth curves and a faint hum of power. Father Pentillion gestured for them to board.

Once inside, the team settled into cushioned seats. The interior glowed faintly, its controls seemingly responding to Father Pentillion's silent commands. With a gentle lurch, it began to move, accelerating smoothly as it carried them deeper into the lunar installation.

"How far does this go?" Carter asked in a wary tone.

"Far enough," Father Pentillion replied enigmatically. "But your journey will not end here."

The tunnel blurred past the windows, the transport's speed steadily increasing. Jenna leaned toward the window, her brow furrowed.

"Where exactly are we heading?" she asked.

"A choice," Father Pentillion said softly. "And an opportunity."

Before she could push for more answers, the transport slowed, its lights dimming as it eased to a stop at another platform. Beyond it, a massive hangar stretched into the distance, its sheer scale almost unfathomable. The walls shimmered with veins of embedded lunar crystal, catching and refracting the glow of overhead panels. The soft, ambient light bathed the space in a silvery hue, giving the vehicles within an almost spectral presence.

Derek froze at the sight, his breath catching. "This is…" he began, his words fading as his gaze swept over the fleet of StarCars.

The StarCars hovered effortlessly above the hangar floor, their sleek bodies a blend of artistry and advanced engineering. Their exteriors shimmered in hues that seemed to shift with the angle of the light — pearlescent silvers, deep cosmic blues, and radiant golds, each swirling subtly with iridescence, like the surface of a living nebula. Their contours were both aerodynamic and sculptural, with no hard edges. Instead, smooth, flowing lines gave them an organic beauty as if they had been grown rather than built.

"These StarCars are your next step," Father Pentillion said, stepping off the platform and leading the group toward the nearest vehicle. His boots clicked softly against the polished floor. "They are equipped for both atmospheric and interstellar travel. You'll need them to leave this facility and continue your mission."

As the group approached, more details came into focus. Each StarCar bore a unique design etched into its hull, glowing faintly with an energy that pulsed like a heartbeat. Their canopies were made of a transparent material that revealed the luxurious interiors within — seats upholstered in a fabric resembling liquid starlight, shimmering and shifting with the colors of the cosmos. The floors beneath the seats glowed softly, the artificial gravity mechanisms humming quietly, ensuring stability no matter the environment.

Carter stepped closer, running his hand along the side of the nearest StarCar. The surface was cool and smooth, almost frictionless, with tiny, intricate glyphs carved into the trim — symbols that seemed ancient and alien. His eyes narrowed. "You're not coming with us?" he asked, glancing back at Father Pentillion.

Father Pentillion stopped and turned, his expression calm but resolute. "My place is here, ensuring that what remains of this sanctuary does not fall completely into darkness. Your path lies ahead, beyond the Moon, beyond this system. There is more to uncover, more to fight for."

Derek's jaw tightened, his voice sharp. "What about the prisoners on the far side? We can't just leave them."

"No, you cannot," Father Pentillion said, his voice weighted with solemnity. "But the tools to free them are not yet within your grasp. First, you must understand the true scope of what you're up against. The StarCars will take you where you need to go."

Jenna stepped closer, her emerald eyes locking onto Father Pentillion's face. "What aren't you telling us?"

Father Pentillion hesitated, his gaze flickering toward the fleet of StarCars. For a moment, he seemed to wrestle with the enormity of his thoughts before speaking. "The reptilians' reach extends far beyond this colony. Their ambitions threaten not just Earth but the balance of the cosmos itself. To stand against them, you must gather allies and knowledge. This… this is only the beginning of your journey."

Carter glanced at his team. Determination mingled with trepidation in their expressions, but no one wavered. Finally, Carter nodded.

"All right," he said, his voice firm. "We'll take the fight to them. But this isn't over, Father Pentillion. We're coming back for those prisoners."

Father Pentillion inclined his head, his eyes filled with a strange mixture of hope and sorrow. "I would expect nothing less."

The team climbed into the StarCars, and the vehicles responded instantly. As Derek slid into the pilot's seat, the controls lit up with a soft glow, adjusting to his touch. The seat cradled him like a cocoon, the sensation both comforting and empowering. A holographic display shimmered to life before him, projecting navigational data and star charts in vibrant, three-dimensional detail.

Above them, the hangar doors slid open without decompression, as if an invisible veil separated the atmosphere from the vacuum of space, revealing the vast, star-speckled void beyond. The silence of space beckoned, filled with infinite possibilities and unimaginable dangers.

Derek gripped the controls, excitement and apprehension coursing through him. "Where to first?" he asked, his voice steady despite the storm of emotions.

Carter's gaze remained fixed on the expanse of space, his jaw set with unwavering determination. "Wherever we need to go to end this."

The StarCars rose gracefully, their engines humming with a melodic resonance, and accelerated toward the hangar's open doors. They slipped into the void one by one, their luminous trails streaking across the blackness like falling stars in reverse. Father Pentillion stood on the platform, his expression unreadable as he watched them disappear.

The hangar doors closed behind them with a low, resonant thud. Father Pentillion turned back toward the long tunnel leading deeper into the sanctuary. His steps were purposeful, his silhouette swallowed by the shadows.

Far above, the faint sound of shattering wood echoed down the staircase, followed by the ominous screech of metal on stone. Father Pentillion's lips tightened into a thin line.

The battle was far from over.

Epilogue: The Rome Lecture

For those interested in the intersection of physics, time, and infinity, this epilogue presents a speech delivered by Professor Elisa Strickland, a renowned science and physics educator who was once Derek Jones's high school teacher.

For readers eager to continue the main story, you may proceed directly to Book 2 of "Derek Jones and the Dark Mirrors."

The lecture at the Vatican Observatory in Rome revisits a thought experiment she once posed to her students — a discussion that may have far more significant implications than she realized.

The Vatican Observatory's main auditorium, nestled within the ancient walls of the Apostolic Palace, hummed with an air of eager anticipation. The audience, composed of high school and university students, physicists, and inquisitive minds from around the world, had gathered under the celestial dome where some of the most profound discussions of astrophysics had taken place. The murals of past scientific revolutions loomed overhead, a reminder that the pursuit of knowledge had always been intertwined with the grand questions of existence.

Standing at the podium, Elisa Strickland adjusted the microphone and smiled at the audience. Her silver watch gleamed subtly beneath the warm stage lights. She always carried herself with approachable confidence, her tone of measured enthusiasm rather than overbearing intellect.

"Tonight," she began, her voice carrying a steady authority, "I want to take you on a journey — not just through space and time, but through thought itself. Some of you may have heard variations of these questions before; for others, this may be the first time you truly wrestle with them. Either way, I encourage you to think freely. Because that is, after all, how every great discovery begins."

A young woman in the front row raised her hand. "Professor Strickland, is it theoretically possible for intelligent life to survive for one trillion to the trillionth power years?"

Punctuated by hushed laughter and whispering, Elisa chuckled softly. "An excellent question that doesn't have a simple yes or no answer. Let's begin with time itself. The universe has a lifespan governed by entropy — the eventual heat death of all matter and energy."

After a pause, she continued, "But what if intelligent beings could move between universes, escaping one as it faded and migrating to the next? If multiverses exist, then a sufficiently advanced intelligence could survive for an unimaginably long period, well beyond the lifetime of any universe. However, that's not truly existence. Even with the ability to jump from universe to universe, there would still be limitations — laws of physics, entropy, or even the sheer unpredictability of quantum mechanics that could eventually make survival impossible."

Derek and Jenna turned in their seats, recognizing a skeptical and nervous voice from the back. "But what if this intelligence was — well, for lack of a better word —? Could it survive indefinitely?"

Elisa nodded. "Jimmy Foster! Thank you for the question. Now, we're stretching beyond physics and into philosophy. If an entity existed that could control not just matter but the framework of reality itself, then survival could extend beyond mere multiversal travel. Such a being could, in theory, manipulate entropy, alter the passage of time, or even exist outside of time altogether. But here's the sixty-four trillion-dollar question: If intelligence existed outside of space and time, could it still be considered 'alive' in understanding life? Or would it transcend into something else entirely?"

Another student, an eager young man with a notepad filled with equations, leaned forward. "Doesn't this mean we can neither prove nor disprove such an intelligence? If something had control over probability itself, wouldn't it have the ability to obscure its own detection?"

Elisa's smile widened. "Now you're thinking critically. That's precisely the dilemma. The scientific method relies on empirical testability—if something cannot be observed, measured, or falsified, it falls outside the scope of science and into the realm of philosophy or metaphysics. Could an intelligence exist beyond our ability to perceive? Theoretically, yes. But without a way to systematically detect or study it, its existence remains an open question rather than a scientific hypothesis."

A murmur rippled through the audience. Some were nodding in agreement, others furrowing their brows in contemplation.

Elisa took a sip of water before continuing. "Let's take this a step further. Suppose such an intelligence did exist — let's call it 'God' for simplicity's sake. Could it create conditions where a human body could live for not just a googolplex of years, but an infinite number of years?"

The room went silent. Even those who had remained skeptical leaned forward in their seats.

"The answer," Elisa said, "depends on whether physics binds immortality or whether physics itself is an illusion. If an entity could rewrite the laws of decay, energy consumption, and entropy, it could sustain life indefinitely. Or it could do something even more radical: transfer consciousness into a non-physical state where time ceases to be relevant as we understand it. But here's the paradox: if this intelligence exists outside of what we define as 'existence,' then by what standard do we say it 'exists'?"

A young woman in the second row raised her hand. "Then it's impossible to prove or disprove?"

Elisa nodded. "That is the conclusion many great minds have come to. And it's why discussions like these are important — not because they provide definitive answers, but because they force us to question the very nature of reality."

She glanced up at the celestial dome, where the painted constellations seemed to glow with an almost ethereal light. "We live in a universe governed by observable laws, but we also live with questions that remain just outside our reach. Pursuing those answers makes us human whether or not we ever find definitive answers."

Elisa stepped back from the podium and let the silence hang momentarily. Then, with a knowing smile, she added, "And if any of you ever find out the truth, do me a favor — send me a message, no matter where in the universe you are."

The audience erupted in laughter, and as they began to clap, many shared thoughtful glances. The discussion had ignited a spark within them, filling them with enthusiasm for the mysteries of the universe and the very act of questioning. As Elisa descended from the podium, she spotted a familiar face in the crowd: one of her students, Derek Jones, watching her with a look of understanding.

And somewhere beyond the walls of this ancient observatory, the stars continued their silent watch over the ever-expanding universe.